PRAISE FOR THE #LOVESTRUCK NOVELS

"Wilson has mastered the art of creating a romance that manages to be both sexy and sweet, and her novel's skillfully drawn characters, deliciously snarky sense of humor, and vividly evoked music-business settings add up to a supremely satisfying love story that will be music to romance readers' ears."

—*Booklist* (starred review) on *#Moonstruck*

"Making excellent use of sassy banter, hilarious texts, and a breezy style, Wilson's energetic story brims with sexual tension and takes readers on a musical road trip that will leave them smiling. Perfect as well for YA and new adult collections."

—*Library Journal* on *#Moonstruck*

"*#Starstruck* is oh so funny! Sariah Wilson created an entertaining story with great banter that I didn't want to put down. Ms. Wilson provided a diverse cast of characters in their friends and family. Fans of *Sweet Cheeks* by K. Bromberg and Ruthie Knox will enjoy *#Starstruck*."

—*Harlequin Junkie* (4.5 stars) on *#Starstruck*

JUST A

Boy

FRIEND

JUST A *Boy* FRIEND

SARIAH WILSON

 Montlake

Published by Montlake, Seattle

www.apub.com

Amazon, the Amazon logo, and Montlake are trademarks of Amazon.com, Inc., or its affiliates.

ISBN-13: 9781542094344
ISBN-10: 1542094348

Cover design by Erin Dameron-Hill

Cover photography by Wander Aguiar Photography

Printed in the United States of America

For Sarah Elizabeth Younger.
To everything yet to come.

CHAPTER ONE

EMBER

"Hey, Mom said to tell you that Bash is coming to dinner."

My little sister, Lauren, stuck her head through my open door with a worried expression, waiting for a response. But I could only stare at her, my mouth hanging open, my newest young-adult fantasy book sliding out of my hand and landing on the floor.

"Ember? Did you hear me? I said Bash is going to be here for dinner. Soon. Doug went to pick him up."

Her voice sounded really far away, like we were at opposite ends of a wind tunnel. Bash? Here? In my house? How was this possible? Somehow I'd thought I'd never have to see him again, and now my sixteen-year-old sister was telling me that I'd been wrong.

My head filled with a howling, rushing wind that made it impossible to think. Or to process what was going on. My stepfather had gone to get Bash. And was bringing him here.

My mother had lured me home from college under false pretenses. She'd offered me a home-cooked meal and said she had something to tell me. Turned out she had someone to show me, instead.

How was I going to face Bash again?

To stand in the same room with him and not fall apart?

"When?" I asked. I had a million other questions, but that one seemed the most important.

She shrugged one shoulder. "I just told you. Any minute now."

A bone-deep paralysis engulfed me. I had to move. To speak. To do something to stop this from happening. But it was inevitable, and although I had delayed it for a long time, today apparently was the day of reckoning.

"You look upset," Lauren said, sitting down on the edge of my bed.

"Well, at least we know my face is still working."

My face. And my hair. I had to do something with both. I couldn't see him with a messy topknot and a shiny nose. I jumped up and ran into the shared bathroom on the second floor. I started throwing open drawers. Did I still have any makeup here? If I did, it would be left over from high school and would most likely give me an eye infection. I didn't care, though—it would be totally worth it. There, in the bottom drawer. A very old stash of some of my makeup that included most of the basics. Including pink eye from using it, probably.

Both Lauren and Marley, my stepsister, kept their makeup in their respective rooms after a screaming, hair-pulling fight over which one of them owned an expensive and hard-to-get tube of Red Hot Romance lipstick. I'd suggested cutting it in half in order to find out who the real owner was, but nobody had been amused.

And given that grudges were nursed for a long time in this household, there was no way either one of them would have helped me out since I hadn't picked their side. *Lipstick* was still a dirty word in these parts. I could have tried to beg and cajole and plead to borrow some makeup, but there wasn't enough time.

So permanent blindness it would have to be.

Lauren had followed me into the bathroom and studied me critically as I dug into the hardened eye shadow. "How long has this weird thing with Bash been going on?" she asked.

I'd never told her all the details, and I had no intention of telling her what had happened. She thought we just didn't get along, and it was easier to let her believe that. I used my right ring finger to brush the neutral beige onto my eyelid. "It's Wednesday, right? So for, like, three and a half years."

She nodded as I grabbed an eyeliner pencil. "Yeah, I thought it was something stupid long like that. You have any embalming fluid in there?"

That made me pause. "What? Is that some kind of crack about me being old?" I was about to turn twenty-one, but to my teen sister, anybody over the age of eighteen was old.

"No. Remember how you said the only way you'd see Bash again would be over your dead body? Mom will be pissed if you start decomposing at the dinner table. So, embalming fluid." She looked so pleased with herself.

"You are not being very helpful right now!" I yelped as I jabbed myself in the eye with the eyeliner. Yep, definitely getting an infection.

"My dad just called. They're almost here!" Marley ran up to us in a blur of blonde hair and bright-white teeth, her voice giddy with excitement. She reached for Lauren's hand. "Come on! I'm so excited!"

Despite the Great Lipstick Wars, Lauren and Marley were the absolute best of friends. Marley had wished for a sister her entire life, and when Doug and Mom married, she was thrilled to be given one exactly her same age. I'd always been kind of an afterthought, not really getting close to anyone in my new family.

Well, except for Bash.

I let my dark-brown hair down and began brushing it savagely. There was a lot of noise and excitement downstairs, including Roscoe, our corgi, barking as loudly as he could. I didn't hear any masculine voices, though, so I still had time. Not enough time to get in the shower and wash my hair, so I settled on a high ponytail and spraying all the frizzies into place.

There. A little bit of lip gloss that tasted like cherries, which seemed hopelessly optimistic, given how unlikely it was that anyone would be kissing me today, and I was ready. Well, readyish.

How could anyone be ready when the love of their life was about to walk through the front door? And after three and a half years of absolute radio silence? Not a text, not an email, not even a like on an Insta post. Nothing.

Maybe seeing him again would be good for me. It would be the closure I'd never gotten. I'd see him, say hello, suffer through dinner with him, and then move on with my life.

I heard the front door open to cries of delight and Roscoe frantically yelping his excitement. I heard men's voices, and my heart dropped to the floor. How was I going to do this? I wasn't strong enough.

Yes, you are, a voice inside me said. *You believed in the tooth fairy for the first nine years of your life. You can believe in yourself for the next two hours.*

Right. I totally could.

And I believed that clear up until I got to the bottom of the stairs and saw him.

Bash.

Still ridiculously tall, with the same blond hair as Marley, the same dark-green eyes, and the same brilliant smile. He was so good-looking it bordered on being suspicious. His football build strained against his white T-shirt as he hugged everyone in the foyer. Roscoe was so excited I thought he was going to throw up.

Which I totally understood, because then Bash directed that smile at me, and I melted. He walked toward me, and giant butterflies formed in my stomach. Not regular little monarchs. But, like, ones that had been grown at a mad scientist's laboratory inside a vat of radioactive goo and then set loose in my stomach, their humungous wings flapping and rearranging my internal organs.

While my insides churned, my heart felt like I had strolled into a time machine and been warped back to my seventeen-year-old self, who had loved him enthusiastically and wholeheartedly. A girl who couldn't imagine the heartache that was waiting for her.

"Hi, Ember."

I couldn't help it. I had to close my eyes, just for a second. His voice. How had I forgotten how much I loved the deep timbre of his voice? Instead of saying hello, it was like he had started performing open-heart surgery on me, exposing all of my hidden emotions to the world. Because I had all of the feels again. All of them.

When he'd run away because he'd been so repulsed by me or by the idea of having a relationship with me, I had very maturely decided that Bash was not the holder and keeper of my self-confidence or my self-worth. That I was beautiful and awesome, and any guy would be lucky to be in a relationship with me. That I was totally fine without him.

Now all those things were being exposed for the lies that they'd so obviously been. All my defenses were being stripped away, and all he'd said was *hi*.

The same thing he'd said to me so many times before in high school, and in the few weeks we'd shared a home, and it caused a pang of nostalgia so powerful I couldn't speak.

Which he, of course, noticed. "Sorry, I guess *hi* was a big ask."

He teased, but I heard something else in his voice. Fear? Of what? I'd never known Bash to be afraid of anything. Was he worried about how I'd respond?

"Nice to see you," I said, hearing how strained my voice was. "You look . . ." I trailed off as I tried to use an appropriate word. Not the ones that were currently whirling around inside my head. Like *gorgeous. Drool-worthy. Jumpable.* I settled on, "Older." It was true. The boy I'd loved was gone, replaced by a man who had somehow managed to improve about a hundredfold with age.

He let out a little laugh. "Time tends to do that to people. You look good, too."

I felt indignant at his remark, like he'd somehow known exactly what I'd been thinking. I hadn't said he looked good. He wasn't allowed to put words in my mouth, regardless of how true they might have been.

Before I could make a proper retort, I noticed Roscoe dancing in circles around Bash's feet. Roscoe had instantly fallen in love with Bash when my family had moved in. Not that I could blame the little guy, having had a similar experience myself several months prior to that event.

But Roscoe quickly added Bash to the list of People Worth Waiting by the Door For. He would sit in the foyer, tail wagging as he waited for Bash to come home from practice. Even after Bash had moved to Pennsylvania to live with his maternal grandparents, Roscoe still expected him to arrive home, not understanding that Bash wasn't coming back.

My heart broke all over again the day Roscoe stopped waiting for him.

That memory . . . just . . . wrecked me. I couldn't stand here and make jokes with Bash or hug him like everyone else had. I found that I couldn't even speak. So I did the only thing that was left.

I turned and ran. Back up the stairs, back to the privacy of my sort-of room, where I could irrationally overreact to my heart's content.

When the Carlson women had moved into the Sebastian home, there weren't enough bedrooms for everyone. It was suggested that Lauren and Marley share, but my mom had worried that all the kids would need their own space in order to better adjust to all the big changes that were happening.

So Doug had taken the game room above the garage and split it in half. He put up some framing, hammered down Sheetrock on one side, and installed a door. It gave the illusion of privacy, and I'd tried my best to make it feel homey, but mostly I'd just put up a bunch of posters. Doug had always intended to finish it off by adding wiring and insulation, and making it sturdier than it currently was. He never did. Every time I closed the door to my bedroom, the entire wall would shake slightly.

Much as it did now. I knew not to slam the door, even though the urge was there. I tried hard to catch my shaky breath and calm my even shakier hands. How had I possibly thought seeing him again would give me closure? If anything, it had given me . . . whatever the opposite of closure was. Opener? All I knew was that it meant reopening old wounds and suffering. Nothing felt neat and finished.

There was a strong knock at my door, making the faux wall shimmy. I knew it was Bash. I also knew that whatever he was going to say needed to be said, and I had to listen. Even though I'd just chosen avoidance as an action plan, it wasn't sustainable. His dad was married to my mom. We were going to see each other on special occasions. We weren't stupid teenagers anymore, running around with our hearts on our sleeves. I had to figure out a way to be mature and civil and polite.

I also didn't want to do anything to add to my mother's stress levels. And fighting with Bash would definitely make her upset.

So while I wanted to tell him to go away, instead I said, "Come in."

Bash opened the door and said, "Hey, do you have a sec?"

"I have lots of secs." It was only after the words left my mouth that I realized how that sounded. "Seconds. I mean I have lots of seconds. As in measurements of time."

He entered the room and shot me a barely suppressed grin, like he wanted to laugh and tease me but was refraining. For which I was grateful.

"I'm guessing no one told you I was coming to dinner tonight."

"No, not until right before you got here. I didn't really have much say in the matter."

"Yeah, I've found the people providing the free food and shelter can usually make you do things you don't want to do."

There was a hint of bitterness in his tone, and as much as I was dying to ask him what it meant, I stayed silent.

Bash walked over to one of my windows with the built-in seat perfect for curling up to read about dragons and witches and valiant princesses. It had been my favorite place when I'd still lived here. He pushed the curtain to one side, looking out into the front yard. The sun had begun to set, and a golden light reflected off his hair and lovingly bathed his strong, angular face, making him look otherworldly.

"Do you remember the last time we were in here together?" He murmured the question, almost as if he hadn't intended to say it out loud.

Did I remember? Did. I. Remember? Was he being serious right now? I felt like I was on the verge of hyperventilating. Someday, when I was a hundred and five and had developed dementia like my great-granny had, the memory of him, of us, in this room would be the very last thing to go. It would be the memory I would cling to for the rest of my life as being the most perfect moment in all of the history of humankind with the worst possible ending.

I would never forget.

But before I could say as much, he spoke again. "There's something I wanted to get off my chest."

That little voice inside my head that usually cheered me on and helped me make right choices had apparently pledged allegiance to all things Bash as it said, *Please let it be his shirt. Please, oh please, let it be his shirt.*

I hissed at it to be quiet. "What?"

"I'm sorry. I know you must hate me after what happened. I shouldn't have just left like that, without any explanation."

In that moment, even though I'd thought I'd wanted an apology, I found I didn't need one. It didn't really matter if he was sorry or if I was. Things had happened the way they had, and we had both moved on.

Or, at least on my part, I was still trying to move on and not compare every guy I met to Bash.

Something I was failing miserably at.

"I don't hate you, Bash. I never hated you," I told him. And it was the absolute truth. Even when I had desperately wanted to, thinking anger had to be better than pain, I couldn't.

Or when I had irrationally and secretly blamed him for somehow causing my mom to have breast cancer by moving out. Even though I logically knew those two events were totally unrelated, one had happened right after the other, and I had somehow held him responsible for it. It seemed silly that I continued blaming him, especially considering she was fine now. Maybe what I'd really blamed him for was not being there when I needed him to be. I had wanted to lean on him, confide in him, and tell him how terrified I was that my mother was going to die and leave me and Lauren alone in the world. I hadn't even hated him then.

Bash turned toward me. "Really?"

His voice caught at the end, and I wrapped my arms around myself so that I wouldn't go over and hug him. I just nodded instead.

Because I had been right. I didn't need his apology. I needed him to go away. To go back to Pennsylvania and out of my life. It felt like I had only recently started filling in the Bash-shaped hole he'd left in my heart.

But he seemed determined to absolve himself. He moved until he was standing right in front of me, so close that we could have kissed. I felt that old electrical surge spark between us, lighting up every molecule in the air around us. Goose bumps broke out on my skin when he started to speak, and his warm, minty breath washed across my face.

I had hoped that when we saw each other again, I'd be immune to him and his charm and his magnetic pull on me.

Not so much.

"I wish we were still friends," he said. "I know it's not fair to ask that of you, but I do miss you."

They were words I'd been dying to hear for so long—*I miss you*—that when he said them I felt totally overwhelmed. So I focused on the other part of what he'd said. I needed him out of my life, not saying things that made me want to cling to him. "I don't know. I think asking an ex to be friends is kind of like your dog dying but saying we could still play with him."

"Maybe the dog didn't die and just went upstate to Grandma's farm in New York."

"Pennsylvania," I corrected him. That was where our friendship had wandered off to.

"No matter where he went off to, we could bring him back."

Did I want that? Could I handle it? Being friends with Bash? We'd never really been just friends. "I don't know. I have a lot of dogs already."

There was a brief flash of his gorgeous smile before his face turned serious again. "I guess I deserve that. Especially since when I left, I should have talked to you first. I should have explained why I was doing what I did."

Then he did something that literally made me jump. Almost out of my skin. He reached for my left hand, enveloping it with both of his. The shaking started up again, only this time it was with excitement and not despair. How could he still have this effect on me? My erratic and too-loud heartbeat was making it difficult to hear what he was saying, and I had to force myself to concentrate.

His voice had gone husky with an emotion I couldn't identify. "We were so young. And I was just . . . immature, and I hadn't realized that—"

I heard someone clearing their throat and turned to see my mother standing in the doorway. I yanked my hand out of Bash's and ignored the way that it still tingled. She had a weird expression, one I couldn't quite place, but it looked a bit like she was worried we were up here about to have sex.

I mean, to be fair, that exact situation had nearly almost happened in this same place, so she had justifiable cause to be alarmed if that was what was bothering her. "Don't we have a no-boys-allowed-in-your-room policy?" She was going for a light, teasing tone, but I could hear the concern. I wasn't sure why, because I'd never given her any reason to worry about Bash since I'd never told her the details of what had transpired between us. "It's time for dinner. Ian, your father is looking for you. Ember, I could use your help in the kitchen."

Bash nodded and left without another word. I, on the other hand, knew something was immediately up, because my mother did not ask for help ever. Even when she needed it. She was determined to never be a burden to her family, even when she was in the midst of treatment.

I found it highly annoying.

Her current expression was also annoying me. "I'm not fourteen. You don't need to kick boys out of my bedroom and embarrass me."

My mother feigned outrage. "Embarrass you? When have I ever embarrassed you?"

I loved this woman with my whole heart, but she had to be kidding. "Um, every single day of high school? My volleyball games? Senior prom? The mall, several times?"

"That's called being a good mother," she said, reaching over to kiss me gently on the cheek. "Come on, help me with dinner."

As I followed behind her, I realized that she probably really did need my help, because Bash could eat like a pillaging horde. Which would be good at dinner because then his mouth would be full the whole time, and we'd get through tonight, and school was starting up in a few weeks, and I had volleyball practices to get to, and I could forget that Bash had ever waltzed back into my room, apologized, and been about to say . . .

What? What had he been going to tell me? For years I had wondered why he had left. Had he been about to confess the reasons? What hadn't he realized? That women came in different sizes? That not everyone had rock-hard abs? That my curvy hips were not a reason to flee across the country?

I needed to stop wondering. I was done giving him the power in our situation. His reasons didn't matter. Especially since he was probably only sharing them to ease his guilty conscience. I shook my head. The past was in the past, and I needed to move forward with my life. It was good that I'd seen Bash and good that our first encounter wasn't terrible and I hadn't screamed and/or sobbed at him.

But after tonight? I was going to stay far, far away from Ian Douglas "Bash" Sebastian.

CHAPTER TWO

BASH

"Everybody, dig in," Tricia said, handing me a plate with pieces of roast chicken on it. Instead of dumping the entire platter onto my plate, I only took some of the dark meat and passed it to Marley, on my right. Ember was seated directly across from me, carefully not making eye contact.

This was not how I had hoped things would go, but I couldn't say I was surprised by it. I deserved her coldness.

Last year, when my university kicked me off the football team for failing a drug test (not once, not twice, but three whole times) because I decided that marijuana was a better medication for my depression than, you know, actual depression medication, I had quite a few offers from junior colleges. My hope was to play a year and then get recruited by another Division 1 school.

When Coach Stan Oakley came personally to invite me to his team at Edwin O'Leary College (also known as End of the Line to Division 1 rejects like myself), I immediately said yes, knowing that it was half an hour from my childhood home. A home I hadn't stepped inside for over three years. Until tonight.

The truth was, I'd missed my dad. And my little sister. I'd been sure to text them and make face-to-face video calls with them almost daily, but it wasn't the same. I'd hoped enough time had passed, that things had changed, and that I could come home again.

But it had only taken thirty seconds for me to realize none of that was true.

She'd been the one I'd been most afraid to see again. Not Marley, who constantly bugged me about coming back. Not my dad, who as a former drug addict had been sorely disappointed in me taking an illegal substance and getting thrown off my team. Not Tricia, who had never really warmed up to me.

Just Ember.

It might have helped if I'd walked into this situation with any information about my opposition. I was fanatical about watching film before any game, but I'd come into this blind.

Mostly because it had been the only way to try to move on from Ember. I was so careful. No deep diving on her social-media accounts. No emailing. No texting. When I chatted with my family, I hadn't asked about her or what she was doing. Total cold turkey.

Which meant that I had suffered some emotional and mental withdrawals that had led to several bad decisions (including the self-medicating), but I had done it. My life had been an Ember-free zone.

Today, when my new coach announced that there would be no alcohol, no drugs, no failing grades, and no women/dating allowed, it had been fine with me. I'd done it before. It had only been the one woman, but I had successfully sworn her off.

Until I saw her again.

As the inside linebacker it was my job to take down offensive players trying to score. I was the one who tackled them and stopped them. When I saw Ember on those stairs, I suddenly had some idea of what those players must have felt. I was stunned. The wind had been knocked out of me. I felt like I couldn't catch my breath, and the only thing I could do was lie on the ground wondering what had just happened.

Because somehow she'd grown even more beautiful than I would have imagined possible.

And I still wanted her with a fierceness that shocked me.

Those feelings probably would have scandalized everybody in the dining room, so I kept that information to myself.

The conversation flowed easily as everyone else talked about their day. I mainly focused on eating. It was one of my favorite things in the entire world to do. I was six foot six, worked out every day, and spent a good amount of time running. I needed lots of calories just to feel normal.

"And, Ian, how did your meeting go today?" Tricia asked with a smile as she passed me the basket of rolls. I only took four, which I thought was admirable. My father must have told her about the meeting, because I hadn't mentioned it.

"Meeting?" Marley echoed, looking confused.

"I had a team meeting today. I'm moving here and playing football for EOL."

"What?" my sister shrieked, and then threw her arms around my neck. Considering that I had just taken a big bite of chicken, she was lucky I hadn't accidentally removed a chunk from her arm.

I saw the alarm in Ember's eyes. "You're going to EOL? I go to EOL."

"Yes, Ember earned a scholarship to play volleyball," Tricia said, the pride in her voice clear.

No one had mentioned that to me. That don't-ask-don't-tell policy of mine was coming back to bite me in the butt. Ember and I would be going to the same college?

"You didn't tell them I was moving here?" I asked my dad, confused.

"I thought you might like to be the one who did."

If I had known it was a surprise, I would have figured out a better way to do it than this. I would have told Ember upstairs when we weren't surrounded by both of our families so that she could have some time to deal with it beforehand.

"Are you going to live here at home?" Marley asked, the excitement shimmering off her in waves.

"Not here. I have a place and a roommate. His name's Logan. He's the quarterback. He seems cool."

My sister hugged me tight one last time and released me. Lauren, whose gaze was still fixed on her phone, asked, "Is this Logan hot?"

Both Tricia and my dad made "whoa" type sounds. "Way too old for you, Little Miss," Tricia said with a warning tone.

"The guys my age suck. It's so much work trying to change them into humans," Lauren grumbled, and Marley nodded vigorously.

"Don't ever think you can change men. Men don't change just because a woman wants them to," my dad said, imparting this fatherly wisdom like it had come from the heavens themselves.

Ember shook her head. "Ha. Says the man who watches every film version of *Pride and Prejudice* with my mother several times a year."

I was eating, and so when I guffawed at her apparently accurate description of my dad (given his sheepish grin), I nearly spewed all over the table. I had to cough several times, and Marley thumped me on the back, afraid that I might be choking. When I swallowed down my food, I grinned at Ember.

There was this . . . moment. Where we were us again. Sharing an inside joke, since watching *Pride and Prejudice* had been one of our very first dates. It was extra credit for English that had turned into something more. But the second I saw that she realized what was happening, the twinkle in her soft hazel eyes faded.

"So," she said, turning toward her mother. "Was there something you wanted to tell us?"

Tricia and Dad glanced at each other from the head and foot of the table, and both put their forks down.

"There is," Tricia said. She let out a little breath, looking to my father for comfort. He smiled back at her. "My latest blood work showed elevated white-blood-cell counts. The doctor wants to run some more tests."

Ember gasped while Lauren put her phone down.

While I was concerned for everyone at the table, I couldn't help but focus on Ember, whose face had gone pale, the color draining away.

I wanted more than anything in the world to get up, walk around the table, and take her in my arms to comfort her. Not like a stepbrother.

Like a boyfriend.

But I knew it was impossible. Not only because of Coach's no-dating rule, but because of my dad's.

He and Tricia had met because of me. I wasn't doing so great in my US Government class, and she called him for a parent-teacher conference. They ended up chatting for two hours, only my father didn't think it was appropriate to try and date his son's teacher.

If only things had ended there.

Instead Tricia used gardening shears to cut a fan belt in her car and called my father, the mechanic, to fix it for her. When he saw all the gouges and marks on the belt and realized that she had probably spent hours trying to slice through that thing with a variety of different tools, he decided to ask her out.

Three weeks into their relationship, they snuck away to Las Vegas. I couldn't even recall what he'd told me about why he'd be out of town, only that I needed to keep an eye on Marley. I remembered being excited because I had hoped to invite Ember over. Only she got sick and stayed home. Meanwhile, Tricia drank all the alcohol from their minibar and decided it would be the best idea in the world to get married, and my normally down-to-earth father agreed.

And they didn't annul it like most people would have. No, they wanted to try and make things work because they were madly in love. They planned to move in together.

Once I mostly processed my shock that my father had not only eloped but had eloped with my girlfriend's mother, and shortly after the Carlsons had moved in, he sat me down and told me his expectations when it came to Ember Carlson. He told me that he expected me to be respectful and keep my distance from Ember because despite the fact that we hadn't been raised together, he and Tricia were trying to create a family.

"It just can't turn out well, son. If something happened with you two, you're still going to have to see each other at Christmas for the next thirty years. Don't mess that up."

He said it like he somehow knew about us, even though I hadn't said a word. He had no idea that Ember and I had been dating for the last few months, and that I had planned on asking her to prom. I wondered if I was just so obvious with my feelings and he'd read it on my face every time Ember walked into a room.

Although I was stupid and basically a giant walking hormone, I knew he was right. I had to end things between us.

Judging by how she'd reacted upstairs when I'd tried to talk to her, I had done a really bad job of it.

Now I was back, looking for a second chance with everybody. I didn't want to screw this up again.

"When will you know, Mom?" Lauren asked. "Whether or not you have a recurrence?"

"The doctor will call as soon as she has more information," Tricia promised, putting her hand on top of Ember's. "But it got me thinking. Remission is not a cure. And really, none of us know how much time we have left. So I made up a bucket list, just in case. I'm hoping that you guys will help me cross some of those things off, because you're the people I most want to spend my time with."

There was a chorus of "yes, of course, absolutely" from the girls at the table. I knew I was going to be busy for the next few months and couldn't really commit to anything just then. More important, I needed to keep my distance from Ember. I felt my father's eyes on me, but I stayed silent.

That brought dinner to an end, even though I could have kept eating. Ember stood up and grabbed her mother's plate along with her own and began clearing the table.

"I can do that," Tricia protested.

"It's okay, Mom. I've got it." Ember left and went into the kitchen.

"What should we do tonight?" Dad asked. "Watch a movie? Play a board game?"

Lauren and Marley discussed possibilities for the evening with Tricia and my dad. I didn't join in. Instead I reminded myself of my resolution to keep away, but I had to know if Ember was okay. I grabbed my plate and thanked Tricia for dinner, telling her it had been a long time since I'd had a home-cooked meal.

When I got into the kitchen, Ember was pressed up against the sink, her head hanging down, shoulders slumped. I wondered if she was crying. And if she was, if she'd be mad at me for interrupting.

I wanted to say, *I'm so sorry about your mom.*

Or, *Sorry I'm an idiot and I'm making your hard life harder.*

I settled on taking the light approach. "So what do you vote for? Movie or a board game?"

She whirled around, and her eyes were bright, as if she'd been about to cry. "What? I don't . . . I don't care."

"You? Not care? The most competitive person I know?" My chest came in contact with her shoulder when I leaned over to put my plate in the sink. Another pang of desire speared through me. I wanted to put my hands on her shoulders and pull her in close, so I took two deliberate steps back. "You're a crazy person when it comes to board games. Like the last time we played Monopoly."

We had played for eight hours straight until I'd finally emerged the winner.

And from the look on her face, I could tell she was remembering it, too. "I don't want to play a game that's about paying rent. I have to play that game in real life."

"Your scholarship doesn't pay for your room and board?"

"It would cover some of it if I lived in the dorms. But since I'm a junior, I'm a little too old to be living in the dorms. I have an apartment off campus with three of the girls from the team. What about you?"

"I'm . . ."

"You're . . ."

"Living in the dorms," we finished together.

"I'm sorry," she said, but she was smiling, and that felt like a win. I was a junior, too. I wondered if it made her think less of me.

"Don't be. I don't mind. I'm going to school to study and play football. I don't need more space than a dorm room."

"And to eat," she reminded me, still sporting her smile.

"Obviously. I plan on eating taking up most of my time."

"EOL's going to regret that scholarship when they realize you can eat your own body weight every day. They have no idea how much money they're about to lose." Ember shook her head, her ponytail flicking over each shoulder. I remembered how soft her hair had been and wondered if it still felt that way. "And speaking of losing, I'm not playing Monopoly with you again. You cheat."

"I cheat?" Was she for real? "The last time we played you launched a communist revolt and tried to redistribute all the property and money."

"That's because it's what's fair." The twinkle was back in her eyes.

"No, it was because you were about to lose. You've always been such a sore loser."

She stayed quiet for a moment, like she was thinking about what I'd just said. I hadn't meant for it to be serious; I liked teasing her. Always had. She said, "I don't want to say you're right because I don't like to give the impression that I might have been wrong about something, but you're somewhat correct. I hate to lose. Anything. Especially people. Especially . . ."

Her voice trailed off, and she stared at me with such intensity that my knees went hollow and my chest suddenly felt too tight. Who had she hated losing? Me? Or was she still worried about her mother?

"Look," I said, my palms suddenly feeling sweaty. Why was I nervous? I had no time to analyze my weird reaction. "Before the whole overprotective-motherus-interruptus thing upstairs, I wanted to clear the air."

"Air clearing is overrated. I'm a fan of a nice thick fog where everyone can stay in a haze of ignorance." She joked, but I could hear a tremor in her voice. "There's nothing to clear. Thanks for the apology, but it's not necessary. Everything happened a long time ago, and we're adults. We've both moved on. I mean, you moved on all the way to the East Coast. So we're good. We can be friends. Just friends."

Why had she said she'd moved on? Was she dating someone? Jealousy flared to life inside my gut. "Yeah. I didn't ask for anything more."

Ember's face flushed, and I realized that I had said the absolute wrong thing. I hadn't meant it like I wasn't interested, because I had come to the realization that I would probably always be in love with her, but that I wanted her to know that I didn't have any expectations and was happy to go along with whatever she wanted.

I reached for her hand. "Wait. I didn't say that right—"

"No." She pulled back and folded her arms. "Don't . . . it's fine. We can be mature and polite, and everything will be fine. We're going to be at the same school. I'm sure we'll run into each other. And we'll be helping my mom with her bucket list, right?"

"Right." Yeah, I had no plans to do that. Especially now.

"Okay. So we're good. Everything's good." She nodded once, as if to reassure both of us that she meant what she'd said, and she left the kitchen.

I balled my hand up into a fist. Both times I'd tried to fix things between us, I'd somehow made them worse.

But this was what I'd chosen. To be back in Washington State, back close to my family. And close to her.

I was going to have to man up and respect her boundaries. Just friends. I looked at my hand. That just-friends thing was going to be difficult if I kept trying to touch her every time we were in the same room.

That meant no more being in the same room together. I was going to have to stay far, far away from Ember Justine Carlson.

CHAPTER THREE

EMBER

Six months later . . .

Staying away from Bash turned out to be surprisingly easier than I would have expected. Mom's test came back clean, and she returned to teaching at the high school in the fall. She'd been tested twice since then, and everything still looked good.

And even though her prognosis was excellent, she still wanted to accomplish things on what she was now calling her survivor list. Our time was limited to weekends and holidays. I spoke with my volleyball coach, explaining the situation to her, and since her own mother had dealt with breast cancer, she was happy to let me have some time off here and there.

I couldn't go to everything; I did miss out on bungee-cord jumping in Las Vegas (which I was very happy to avoid because, while I hadn't tested the theory completely, I suspected that I was afraid of heights). We did a 5k run to support breast-cancer research. We spent an entire day in a high-end luxury spa in Seattle, being pampered and catered to.

We also spent Thanksgiving in Indonesia, which was strange because my mom had always been so big into traditions, and it was beyond weird not to be at home with a game on and the kitchen smelling like turkey and pumpkin pie. We did find a restaurant serving an American Thanksgiving dinner, only they had substituted duck for the turkey. It was fun experiencing new things, but part of me wished we were back home.

Although if we'd stayed in Washington, there was a chance Bash might have joined us. He had a home game Thanksgiving weekend that prevented him from going out of the country, and I was secretly relieved. I also didn't have to deal with him at Christmas. His grandparents had missed him and asked him to spend half of his winter break at their house, and the plan was for him to return home in time for the holiday. Doug and Marley had been so excited, hanging up his stocking and setting aside the ornaments with his name on them so that he could put them on the tree himself.

But a terrible blizzard had closed the airport, and he wasn't able to get back until after Christmas Day.

Then my mom, Lauren, and I left to go to Michigan to visit my mother's extended family, and a supercharged version of the same storm that had hit Pennsylvania hit us, too. No power for several days, roads impassable. We stayed a week longer than we had planned.

Which meant I had missed the first week of classes. Most of my new professors were understanding and helped me get the materials I needed to catch up.

The lone exception was my biochemistry teacher. After class I'd explained my situation, and he wished me luck and said that he didn't make notes available for students who failed to show up for class. And that he advised the ones who did respect his time not to share their notes. Which would be to my detriment because things he'd already taught would be on the midterms.

Obviously, I was going to hate that class. I left in a huff, nearly flattening a little blonde woman who had been a witness to our whole exchange as she waited for her turn to speak to the professor.

My next class was college algebra. It was on the easy side as far as math classes went, and it was my one math requirement to get my bachelor of science in nursing. When my mom had fallen sick, I'd decided that I wanted to help other families the way that ours had been helped. I wanted to be there for other teen girls worrying about losing their mom, so I decided to become an oncology nurse. My mom had been so proud of my decision.

It hadn't been easy, but I was determined. I had much harder classes scheduled for next year, so I thought it would be better to get math out of the way now.

The algebra class was in a large lecture hall filled mostly with freshmen. I settled into a seat near the back, pulling out my laptop to take notes and a pad of paper for working out any problems the professor might put on the board.

"Is this seat taken?"

My heart twisted and turned in my chest as the air inside my lungs solidified.

Bash.

Without waiting for me to respond, he sat next to me. His leg brushed against mine as he settled in, and a lash of electricity burned its way up to my stomach. I moved both of my legs away, not making eye contact.

"What are you doing here?" I asked.

It had been surprisingly easy to keep all things Bash related on a low simmer in the back of my brain. Sure, I had twinges where I missed him. That was nothing new—it had been going on for nearly four years. And maybe they were a bit worse since I knew he was so close by. Especially when I was in the athletics building, training or practicing.

When I could hear the football team lifting weights next door and knew that he was there, just out of reach.

And sometimes those twinges turned into full-blown I-miss-Bash attacks. It happened mostly when I let myself overworry about my mom. Even after all this time, he was still the first person I wanted to call when things got hard.

But that was only occasionally. For the most part my life was steady. Peaceful. Just the way I liked it.

Alas, all good things had to come to an end.

And I was feeling one of those full-body attacks right now. He was so close, and he had obviously just showered, because he smelled like soap and his favorite brand of shampoo, and it was such an intoxicating and familiar blend that my mouth actually went dry.

"What am I doing here? I'm here for algebra class. Just like you." He said it with a smirk that on anybody else would have been annoying, but on him was just totally endearing.

It felt surreal to be sitting here, just having a conversation with him, like we'd done it a million times before and would do it another million times. As if we hadn't spent the last few years not having conversations.

I tried to come up with some clever retort, but I had nothing.

"Hey, Bash." A tall girl with chestnut-brown hair and an athletic frame sat down on the other side of me, leaning over to say hi to him. She offered him her fist, and he bumped it.

"What up, Sabrina? Hey, have you met Ember? She's . . ." His voice trailed off as he looked at me, obviously not sure what to say next. "An old friend."

Sabrina had a bright smile, and she gave me a little wave. "Hi. Nice to meet you."

"You too."

My brain had immediately flipped into jealous-girlfriend mode. *Who is this woman? Is she dating Bash? Why is she so pretty? Does he love her?*

"Sabrina's on the team and is completely awesome. Coach just recruited her to be our starting kicker. And she's already killing it," Bash said.

"Wow. That's really impressive," I said. I didn't want to give her any cool points, but even JUCO football teams were highly competitive. Very few women got football scholarships.

She shrugged. "I love the game. And EOL is actually going to let me play, unlike my last school."

The professor at the front of the room held a stack of papers aloft. "This is the study guide for your first test, which will take place in two weeks. Come down and grab a copy!"

"I'll get them for us," Bash offered, running down the steps to reach the teacher's table at the front of the hall.

"Are you two dating?" Sabrina asked. Ruh-roh. Was she in jealous-girlfriend mode, too? She didn't look envious. Just curious, her expression honest and open.

"No!" The word exploded out of my chest. "No. Nope. Definitely not. No."

"So that's a maybe, then?" she teased, and given her sense of humor, I could see why Bash thought she was awesome.

"What about you?"

"Me and Bash?" she asked. She raised her eyebrows briefly, as if considering. "We're not. Could we? No. Don't get me wrong, he's a great guy and is one of the few in my career who hasn't tried to harass and/or hook up with me. But I learned a long time ago to never date teammates. It gets messy."

Bash chose that moment to return, and I thanked him for getting me a copy of the study guide. His long fingers brushed against mine . . . and I dropped my paper. Which slid across the floor and under the seat of the student in front of me. Humiliated, I tapped on her shoulder and asked if she could return it. I didn't need to look at Bash to know that he would be grinning.

Other than the current embarrassment, the strange thing was how normal this all felt. Yes, I was totally aware of Bash's body and its proximity to mine, the heat pulsing out of him that beckoned me closer, the way his clothes strained against him, as if they could barely contain all that muscular hotness. But other than that, I was just sitting in a class that I apparently shared with him, and it was . . . okay.

"How are your other classes going?" Bash asked.

I filled him in on my delayed return, and since I was still upset about it, the story about my biochem professor's refusal to let me have any notes from the first week came tumbling out. Both Bash and Sabrina made sympathetic noises and threw in a couple of "that sucks" for me.

"If you need help catching up in here, I have a friend named Jess who is really good at math. I could get her number for you," Bash said.

Another her? Crazy Jealous Girlfriend Brain returned. *Who is this Jess? Does Bash like her? What did he mean by* friend? *How hard would it be to destroy her?*

The professor called the class to order, and while I was still totally distracted by all things Bash, I did manage to listen and even understood some of what he was saying. But they must have gone over some of the concepts the week prior; I wasn't quite getting everything. I didn't know about this Jess person, but I could go to the athletic department's academic adviser, Keilani, and have her point me in the right direction for some minor tutoring.

Bash held his pencil against his lips. His very masculine, delicious lips, if I recalled correctly. Firm and perfect. Bash was good at a lot of things, but he'd been a genuine All-American at kissing.

His gaze caught mine, and I quickly looked away, feeling the heat rising to my cheeks. What was wrong with me? Why couldn't I just put Bash squarely in the Friends and People I Don't Get to Date categories?

Class finally came to an end, and I'd only fantasized about climbing into Bash's lap and kissing him four times, so I was counting that as a win.

"I'm heading over to the Smithson to grab some lunch," Bash said, naming the student center that held our food court. "Do you guys want to join me?"

Yes. The word crashed into the back of my lips so hard I had to purse them shut to keep it from escaping. I shouldn't want to go, but I did.

"Sure!" Sabrina said, standing up and sliding her backpack on.

Bash also stood. "Ember?"

My throat was inexplicably tight. I swallowed and then coughed. I was not one to turn down food, ever. But I'd had enough Bash nearness for one day. "I have some other stuff to do."

"Okay. See you around."

I watched him and Sabrina leave, my stomach curling up when she nudged him in the arm and he let out a laugh at whatever she'd said. Sighing, I packed up my own bag, careful to slide the laptop into its protective case.

As I headed out of the classroom and into the bustling hallway, I felt a tap on my left shoulder. I turned around to see someone who was like the photo negative of me. Petite, blonde, expensive clothes, and a smile that made it look like she was perpetually happy. She looked like the kind of girl who had a pet unicorn and a goblin bodyguard at home. She literally smelled like cupcake frosting. It was making me hungry.

Then I realized she was the same woman I'd seen in my biochem class after the professor had reprimanded me. "Can I help you?" I asked.

"You can, actually. I have kind of a strange proposition for you. Can we sit?"

CHAPTER FOUR

EMBER

The tiny blonde gestured toward a pair of padded stools situated in front of long windows. I nodded and walked over to one of the seats. I was curious as to what she had to say, and I instinctively trusted anyone who smelled like baked goods. I noted that it was snowing again as I grabbed one of the stools, sitting cross-legged.

"So, I'm Bethany." She formally offered me her Lollipop Guild–size hand, and I shook it, taking care not to crush her.

"I'm Ember."

"Are you in the nursing program, too?"

"I am."

She nodded. "That's why we have a couple of classes in common. And you know that guy you were sitting with in algebra today? Bash?"

"Yeah. He's my . . ." What I wanted to say was *his dad is married to my mom, but we're not related and have never even really lived in the same house together, so I don't consider him to be my stepbrother, although I guess technically he is, and we used to date when we were in high school, and we're only sort of friends so not really close or anything like that.* I settled on the same phrase he'd used. "He's an old friend. Why?"

She looked uncomfortable. "Do you like cookies?"

I hadn't expected that. "I freaking love cookies."

She opened up her purse and pulled out a Ziploc bag with two giant chocolate-chip cookies. At least, they'd better be chocolate chips. If she was trying to pull some oatmeal-raisin situation on me, we were going to have words.

I questioned my lifelong stance on not carrying a purse. I'd never seen the point. My cell phone case had slots for my ID and debit card, and I could stick it in my backpack or my pocket. Why bother with a whole other bag?

I knew other women used purses for things like lipsticks and tampons and wallets. But as a cookie-transportation system? That idea had definite merit.

"Thanks." I took a bite of the chocolate-chip cookie, and it was divine. Soft, chewy, with huge chocolate chips. "Seriously, again, thank you. This is amazing."

Was she just some kind of cookie fairy, lifting the spirits of depressed college students? This was another idea I could get behind. If this was a Pied Piper situation, and she was planning on luring me away, I was pretty sure it was going to work.

"I'm good at making cookies, don't you think?" Bethany asked.

I nodded. "You're fantastic at it. You should open up your own shop. Or I'll kick out one of my roommates, and you can move in and bake as much as you'd like."

She waved my suggestion away. "Since I've proven to you that I'm good at something I say I'm good at, I'm also amazing at taking notes. Like, exceptional. I record the lectures and then go back and fill in my outlines with any details I might have missed in class."

Bethany took out a notebook and placed it on her lap. "Sorry for eavesdropping, but I heard you saying you needed the notes from Professor Kozwolski's class. You can copy my notes, and you won't miss anything he said while you were gone."

Whoa. That was a level of academic dedication I was unused to witnessing. This whole thing was confusing. "But he said he told the students not to share notes."

"He said he 'strongly encouraged' us not to. That's not a rule."

"I think he still meant 'don't do this.'"

"Then he should have used his words more precisely," she said in a prim tone. "Are you interested?"

What kind of sorcery was this? She was offering me incredible cookies and was willing to lend me excellent notes? "What's the catch?"

"It's not really a catch. More of a . . . quid pro quo."

"What can I offer you? I'm pretty much *quo* free."

"You can set me up with your old friend Bash. I've had a bit of a crush on him since football season. I just haven't worked up the courage to talk to him. And trust me, I know how pathetic and desperate this sounds. But I broke up with my high-school boyfriend a month ago and realized that I have no idea how to talk to a new guy or get him interested in me other than sending a kissy face or winking emoji. But if you could talk to him . . ."

This was what I was willing to do for baked goods and a passing grade. Pimp out Bash. Even if it felt like she'd just sucker punched me.

But I really needed those notes.

"Leave it to me," I said, hoping my smile didn't look fake. "I'll make the introductions, and we'll get it set up. I even know where he is right now. You should come over with me and meet him." It shouldn't be that hard to convince him. Bethany was pretty, seemed hardworking, and could bake. Bash would probably marry her if I saved one of these cookies for him. I crammed the leftover one into my mouth instead.

"Thanks. This whole thing is so weird. I can't believe I even talked to you about this. It's very unlike me. It's actually kind of stressing me out," she said with a laugh as she began to dig through her purse. More cookies? Yes, please. "And if I'm going to actually talk to him, I probably need to, you know."

She pulled out a package of Tic Tacs and opened it up. "Do you ever stop and wonder how many calories there are in these things?"

Was she serious? I looked at her face. Oh no, she was. It was in that moment that I knew we could never be friends. Some things in life you just know with a hundred percent certainty, and this was one of them.

I didn't need to be her friend. I just needed her notes. "Yep. Okay. Let's head over to the Smithson, and I'll get this set up. You hang back, and I'll arrange everything."

We walked over to the food court, crunching through the snow, and we made small talk, comparing our other classes, since we shared a major. My mind was somewhere else, though. Here I'd made up concerns about Sabrina or Jess when there was someone else waiting in the wings to try and claim Bash's heart.

It shouldn't have bothered me, but it totally did.

Bash was easy to find in the midst of the food court. He was the best-looking, tallest, and broadest guy in the place, with the biggest mountain of food in front of him. And he was digging into it like a pack of lions attacking a zebra. It was one of the things I'd always liked best about him. How he ate like they'd just invented it. Because it meant that when we went out to eat, he was never one of those guys who was like, *Are you sure you want to order dessert?* as they looked you up and down.

I grabbed a bag of vegetable chips so that I had a reason to be here and paid a ridiculous amount of money for them to the nice man at the register. I wondered what had happened to Sabrina. Maybe she'd taken one look at Bash's carnage and fled.

"Hey," I said as I sat at Bash's table. "I see you didn't leave anything for the rest of the student body."

He swallowed quickly and then said, "First come, first gets all the food. I decided to go ahead and have second lunch while I was here."

"As one does." I opened my bag of veggie chips and ate a few. I didn't gag this time like I had the last time I'd eaten these.

"Twice in one day, huh? Are you stalking me now?" he asked with a wink as he settled a plate of spaghetti in front of himself.

If anything, I was rather adept at doing the opposite. "Hardly. I just needed something to eat." I shook the bag.

"That doesn't seem like something you'd eat. More like something they'd give to the hamsters at the pet store."

"Shows what you know. Don't mock my nutritionally woke food. One of my New Year's resolutions was to eat healthier." I did not tell him that I had broken this resolution only minutes earlier, or that my other resolutions were mainly about not doing what I was doing right now. Being around / talking to him. "These are chips made out of vegetables. Which basically means I'm eating a salad."

"Check the label. Those aren't healthy."

"Says the man downing enough carbs to feed an Olympic swim team." I turned the bag around and read the ingredients. "This is made from, like, spinach and beets. Anything that comes from the ground is basically healthy, right?"

"Potatoes come from the ground. If you're going to eat something like that, at least enjoy yourself. Like me. I'm enjoying myself. I feel like I owe fealty to the Smithson for all the delicious food."

"That's what the money's for," I told him.

"Maybe I should name our firstborn child after it. Smithson Sebastian."

Our? Had he actually just said *our* firstborn child? I was low-key hallucinating. Add to that the fact that I'd spent the last two and a half weeks eating those bad-for-you vegetable chips and today was becoming rather disappointing. I threw the bag on the table and reached over to grab some of Bash's fries, which were at the opposite end. We ate in silence for a couple of minutes while I tried to figure out a smooth transition for the Bethany situation.

"This is nice," he said.

"What? Me stealing your food?" I stole some more.

"No. Today's been nice. It was fun sitting next to you in class, being able to talk like friends again."

Well, I'd been all for ignoring the your-dad-married-my-mom-and-we-haven't-talked-in-years elephant in the room, but he wasn't wrong. "It was nice." It was one of the things I'd always liked about hanging out with Bash. The camaraderie that happened without us even trying. I had always felt like the best version of myself when I was with him.

So, obviously, I had to find a way to take away nice and normal and make it all stupid again. "Are you dating anyone?"

Bash froze. Like, pigeons-could-have-landed-on-him level of freezing. And he stayed that way for longer than was comfortable. He gulped down whatever had been in his mouth. "No. Why? Are you seeing someone?"

"Only if I close my eyes and concentrate real hard." Why was he being so weird about this? It wasn't like I'd asked for the password to his phone or something. I was just . . . making conversation. To find out if Bethany, Giver of Sweet Things, had a shot.

Okay, I was doing it badly, but still.

"I meant, are you dating anyone?" he asked. Then his lips did that little sardonic twist that I'd always loved, and I just barely prevented myself from sighing.

"Nope. I'm single and ready to act awkward around anyone I find even a little bit attractive." I grabbed more fries. How could I have ever thought I could give up fried potatoes? I must have been in a vegetable-chip-induced madness.

"You were never awkward," he said in a way that made my stomach flip. Or maybe it was the veggie chips staging a coup against the tasty food I was eating. Regardless, he was a big old liar.

And now I was feeling plenty awkward. "Look, I was going to try and be slick about this, but here's the truth. My new friend, Bethany, much to my surprise, is interested in going out with you."

"How well do you know Bethany?" He had a weird expression on his face, almost like he'd eaten something bad. Which didn't make any sense because he once ate almost an entire pound of potato salad that gave everyone else on the football team food poisoning. He had an iron stomach, both inside and out.

"How well do I know her? Not as well as you're going to." Ugh. I was grossing myself out. I could not be his wingman. What was I thinking?

He seemed to share in my sentiment as he didn't even crack a smile. "Seriously."

"Don't look a gift hot chick in the mouth. I'm sure she fits all of your superhigh standards. Like, she's alive, and she's interested in you." She also lacked curves of any kind other than the ones on her chest, and I had my suspicions about those.

While I was pondering whether or not to mention the chocolate-chip cookies, he asked, "Why didn't she come talk to me herself?"

"I don't know. There was this whole thing about how she broke up with her longtime boyfriend and wasn't sure how to approach you, and she said she'd lend me her notes for biochem if I would just talk to you, and . . ." Again, my mouth went faster than my brain could keep up, and I'd probably just ruined everything.

He blinked slowly. "You're whoring me out?"

"Nobody's getting paid. It's more of a tradeoff. And it's good for you. She's cute, and when you ask her out, she's going to say yes. Please?"

Something in my tone must have affected him because he just shook his head, and that good old Bash smile was back. It meant things were okay between us. "I haven't asked a girl out in so long, I'm not sure I remember how it's done."

"Just use that charm you think you have and those things called words, and you'll be fine." I grabbed his melting chocolate milkshake and took a big gulp.

He leaned back against the booth, crossing his arms. He studied me while I slurped down the rest of his milkshake. Resolution broken again.

"I have an idea," he announced, and something in his expression set off warning bells.

Excellent. I just knew that somehow Bash was about to make everything stupider.

"I'll do it on one condition."

"What's that?" I asked.

"You let me set you up with a guy from the football team."

"Why?" It was bad enough that I was setting Bash up. I didn't want him to do the same. Even though I knew he didn't want me and we had a weird family situation, as long as he didn't do stuff like set me up with his friends, I could still daydream.

"You do something nice for me, I do something nice for you. It's what friends do. An even trade."

I pushed the metal milkshake cup away and let out a groan of disgust. "When did this school turn into one giant bartering system?"

"What?" he asked, understandably confused.

"Nothing," I said with a wave. "But I'm running out of stuff I can trade. I mean, if we keep going down this road, I'm going to have to start doing unspeakable things to the guy at the register just to get some ice cream."

He continued to seem confused, and I wisely refrained from explaining my trade tirade and kept the details of the cookie bribing to myself. No need to add gasoline to the fire.

"Is that your bizarre way of saying yes? And that we'll make this a double date so that it'll be less awkward for everyone?"

What? How on earth could a double date possibly be less awkward? I so did not want to agree to that. I looked across the cafeteria to where Bethany was watching us with a hopeful look on her face, and I really wanted the nice cookie lady to feel better. I also still really wanted her notes.

"I think it might make it more awkward, but whatever. I'm in. That's Bethany over there." I waved to her, and she gave me the most enthusiastic wave back that I'd ever personally witnessed. Like a beauty queen on meth.

"Wish me luck," he said as he got up and made his way over to her. She jumped out of her seat, nervously shifting her weight back and forth as he approached.

Like a glutton for punishment, I watched it happen with a heightened heartbeat. I wanted her to say no, even though I knew she wouldn't. I wanted him to botch it so badly that he had to slink away in shame. But given his charm and sense of humor, there was nothing he couldn't bounce back from. Even if he did mess up, he'd make it cute and adorable somehow.

They greeted each other, and I wished I could hear what they were saying. He smiled, she smiled. I could see her nervousness seeping away. They looked like a short Barbie and an overgrown Malibu Ken. Even in boots with heels she barely reached his bicep. Then she put her hand on said bicep, laughing at something he'd said.

Why was my heart clenching so hard? Why was it suddenly so difficult to breathe? I mean, Bash had to have dated other people while we were apart. I certainly had. But I'd never had to watch one of his dates happening in front of me in real time. Like a slow-motion car wreck that I couldn't look away from. Then they exchanged their phones to give one another their contact information.

OMG, this was it. They were going to get married, and I'd have to see her at holiday dinners where she'd wonder out loud how many pesticides were on the lettuce because they were obviously going to get married, and their wedding invitations would have intertwined *B*'s on them, and the theme would be "meant to bee" with those honeypots and mason jars everywhere, and they'd have little blond babies and get a golden retriever and live happily ever after.

It was possible I was overthinking this.

Bash returned and sat back down. "She said yes. I'll get everything set up and text you the date and time. Is your phone number still the same?"

Still the same as it had been back when I thought I was the one who would have his blond babies someday? "Yes."

"My number's the same, too. We'll talk soon. And maybe after the date we can have a post-game recap. As friends."

"Okay."

He walked away, and I stayed at the table, sadly surveying the left-over wrappers and whole chicken carcass he'd left behind.

What had I done?

CHAPTER FIVE

BASH

What had I done?

Why had I asked Bethany out on a date? Was it some immature thing where my subconscious mind was acting out, like, *If Ember's over me and can push me off on someone else, then I'm going to show her that I'm in the same place emotionally and it wouldn't bother me at all for her to go out with one of my teammates?*

While I was supposed to be wrestling with the fine art of astronomy, instead I was thinking about Ember and why I'd gone along with her scheme. It couldn't have been a petty I'll-show-you situation because Ember had told me months ago at the house that she had moved on. That she wasn't looking for an apology or an explanation and that she wanted us to be *just* friends. It was hard to forget the emphasis on the word *just*.

She'd made it painfully obvious that there was nothing between us. Finding out that she'd had the same phone number she'd had back in high school . . . it stirred up a mixture of nostalgia and regret. It was a good thing she'd never called me after I moved. I probably would have picked up. But she hadn't called. I'd always assumed it was out of anger. And maybe it was in the beginning, but now . . . now I knew better.

When I'd accepted Coach Oakley's offer, I hadn't known that Ember was at EOL. But I did know where her mom and younger sister would be. I knew that I was going to have a way to get in touch with her. And I wanted that more than anything, to see her again. To see if we could be friends moving forward, once I'd cleared the air and apologized for my stupid teenage behavior.

I had to accept that the decision I'd made all those years ago was still the right one.

But even now . . . even after I'd stayed away and reminded myself that we couldn't be together, I still wanted her. I still felt that spark when we touched. Felt totally enthralled whenever she was speaking and couldn't wait to hear what she was going to say next. And when she'd talked about doing unspeakable things to the guy in the food court, my mind had wandered into not-suitable-for-work territory.

I liked being with her, hanging out with her. I always had.

And friends was better than nothing. Which I knew for a fact because I'd had nothing for almost four years.

So I was going to have to set her up with one of my teammates. I ran through a mental checklist of who was actually single, and who I would trust to take out Ember.

Only one name came to mind. Once class ended, I pulled out my cell phone and called Todd Woodby. He was the slowest texter I'd ever met, and I didn't currently have the patience to wait for his response.

Woodby picked up right away. "Yo, what is up, you mother flipper?" he asked.

Coach had a no-swearing rule, and while I was typically fine off the field, on the field was a different story. I got . . . passionate about the game. And I expressed that passion. Forcefully. So I had to come up with some . . . creative means of expressing my frustration, which consisted of substitute words. Which my teammates found totally hilarious and mocked me constantly.

My roommate, Logan, had once told me that whenever we were watching international sports and they started playing the Canadian national anthem, he always felt slightly scandalized since one of my favorite angry expressions was *O, Canada!* I couldn't explain why, but saying it angrily was really satisfying.

"Hey, Woodby. So, I have this girl—"

"Woodby likes where this is going already."

Too bad he couldn't see me rolling my eyes so hard I almost gave myself a concussion. "Come on, dude. Be serious and just listen for a second. There's this girl I know, Ember. I want to set you up with her."

"Oh, yeah? Is she hot like her name?"

I was beginning to rethink this entire situation. Woodby was being an idiot. "If you don't want to take this seriously, then . . ."

"No, I'm taking it seriously," he said with a laugh that negated his statement. "Tell me about her."

"She's . . ." At that I let my voice trail off. How could I describe Ember and everything that I loved about her to somebody like Woodby?

She had all of what I'd call "the basics" of what attracts you to someone. She was smart, beautiful, funny, hardworking, kind, generous. But then there were the other aspects of her that I adored. She was an athlete, like me. So she got how important that part of my life was. She loved food almost as much as I did, which I'd discovered was kind of intoxicating. She was fun to talk to and always made me laugh. I loved the way her mind worked, the weird things she'd come up with and share with me. She had this, I don't know, calming presence that made silence comfortable and made me feel better. Especially when things got tough. She didn't take herself too seriously and always seemed to roll with the punches.

"Ember is a lot of fun," was what I settled on. "You'll have a good time."

If he'd noticed how long my pause was, he didn't say anything about it. "Woodby's in. Just tell me when and where."

"I'll text you when I have all the details. Talk to you later."

During our conversation I'd managed to make it back to my dorm. I put my key in the lock, but to my surprise, Logan was in our room. I hadn't seen much of him lately as he was either in class getting ready to graduate, with his girlfriend, Jess (they'd been together since Coach Oakley had lifted his no-dating rule), or training in the weight room or out on the field. At the end of next month he'd be going to the NFL Scouting Combine, and he was trying to get in as much training as he could before he went.

He had wanted to put in a good word for me and see if he could get an invite for me as well, but I told him maybe next year before I graduated. My father hadn't gone to college, so it was always really important to him that Marley and I graduate. I wasn't going to let him down, again. Even if playing professional football was my dream.

"What are you doing here?" I asked. "Did that girlfriend of yours finally come to her senses and break up with you?"

He let out a short bark of laughter as I dropped my backpack onto my desk. "You're hilarious. No, she's on her way over. But I have a test this week, and I'm attempting to study in what little time I have."

"Have fun," I told him as I flopped onto my own bed, still wondering whether or not this double date was a good idea.

Logan put his book down. "What's going on with you? You look like you need to talk. You have but face."

"Did you really just call me a butt face?"

"No. You have the I-want-to-talk-about-my-feelings-*but*-I'm-a-man-so-I-can't face."

I probably should have been surprised, but ever since Jess came into his life, he'd been super in touch with his emotional side. I had mocked him for it on more than one occasion. "You should know all about that face."

"Yeah, I might have originated that face while I was busy being 'just friends' with Jess. Come on, lay it on me. I owe you."

He did owe me. Not only for all the feelings talks I'd endured previously from him, but also because the only reason he and Jess were together now was that I'd protected him and his secret. While I'd fought off my natural inclination to tease him endlessly for doing something so stupid as falling in love with the coach's daughter back when all dating had been declared off-limits, I'd also wanted to protect him and keep him at school. And on the team. He loved playing almost as much as I did. Not to mention that he was a big part of the reason why we'd won the junior college national championship. Logan had probably been the most excited of us all when Coach allowed the team to start dating again.

"There's a girl named Ember. We met our junior year in high school, and I fell for her hard and fast. We dated for months, and somehow in the midst of that, my dad and her mom met and fell in love and eloped."

"Uh-oh." I had his full attention now. "I think I can guess where this is going."

"That's where it went. She moved into my house, and my dad told me to steer clear. He didn't know we were together because I'd never told him. He had been heartbroken over my mom leaving him for a long time, and I didn't want to hurt him by telling him how in love I was. Anyway, I saw that he had a point. That odds were Ember and I wouldn't work out, and it would make it awkward for the rest of our families. About three weeks after her family moved in, I realized that the only way that I could stay away from her was to move out. I asked my maternal grandparents if I could come live with them, and that's what happened. My dad was sad, but he didn't try to stop me. I think he knew why I was doing it. And it sucked, and it was hard, and I missed her, but I did it. Anyway, it was probably the most mature decision I've ever made."

"Definitely." He nodded. "I can vouch for that."

"Shut up, man. I was trying to do the right thing. For me and for her."

"I've heard the road to hell is paved with girl intentions."

I chucked one of my pillows at him while he laughed. He sat up, tossing my pillow back. "Did you ever tell her that's why you moved out? Does she know?" he asked.

I shrugged my shoulders. "I'm not sure. How could she not, though? It was pretty obvious."

"Just because we think stuff is obvious doesn't mean other people perceive it in the same way. Maybe that's something you should share with her. And how did I not know any of this about you? You've always seemed like a bit of an oversharer."

"There's things I share because I don't really care about them and it doesn't matter who knows them."

"But Ember's different?"

She was. "But we're just friends now."

"Ha. Tell me something I didn't invent and fail miserably at," Logan said.

"What? It's true." I had to make it true. I didn't want to lose Ember again. She was too important to me.

"Yeah, that's what I spent months telling myself, too. It's obvious that you still have feelings for this girl."

He didn't get it. "This isn't about breaking some rule of Coach's. This is about my family. I mean, I don't think of her as being part of that, but I don't want to do anything that would wreck things for my dad and my sister."

"I'll admit, it's kind of a weird spot to be in, but it's not like you'd be the first person in the world this has ever happened to." He paused, as if considering whether or not he should say the next thing. "How often do you think about her?"

"What?"

"Just from personal experience, I've found that when you think about somebody constantly, when they're on your mind first thing in the morning and the last thing you think about before you fall asleep at night, either you're in love or dealing with some incredible heartache."

Both. It was both.

"Wow, that was deep for me, don't you think?" he asked with a laugh, going over to the mirror above his dresser to fix his hair.

"Yeah. Very uncharacteristic. But I was serious about the friends thing. I have to find a way to make this work. I mean, she told me she's over it. And she must be, since she's setting me up with someone else."

"Really? So you think that's proof?"

"It seems that way to me."

There was a knock at our door. "Let's ask Jess, shall we?"

I tried to say, *Don't drag Jess into this*, but it was too late. He greeted his girlfriend with a seriously thorough kiss because they were in a perpetual quest to finally take that gold medal in the PDA Olympics. They were literally joined at the tongue these days.

"I'm still in here. I didn't leave, just so you guys know."

Jess broke the kiss off, sheepishly saying, "Sorry. What's going on with you guys? Did I interrupt something?"

She made herself comfortable on Logan's bed, and he sat so close to her that they were basically conjoined twins.

"Don't worry about it. It's nothing," I said, right as Logan launched into a summarized version of what I'd just told him.

When I shot him a dirty look, he said, "What? I don't keep anything from my girl. And we need a woman's perspective. Do you think she set him up with someone else because she's over him?"

"It's hard to say without knowing her. But I think we're in a pretty strong either/or situation. Either she doesn't have feelings for you and is completely over you and has set you up with someone because of those non-feelings, or she does have feelings and knows you can't be together so she's making you off-limits to herself and encouraging you to date other people. I know how hard it is when you're falling for someone but can't date them."

"Then how come you didn't encourage me to date other people?" Logan asked in mock outrage.

"You weren't allowed to date anyone at all, and even if you had been, I still wouldn't have set you up with anyone. Because I wanted you to keep playing football, and you couldn't have done that with two slashed Achilles' heels."

Apparently amused at his girlfriend's jealousy and empty threat, he kissed her on the nose. They were so saccharine sweet it made my teeth ache.

"I set her up, too." I'd forgotten to mention that earlier.

"With who?" Jess asked.

"Woodby."

"Dude, mistake," Logan said with a grimace. "Woodby's a good guy. I mean, he tries too hard to be funny and wants to convert us all into vegetarians, but he's decent."

"Why is that a bad thing?" I only wanted the best for Ember.

"You should have set her up with somebody like Johnson. That guy's an a—idiot," he quickly corrected, "and she'd definitely never go out with him again."

"Yeah, but Johnson would never keep his hands to himself, and then I'd have to kill him, and I am not getting kicked off the team for it because I'm pretty sure that's one of Coach's rules. Thou shalt not kill."

"You're confusing him with the Bible," Logan said. "Which is a common mistake, given Coach thinks his rules were handed down from on high."

That made Jess giggle. She murmured something to Logan, and I was getting more grossed out by the minute.

"Just so you know," I informed them, "neither one of you has been any help."

Jess made a sad face at me. "I'm sorry. I wish I could do more. Maybe you should introduce us, and I can get to know her better and find out why she's doing this."

That idea had some merit. "She was saying that she's a little behind in algebra."

"Perfect! Send her to the math lab, and I will get to the bottom of this."

"I like when you get to the bottom of things," Logan said as he nuzzled behind her ear.

"I'm going to go and . . . vomit somewhere that's not here. My innocent eyes can't take any more of this," I announced, grabbing my keys and my phone before I left them to whatever shenanigans they had planned for the day.

I was going to keep telling myself that I thought they were disgustingly sweet and that nobody should have to witness it, but I suspected the truth was that I was more than a little jealous of what they shared.

And I wanted it for myself.

But not with someone like Bethany.

With Ember.

CHAPTER SIX

EMBER

I texted my mom, checking in with her as I walked across the campus's main quad. She sent me back a short message that said, I'm fine, Ember. I could practically hear her exasperation. I figured she should be happy that I was limiting myself to one text to her a day. I worried about her all the time. I couldn't help it.

Entering the math lab, I found the person I was looking for.

"Hi, Keilani," I said.

She smiled at me, but her smiles weren't like anyone else's. All of her infectious optimism seemed to bubble up inside of her and shined out from her face. You couldn't help but feel happy when you were around her.

"Hey, Ember! How are things going with you catching up?"

I filled her in on each class, telling her I had some concern about algebra. The teacher had told me what chapters to look at, and I'd decided to take Bash's advice (there was a first time for everything, right?) and head over to the math lab.

"Funny you should say that. I actually had a tutor request you, in case you came in."

"What?" That seemed strange.

"Her name is Jess Oakley." She stood up from behind her desk and waved to someone behind me.

Suddenly everything clicked in my brain. Jess. The girl Bash had told me about. Which meant he had to have talked to her about me, and I wasn't sure how to feel about that particular piece of information. But why would she request to tutor me?

She had dark-blonde hair and dark-brown eyes, and objectively, she was average. Okay, she was gorgeous, and I was already envious. "Hi, I'm Jess. It's so nice to finally meet you. Ember is such an unusual name. Where is it from?"

Inwardly I sighed. You'd think by now I'd be used to answering this question. "My dad was an award-winning poet, and they named me after his most famous poem, 'Embers of Our Dying Love.' Which probably should have been my mom's first clue that their marriage wasn't going to last."

"Was?" Keilani asked.

"About a year after he divorced my mom, he died in a car accident."

"Oh, I'm so sorry," Keilani said while Jess nodded sympathetically.

What I wanted to say was, *Don't be*, because he was a total deadbeat dad who had nothing to do with us and left all his prize poetry money to some scholarship foundation for poets. But then I remembered that it was the kind of thing I couldn't say out loud if I wanted people to think that I was normal and didn't have extreme daddy issues. So I said, "Thanks. It was a long time ago, and I'm okay."

A shadow passed over Keilani's face, which seemed strange since I'd just told her I wasn't upset about my father, but I realized her gaze was trained behind me. There was a tall, good-looking guy, a little older, talking to one of the students. They were laughing, and then they walked out of the room.

"What was that?" I couldn't help but ask.

"Someone who forgets about boundaries and where he is and is not supposed to go," Keilani muttered under her breath before turning back to her computer.

Feeling dismissed, I turned toward Jess, silently questioning what was going on. "Come with me," she whispered. "I will spill all the delicious tea on that particular situation."

We hurried over to an empty table, and I had only just sat down when Jess began to speak. "Okay, so that's Ford Blackwell. He's the quarterback coach for the football team. And I think he's secretly in love with Keilani, and even though she denies it, I know she's in love with him."

"How do you know?"

"Just some stuff she's said. And at Halloween last year they ran into each other at a party, but they were both in costume, so they didn't know who the other one was, and they had this fantastic conversation where they found out they had so much in common and were finishing each other's sentences. She really liked him, right up until he took off his mask."

"So what is up with them now?"

"Well," Jess said with a sigh, "I keep trying to get Keilani to admit how she feels, but she's a lot more stubborn than I'd realized. Apparently something happened at a Christmas party for the athletics department. I've heard rumors of mistletoe and a quick kiss, but Keilani refuses to confirm or deny, which is infuriating."

I found this all way more fascinating than I probably should have, but I'd always enjoyed harmless gossip. I took out my algebra book and laid it on the table. "We should probably get started. I'm a little lost. I did okay in math back in high school, but then Satan put the alphabet into algebra, and I've been floundering ever since."

Jess laughed as she took my book. "It's not as hard as it looks. We'll get you caught up in no time. I'm so glad that we're like roommates-in-law."

"Roommates-in-law?"

"Didn't Bash tell you? I'm dating his roommate, Logan. We've been together for a few months now."

I should probably stop jumping to conclusions that every woman in Bash's life was after him. "I didn't know that."

"Yeah. I've learned recently that Bash does keep some things to himself. Like he told us a little of your history with him." She looked distinctly uncomfortable, and I wondered if what he'd told her was bad. If we were really going to be friends, I felt like I needed to explain my side. To defend myself. I wanted her to have the whole story.

"I don't know what he said, but here's what actually happened."

~

I had a beyond-serious crush on Ian Sebastian from the moment that I'd moved to my new school. My mother had accepted a much better paying job at a high school about an hour away from our home, and we packed up and moved. I'd been really angry at the time because I'd had to leave my friends, but when she showed me the girls' volleyball team's stats for my new school, I'd been more on board.

I'd been able to join the team and practiced with them all summer and made new friends. As soon as school started, I immediately began scouting out which boys were actually tall enough for me. There were a couple on the basketball team, but they had that superlanky, skinny build. The only other guy was Bash.

He was perfect. And I fell hard without ever even speaking to him.

The thing is, when you become that obsessed with someone as a teenager, you manage to learn a lot about them. I don't mean just, like, their schedule (which I had memorized, naturally), but you watch them interact with their friends. In class. Hear them talking and find out what they like and don't like.

He was like a religion to me, and I was one fanatical cultist.

My friends were also constantly feeding me tidbits about him and supporting my delusion—"Bash is going to Jason's party this weekend, and he said he loves club music," or "Bash was so cute in English today where he talked about this time in third grade when he fell and broke his front tooth." They were the kind of friends who understood that when I said, "I saw my boyfriend today," they all knew that I meant Bash, who had no idea I existed.

Or when I said, "We ate lunch together," that no, we hadn't sat at the same table and had a conversation, but since we were in the same giant room at the same time, it counted.

And things stayed that way up until one day in my junior year. It was a couple of hours after school had let out, and I was in the process of trying to break into my mom's classroom.

Bash found me, kneeling in front of the door with the lock-pick tools I had ordered off the internet. "Hey, Ember. I never figured you for a cat burglar."

The entire world came to a screeching halt. My blood turned slow and thick while my heart hammered so hard against my chest, it was like a hummingbird trying to break out of a cage.

Bash.

Talked.

To.

Me.

And he knew my name.

And instead of having some witty response, I actually said, "You know my name?"

He leaned against the wall, all sexy-like with a charming grin. "I make it a point to know the names of all the pretty girls at school."

I died. Literally died and left my body and hovered above our conversation watching it happen like some scene out of a movie that could not be real.

"Why are you breaking into your mom's classroom?"

"You know who my mom is?" This was all starting to feel a bit like a fever dream. Or a hallucination.

If so, my imagination was *awesome*.

"Yeah." He said it like I had asked a really weird question. "And you still haven't answered me as to why you're breaking and entering."

My brain started to function again, which was very helpful. "Well, so far I'm just messing around with the lock, so I haven't broken anything and I definitely haven't entered yet. But it's because my mom took my cell phone a week ago, and I'm on a mission to liberate it."

"Why did she take it?"

"Annaliese texted me, and I was responding because that's just good manners. I mean, my mother is the one who taught me to be polite. But did she see it that way? Noooo."

"And where did you learn to pick locks? Or attempt to pick locks, since you haven't actually done it yet?"

"Duh, YouTube." And the patron saint of unrequited love must have been smiling down on me because I heard that clicking sound that meant I had unlocked the door. I shot a smirk at Bash, as if I'd known exactly what I was doing and was actually that cool.

He was suitably impressed, letting out a low whistle as we entered the room. I was floating around on a runner's high and went over to my mom's desk. I opened her bottom drawer and saw my phone. I grabbed it, feeling a sense of relief. Similar to how I figured a drug addict would feel if they'd opened the drawer and found a big bag of cocaine.

"Won't she get mad?"

The sound of his voice shocked me as I'd momentarily forgotten he was in the room, since I was so excited to be reunited with my phone. I knocked a jar of pens and pencils to the floor.

I crouched down to pick them up. "Better to ask forgiveness than permission, right?"

As he bent down to help me, his fingers brushed against mine, and I jumped, as if he'd scalded me. It wasn't something I could play off. It had been really obvious.

"Sorry," I said. "I guess I'm feeling a little flustered."

He gave me a half smile. "Flustered? Are you saying I fluster you?"

Why was he like this? Boys in high school were supposed to have acne, braces, dandruff, and questionable body odor. They were supposed to be in the AV club and really into some online game. They were not supposed to be handsome and charming and flirt with you like they'd been taking classes in it.

Then he reached for my hand, and my whole hand pulsed and pulsed, like a giant heartbeat, while tingles ran up and down my arm.

"Maybe," he said, "we could go out some time and see if the fluster is just school related, or if I can fluster you in the real world, too."

The fluster was real in every situation. We watched a Jane Austen movie for English. I'd used it as an excuse to contact him, and we started dating from there. I'd always been close to my mom, but I didn't tell her about Bash. I didn't tell my friends, either. They would have thrown me a party if they had known. They would have created a holiday called Bash Day to commemorate the momentous occasion of us going on a real date.

But I kept him to myself. I didn't want to share him with anyone else. I didn't tell anyone that we had cutesy nicknames for each other. He called me *E* and I called him *B*. Yes, they were for the first letter of our names, but they were also short for *breaking* and *entering*. Which was when Bash said he started to fall hard for me.

I knew eventually I would have to tell the world, but I liked it being just the two of us.

We dated for months, and I was grateful that I hadn't told anyone about us dating because I didn't have to deal with their pity when it all fell apart.

It was nearly prom, and we had decided it would be our coming-out as an official couple. Bash planned to ask me in a really extravagant way, in front of the entire school. He wouldn't tell me what he had planned, but I was excited to spring our surprise on all our friends.

Only, we were the ones surprised when our parents told us they had met, fallen in love, and eloped after dating for three weeks.

And that I was moving into Bash's house.

I tried calling him that night, but he didn't answer.

Two days later, when I moved in, suddenly he was never around. There was no more mention of prom, no response to my texts or emails. He basically ghosted me even though we were living in the same house and going to the same school.

For three weeks, the same amount of time it took our parents to have an entire relationship and decide to get married, Bash ignored me.

Until one night when I was supposed to have been home alone. Bash was out with his friends, like always. Doug and my mom had gone to see a play in downtown Seattle. Lauren and Marley had gone to a sleepover birthday party. And I had plans with my friends but at the last minute begged off so that I could stay home and enjoy having the house to myself for once.

I decided to eat a sleeve or two of Oreos and take a bubble bath. I was a pathetic excuse for a teenager. I had an empty house, and the worst thing I could come up with was bathing and being reckless with sugar and gluten.

It was nice, wearing my earbuds and listening to my favorite songs while I blocked the whole world out. I didn't have to think of the crushing heartache that had become my daily companion because my boyfriend had ditched me, or how uncomfortable I was in the Sebastian house that did not feel like home. I could just zone out and relax.

I finished my bath and my Oreos and wrapped a towel around myself to go back into my room.

Only when I got there, Bash was in the game room with three of his buddies. I hadn't heard them come in, and I could tell from the look on Bash's face he had no idea I was home. I had to walk past them to reach my room. For a second I just froze, taking in his friends' expressions. They were mocking me, but there was a hint of interest there. Holding my head up, I hurried as quickly as I could into my room and locked the door. I still had my earbuds in so I couldn't hear exactly what they were saying, but I knew I didn't want to find out.

I waited a minute or two before I removed my earbuds, hoping that they would have forgotten about me and gone back to their games. I heard noises, but it sounded far away. Like, downstairs. As I hurried and got dressed, the front door slammed shut. I went over to the windows and saw Bash's friends leaving.

I didn't see Bash.

When there was a knock on my door, I realized why.

"E, please let me in."

I had a moment where I wanted to refuse. To say nothing so that he could see what it felt like to be frozen out and ignored.

But my heart couldn't resist him. I unlocked the door. "What do you want?"

"To apologize. I'm so sorry. I didn't know you were here. If I had—"

"If you had, you wouldn't have come home," I finished. "Or, more accurately, back to your house. This isn't my home."

"But it should be. I want you to feel comfortable here. We have to figure out a way to make this whole thing work."

I turned around and walked over to my bed, sitting down. "There's no way for any of this to work."

He followed and sat next to me. "There has to be."

Sitting so close to me, he smelled so good and was so big and taking up all the space in my room. My heart had gone light and fluttery, like a giant butterfly, beating inside my chest. All I wanted to do was turn to him and have him hold me like he had so many times before. Without thinking, not able to help myself, I twined my arms around his neck and buried my face there.

I felt his hesitation, but it only lasted for half a moment before his arms were around me, squeezing me tightly. I had missed this so much.

"E. Ember. We can't."

We could. I pressed my lips against his throat and felt his Adam's apple bob, hard. There was some token resistance, and then he turned his face to mine, capturing my lips in a kiss. My entire body rejoiced in the feeling, like an internal chorus of angels sang in celebration of his mouth against mine.

It escalated quickly. I hadn't touched him or kissed him in weeks, and I was desperate for him. We went from zero to sixty in about one and a half seconds. There was no slow ramping up, just foot to the floor, immediate acceleration and speed.

Then he started to pull his head back, as if he intended to stop. I wasn't going to let him. I deepened the kiss, and he instantly responded, his mouth hard and driving and amazing. I had missed him, and I wanted to show him how much. He wouldn't talk to me, so this was the only way I had to communicate that to him.

We'd made out before. Lots of times. But it had never felt like this. There had never been so much . . . ferocity. Intensity. I reveled in it even as part of my brain whispered this probably wasn't a good idea.

I told it to be quiet.

Instead of listening to reason, I crawled into his lap so that I could kiss him better. He ran his hands up and down my back, and I could feel the strength of his touch, the warmth of his palms through my thin hoodie.

He hadn't shaved since that morning, and his stubble was scraping against my chin. It was rubbing my skin, turning it extra sensitive so that when he began to kiss along my jaw I nearly passed out from how good it felt. He had the world's most perfect lips, and I loved every single kiss I ever got from him.

As he moved his mouth down, I leaned my head back so that he could nibble along my throat. I let out a low sound of appreciation and pleasure and felt his hands tighten against me in response. Bash might not have been the world's best student, but he was a freaking genius when it came to kissing.

"E." He said my nickname against my collarbone, and that pleading sound was gone. Instead there was nothing but confidence there and a promise. A promise of things to come.

And I wanted those things more desperately than I'd wanted anything in my entire life.

He broke off the kiss, his breathing fast and uneven. "Why can't I stay away from you?" he asked.

"Why would you want to?" My lips felt swollen and neglected.

Bash shook his head. "Everything's changed."

"This hasn't." It didn't take much to get his mouth to return to mine, and his kisses became more deliberate. More exacting. Like he knew exactly what he was doing to me. He was drugging me with his touch. My limbs turned heavy, my brain turned completely off. Bash was the only thing in the world that mattered.

He leaned me back on the bed and then braced himself over me. I opened my eyes to see him looking at me, and he looked at me like . . . he loved me.

I loved him.

I pulled him to me, letting his weight crush me in the most delightful way possible. I intertwined my legs with his so that I could keep him in place, but he wasn't going anywhere. He kept drugging me with fire and pleasure until I became mindless with need.

I wanted more of his warmth, more of his touch, more of his skin.

Tugging at his shirt, I whispered, "Take it off."

He pulled back. "Are you sure?"

It was further than we'd ever gone. "Yes."

That was all he needed, and he reached over his shoulder to tug his shirt off with one hand, leaving his impressive chest on display. I'd never seen him like this, and I was fascinated by his muscles, by the planes and ridges that curved and straightened back out. I ran my fingers over them, loving his harsh breaths and how his breath would catch when I touched a sensitive spot. There was so much strength under his soft skin. His abdomen clenched when my fingers brushed against it.

"You're so beautiful," I said, my voice full of wonder.

Then his mouth was on mine, and I continued my exploration, the smooth but strong warmth of his skin heating up my palms. Fire coursed through my veins, a fire that burned hard and strong but didn't die out. It just burned and burned until I knew that the fire was going to consume me. I didn't care. I wanted it. I wanted him, like this, forever. And in that moment, it was enough.

Until it wasn't. Until I wanted his skin against mine.

As if he'd read my mind, it was his turn to explore. His hands moved over me like liquid flame, burning and igniting my skin everywhere he touched. I felt his fingers against my stomach, trailing a path down to my hips. He lifted the band of my yoga pants and took my hip in his hand, squeezing tightly and rocking me against him.

The sensation was incredible. I gasped.

"Is this what you want?" he asked in a voice so low and sexy it was hypnotic.

"I want you. Just you. I love you."

I was breathing so hard I wondered if I might actually pass out.

But it stopped.

Everything just stopped.

I opened my eyes and couldn't focus for a second. Bash was sitting at the foot of my bed, his head in his hands. It took me a minute to get control of all my limbs.

"B?" I moved over to him and put my hand against his shoulder. He jerked away from me. Without even looking at me, he grabbed his shirt and left.

I was too stunned to chase after him. I sat there, unable to catch my breath, my entire body pulsing with need for him. What had just happened?

I never got the chance to ask him.

He moved out the next day.

~

"Wow," Jess breathed. "That's like Greek suburban tragedy stuff right there. Didn't you ask him why he stopped?"

"No, it never came up in the three and a half years we weren't speaking to each other." I tried but couldn't keep the sarcasm out of my voice.

"You are beautiful and snarky, which is my personal favorite combination. We are going to be really good friends. And as your future good friend, I think you and he should have a conversation."

"Nope. I prefer the let's-pretend-everything's-fine-forever method of dealing with this situation." My frontal lobe had been so young and stupid back then. The best thing was to just move on.

Jess gave me a serious look. "Trust me on this one. Avoidance is never the way."

"It has been so far."

She nodded and then said something totally unexpected. "I've never had a stepsibling before, and I'm not much of an expert on those kind of relationships. Like, the only thing I can think of right now is the story of Cain and Abel."

"What? You want me to kill him?"

"No. I mean when I heard that story in church last week, I thought maybe if they'd talked out their issues, the bad stuff wouldn't have happened."

"I don't know how you came to that conclusion, but I think something may be a little off with your religious education. Also, he's not my brother."

Jess didn't look the least bit offended, for which I was grateful as my mouth had often landed me in hot water when I spoke before I thought.

"Do you still have feelings for him? Or are you over him?"

Wow, that was a loaded question. Part of me wanted to shrug it off and remind her about the tutoring, but the other part figured I'd already told her the whole sordid story so I might as well be honest. "I do. Is that crazy, given everything that's happened between us and our current family situation?"

"I mean, there are probably some psych majors who'd have fun with that."

I smiled at her gentle teasing. "But our situation makes it so that it doesn't matter. I have to move on. You can't start the next chapter of your life if you keep rereading the last one." There was no need to confess that I'd been stuck in the old chapter and couldn't figure out how to turn the page.

Jess had fallen silent, and I wondered why. I had to ask. "So, what do you think about all this?"

"I was just thinking you're amazing, and you're awesome, and I'm so impressed by how willing you were to be open and share your story with me. And I was also thinking . . . poor Bash. He is so screwed."

CHAPTER SEVEN

BASH

While the NCAA didn't allow us to have practices run by the coaches, we could have our own pickup games on the empty field. And we could wear our padding and helmets if we wanted to. We ignored the snow and ran our plays as if Coach Oakley and his staff were watching, because they probably were. Just not "officially."

Logan called out the next play, and I was up with the other three linebackers at the line of scrimmage, not knowing what he planned on doing. He lived for trying to confuse me. It was my job to watch the offense and especially the quarterback. I had to figure out their play as soon as it was in motion and call out to the defense what was going on. If I messed up, if all of the linebackers failed to correctly and instantly read the play, it took just one mistake to let the ball through and miss the tackle.

The ball was snapped to Logan, and he moved into position. Unfortunately, the entire defensive line seemed to be surprised by what was going on and missed their blocks. Which made it so Logan could complete his long pass to Johnson and score a touchdown.

"Are you kidding me?" I screamed. "How hard is it to block your mother-funding-cotton-candy-licking blocks? O, Canada! We weren't running a zone defense! That was man to man! Pay attention!"

The snow was limiting our visibility, but that was no excuse. I was about to unleash another tirade since our defense coach wasn't there to tell me to calm down before I worked myself into a frenzy. Fortunately my roommate knew just how to get me to chill. Logan removed his helmet and walked over to me, putting his hand on my shoulder. "Hey, big guy, sun's getting real low."

"I'm not the Incredible Hulk," I muttered to him.

"Yeah, more like the Incredible Sulk. We should pack it up. Everybody's tired."

I was about to protest when I saw a familiar figure off on the sidelines.

It was my dad. He raised his hand to wave at me.

"Sure, that sounds like a good idea," I told Logan, who seemed surprised at how quickly I'd given in. I couldn't blame him; if not for my father on the sidelines, I would have demanded we keep going until the defense could get their heads out of their butts. Not to mention that our official off-season was fast approaching and we'd be forced to focus on strength training and conditioning and there wouldn't be any more of these loosely structured practices. And we obviously needed all the help we could get.

But there were more important things going on.

Logan called out that the practice was over, and while everyone else went over to the locker room, I trotted over to the sidelines.

"Dad, what are you doing here?"

"There's something important that I need to talk to you about. Do you have some free time?"

"Um, yeah. Let me go get changed. Can I meet you over at the Smithson building? We could grab something to eat."

He nodded. "I'll see you there."

I jogged over to the locker room, wondering what could be bad enough that my dad would come out here in the middle of a snowstorm to talk to me. He could have just called or texted. Which meant it was something big.

For one awful minute, I wondered if he was going to tell me that he and Tricia were getting divorced. Not that I'd want him to go through that pain again, but if they broke up it would clear a path for me and Ember.

It was entirely selfish, and I felt bad as soon as I thought it.

I hurried and changed, not bothering to shower. I would do it later. My mind was coming up with terrible scenarios, each one worse than the last. I'd even worried that maybe Marley was hurt, but my father wouldn't make me wait if that was it.

Just as I reached the locker room door, I heard, "Hey, Bash!"

Woodby came over, still wearing his gear. "Tomorrow night?"

"What about tomorrow night?" I asked.

"We still on for our double date?"

I had completely forgotten about it since my mind was somewhere else. "Yes. Tomorrow night."

He held out his fist and I bumped it. "Cool. See you at the movie theater."

I headed out of the locker room, pulling up my coat's hood. I'd made plans for the four of us to go see a movie and then head over to a restaurant for dinner. I figured that if everything went badly, we'd spend the first part of the date sitting quietly in the dark, and then we could spend the second half discussing what we'd just watched so the conversation wouldn't lapse into awkward silence. Built-in safety net.

I almost ran over Jess, who was obviously waiting for Logan. "Jess! How's it going?"

She walked over to me and smacked me hard on the shoulder. "You're a jerk," she informed me.

"Ow! What did I do?" I asked in protest, rubbing my shoulder. For someone her size, she really packed a punch.

"You know what you did," she said in that female way where no, I did not know what I had done, and she had no intention of telling me and planned on just being angry about it instead. I tried to think over what recent heinous crime I could have committed. Would she really be this mad about me putting Vaseline on the inside of Logan's helmet? Even he had thought it was funny.

Then it struck me. "Did you talk to Ember? What did she say?"

Jess wagged her finger at me. "Don't ask me if I talked to her or what she said. She's my friend, and I'm not telling you anything."

Logan chose that moment to arrive, just as surprised to see Jess reprimanding me as I was. "What's going on?" he asked.

"I'm not telling you what she said, either," she informed her boyfriend. "Because you'll run off and tell him, and if he doesn't already know what he did, he doesn't deserve to."

"I wouldn't say anything!" Logan protested as she began to stalk off. "Jess!" He glared at me for getting him in trouble with his girlfriend and then followed after her.

Although she hadn't said anything substantial, Jess wouldn't be so riled up over Ember unless Ember had been riled up, too. Which meant that she wasn't indifferent to me.

Ember might even be angry with me, despite what she'd said to the contrary. And if that was true . . . then what? She didn't think of me as just a friend? Would just a friend make her new friend mad enough to smack me? A totally innocent and undeserving guy who didn't do smackworthy things?

Huh. That put me in a good mood. A much better one than I'd been in just a few minutes ago. Maybe I was overthinking this thing with my dad. Maybe it was more good news.

I smelled the meat cooking on the grill as I approached the Smithson and wondered how many hamburgers I should order for my late afternoon snack. My dad was waiting by the south doors and opened one as soon as I arrived. He'd been watching for me?

I could see on his face that it wasn't good news.

Suddenly I wasn't hungry, and that never happened.

"Whatever it is, I need you to tell me. Because it can't be any worse than the stuff I'm coming up with."

His whole body sagged, and he suddenly looked years older. "Let's go sit down first."

We found a table, and I felt like my chest was going to explode if he didn't explain himself soon.

He reached inside his coat and pulled out an envelope. He put it on the table and slid it over to me.

My mind tried to go to happy places. Maybe it was a recruitment letter from a Division 1 college. Or I had inherited a fortune from an unknown relative. Or he'd enrolled me in the Cheese of the Month club, and I could look forward to receiving twelve delicious different cheeses next year.

But I knew. Before he had even turned it over and I saw her handwriting, I knew.

It was a letter from my mother.

"She sent this as certified mail," he said.

I looked at the envelope. It might as well have been filled with anthrax; that was how unexcited I was to see what was inside. "What is certified mail?"

"It's a legal way of mailing things so that the sender knows the letter was delivered."

Why did she need to know legally if the letter was received? Was this where he was going to tell me that she had died? I hadn't felt afraid in a long time, but I was too scared to pick the letter up. "What does it say?"

"I don't know. She sent one to Marley, too. I thought it would be better to have you open yours first and see what's going on."

My dad had some serious willpower. I couldn't believe that he hadn't opened it. If I'd gotten Marley's letter, I probably would have opened it just so that I would know the content and could plan out the best way to protect her. I still didn't want to open mine, though. But I had to. For Marley's sake, if nothing else.

There was a green line along the top of the envelope that read *certified*. I reached under the flap to rip it open. I pulled out a single sheet of paper and a picture. I looked at the picture first, and it was like someone had thrown an anvil against my stomach. It was my mother, looking happy, healthy, and older. She was with a man and two small children who had the same bright-blond hair as Marley and me. The same hair as our mom.

I passed my dad the picture and opened the letter. I read it out loud. "Dear Ian, It's been so long I'm not even sure what to say to you. I'm so sorry I left. It was wrong, and I regret walking out on you and Marley. I'm sober now, and I have been for the last seven years. I've met a wonderful man and have married again. You have a half brother and a half sister who want to get to know their big brother. I want to get to know you again. I hope you'll find it in your heart to forgive me for everything I've done. I want to be a part of your life, but I understand if you don't feel the same. So I'm leaving it up to you. I've written all my contact information down at the bottom; I really hope to hear from you. I never stopped loving you. Mom."

Her email address, phone number, and home address were listed at the bottom. She was still in Washington State. I wondered how far away Ironwood was. Letting out a shaky breath I hadn't realized I'd been holding, I handed my father the letter, too. We sat in silence, both of us contemplating what a big deal this was.

What a big deal it would be for Marley, who had really missed our mother. She wasn't old enough to remember how bad things got. How Mom would lie in bed all day every day. That I was the one who had to feed Marley and keep her safe. How when I was nine years old I swore to myself that I would never drink alcohol or abuse drugs because I would never be like my mom.

My dad had gotten sober when my mom became pregnant with me, because she didn't want to use anything while she was pregnant, and he wanted to support her. He said he took one look at me and promised himself he'd never get high again. And he never had.

My mother went off everything again when she got pregnant with Marley, but that was the only good thing she ever did for either one of us. I didn't know why my dad—an addict himself—could never see that my mom was still using. She lied to him and said she wasn't. And he must have loved her so much that he was willing to believe her lies. Sometimes I wished he'd loved her a little less and us a little more.

I shook my head. I wasn't being fair. My dad did the best he could, and that was all anyone could ask for. He was probably overwhelmed, too, trying to provide for us and keep our home and help my mother while maintaining his own sobriety. And he stayed. She abandoned us, and he stayed and loved us. That was enough to override everything else.

"What are you going to do?" my dad asked.

"I don't know." It was the only honest answer I could give him. It was too much all at once. Radio silence for ten years, and now she wanted to have a relationship with me? Had she never heard the words *too little, too late*? "I need to think about it. Figure out what I should do next. Could we maybe talk about something else?"

He looked as uncomfortable as I felt. "Sure. How's school?"

"Fine. I mean, it's school."

"What about your social life? You dating anyone?"

"Not really." And that included the daughters of people he was married to. "I mean, I do have a date planned soon. A double date, actually. With Ember."

Somehow this news seemed to make him even more upset. "With Ember?"

I realized how that must have sounded. "She set me up with her friend, and I set her up with one of mine. We thought it might be less awkward if we hung out together."

His relief was evident. "That's good. It's good for the two of you to get along. It will be easier on everyone. Tricia has some big plans for her survivor list coming up, and she's hoping you'll be part of it."

"We'll see."

"We all miss you. We'd like you to be around more."

Guilt gnawed on my insides. "I know, Dad. I'm just really busy with school and football."

"Your cousins are coming up next weekend. They're upset that they weren't able to play our traditional Sebastian game of football on Thanksgiving."

I grinned. "I didn't know they were that excited for a beatdown. Do they not remember how everyone opposing me loses?"

"Just promise me nobody will break any bones this year."

"I can make no such promise." I knew for the last few years they'd held it at my Uncle Darren's house, and it was kind of nice that they wanted to play at my home again, even if it was a couple of months late. I loved the Sebastian family annual Thanksgiving football game. Thanks to our genetic competitiveness, it was a game that didn't follow the supposed "touch only" rules and quickly turned into thrown elbows and busted teeth and only one minor (okay, major) concussion.

Ember was just as competitive. I wondered if she was going to play. "Do you want me to bring Ember with me? I think she'd like it."

"Maybe. We'll see what Tricia thinks." He patted his pants pockets, like he was looking for something. "Oh. I should probably warn you. Tricia's dyed her hair bubblegum pink. It was on her list. Try not to stare when you see her."

I had to laugh. "Seriously?"

My dad cracked a smile. "Yep. When she wears black high heels, she looks a little like a number two pencil."

70

I laughed again, and it was good to laugh and not think about the fairly traumatic thing that had just happened to me.

"It's good to see you happy," my dad said when I calmed down.

"Are you happy?" He'd been so sad when my mom left. For a really long time. Even when things felt normal and like we were living our lives, I could tell he missed her. That was the main reason why I didn't want to do anything that might mess up his relationship with Tricia. He deserved happiness more than anyone else I knew.

"I am. Very happy."

"Good. I'm glad." I was, considering what I had sacrificed to make that happen.

"I should probably get going. Greg Walker's old Mustang is giving him troubles again, and I said I'd stop by and take a look at it."

"Okay. Hey, before you go, what are you going to do about Marley's letter?"

My dad took in a deep breath and slowly let it out. "I think she's old enough to make the decision about your mom herself. I don't want to keep her from her mother."

"No, why would you want to do that? Especially considering that Mom's done a fantastic job of it all by herself."

In an uncharacteristic move, my dad reached across the table and put his hand on top of my arm. "At some point you have to forgive and move on. You can't let your anger at your mom define your life."

He got up and I stayed put. Was he right? How much of my life had I given over to a woman who had abandoned me when I was eleven years old?

I picked up my phone. I wanted to call Ember. To talk this out with her.

But I couldn't. Another thing my mom had inadvertently caused by leaving us. Because it led to my dad marrying Tricia and making it so Ember had to be just a friend.

Years had passed, though. And I hadn't found anyone in that entire time that I wanted to be serious with. Was it because no one compared to Ember?

Or was it because my childhood experiences had led me to believe that no relationship was ever permanent? Especially the one I most wanted?

All that hope I'd felt when I ran into Jess was gone. Instead, I felt cursed.

CHAPTER EIGHT

EMBER

It was the day of our double date. A blind date for me since Bash hadn't even bothered telling me his friend's name so that I could stalk him on social media, like a normal person. Thankfully Bethany had emailed me her notes from class, which I thought was cool of her, given that Bash could have called off the date at the last minute (something I might or might not have been praying for all day) and I would still have what I wanted out of the bargain. Without paying the price. Instead I was going to have to go out with whatever rando Bash had chosen.

I was at home in my apartment lying on the bed in the room I shared with Ximena. Like always, she was off at the library because she said our place wasn't "conducive" to studying. She wasn't wrong.

Knowing I had nothing to wear and that my other roommate Deja would, I ventured out into the main living area. If Ximena was our resident bookworm and lover of all things academic, Deja was her total opposite. She never met a gathering she didn't like or a boy who wasn't interesting. She was our in-the-know fashionista and a whiz in the kitchen, where she was currently making something out of leftovers in the fridge that smelled divine. She played volleyball because it gave her unlimited access to college parties and college men, which were her two best events. But she fed me, which made her my favorite.

I'd only chosen to share a room with Ximena because she was never home. If she did come home, it was under the cover of darkness, long after I'd gone to bed. She would leave before I woke up. That was her story whenever I talked to her at practice or at training. I wasn't sure whether or not I believed her. But it didn't really matter since I basically had my own room.

Our final roommate, Molly, was like having a guy living with us. To say she was a slob would have been underselling it. For example, I don't think she'd done a load of laundry the entire year. She didn't seem to believe in it. Instead she believed in leaving her clothing on the floor long enough so that it somehow cycled from dirty to clean again. Showering also seemed to be somewhat optional. Things none of us had realized until we moved in with her. We loved her to death, she was our teammate, but Deja kept threatening to forcibly hold her down in a shower and to clean all her clothes while she was out. Molly would then yell about how Deja better not disrupt her system, and I usually left the apartment before things got uglier. Anyway, Molly spent much of her time playing whatever new game had come out on her Xbox and was the only girl I'd ever met who could eat and drink me under the table.

"I need to borrow a shirt," I told Deja.

"Occasion, location, people attending."

Trying not to sigh since I needed her help, I said, "A blind/double date, movie theater and a restaurant, I don't know which one, and it will be this girl Bethany I know from class, and two guys from the football team."

She stopped stirring the food in the pan and stared at me. "What do we say about football players?"

Molly piped up from the other room. "Football players are just for fun, not for boyfriends!"

"That's right." Deja nodded in agreement. "They're not relationship material. You take them to the club for fun and then you leave them there. This is the problem with most athletes—no guy spends time getting six-pack abs to date just one girl."

Even I had to concede that she was a little bit right. I liked an athletic build and a broad, well-defined chest. I still had very fond and pleasant memories of Bash's. But it could mean trouble. I was a case in point.

"Speaking of men who can't date one girl at a time, did I tell you I caught Fisher cheating on me?" Deja poked violently at her stir-fry with a spatula.

"Already?" At the look on her face, I shifted gears. "I mean, oh no. That's terrible." Like we all hadn't seen that coming. Even Ximena knew it was doomed to failure. Fisher had quite the reputation. "Did you beat him up?"

"I considered it, but I just broke up with him instead."

Good. "I'm sorry that you guys broke up." It seemed like the appropriate thing to say.

Molly had wandered into the kitchen, looking for something to eat. "I'm not sorry. Fisher was the worst. I think we should throw you a party to celebrate." When she reached into Deja's pan, Deja smacked Molly's hand with the spatula.

"Don't worry," I told Deja while Molly gave up and went through the fridge instead. "There are plenty of Fishers in the sea."

"Men. Can't live with them," Molly announced, having settled on some slices of bologna as her snack.

I waited for her to keep talking. "And?"

"Nothing. That was the end of my thought."

"Easy for you to say." Molly had been in a serious relationship with the same guy since she was twelve. They planned on getting married. He was in college in California, and I'd met him a couple of times over long weekends when he'd come up to visit Molly.

I wondered if Ximena was dating anyone. I should ask her the next time I saw her. Which might be weeks from now.

Deja turned off the heat and set the pan to one side. "Come on, let's go find you something to wear."

I followed her into her room and sat on her clean, made bed. Molly's half of the room looked like the city had claimed it as a new dumping zone.

Deja went through her clothes one by one, considering each before moving on. "So is this just dinner and a movie, or is it a *date* date?"

"What's the difference?"

"Usually where your hands and mouths end up," she said with a wink.

"It's not a hang. It is, like, officially a date, I think."

"A date on a school night. You know that's serious. Who are you going out with again?"

I deliberately hadn't mentioned any names because Deja had a brain with its own personal filing cabinet where she kept dossiers on every man on campus. "I don't know my date's name."

"And the other guy?"

She also knew when other people were lying. It made it difficult for her flavor of the week to cheat on her, but they kept trying. "Bash."

Deja stopped, turning slowly on her heel to stare at me. "Your Bash? Your ex, Bash?"

Of course. It wasn't bad enough that she had probably already gathered intel about exactly what kind of date he'd be and how good of a kisser he was, but she also remembered that night two years ago when we were at our first away game and I'd been really missing him and had broken down and told her most of the story.

Frankly, I'd been hoping she'd forgotten.

No such luck.

"Yes, that Bash. We're trying to be friends now."

"But dating your ex's friend . . . that's just ex adjacent. More of the same."

"Maybe," I said with a shrug. "Maybe not. I don't even know who it is."

She gave me a superior look. "You know my stance when it comes to exes."

I did. There was no forgiveness and no forgetting, and striking an ex out of her life would often mean his social group as well.

She was going to run out of people to date really soon.

"Hanging out with your ex is like failing a test you had all the answers to," she informed me as she pulled out a black blouse. It had slightly puffy sleeves and gathered in right under the chest. It was adorable. "But if you're going to put yourself in the line of fire, you might as well have the right uniform. Try it on."

I yanked off my T-shirt and slid on the blouse. The material was soft and warm at the same time, and there was a delicate embroidery around the neckline. It was perfect. "I'm not going to war."

"That's not how I remember it. Didn't you tell him you loved him first?"

"So?"

"You never pull that trigger until you've been fired upon!"

Fisher had been a World War II buff and it was the only explanation for all the fighting imagery. Or else she was really mad at him for cheating on her and was considering some unsavory methods of dealing with said anger.

Problem was, I didn't hate Bash. He wasn't a jerk or a liar. He hadn't cheated on me. He was someone who had once made my life feel like an actual fairy tale.

"You don't have to worry about me," I told her. "Bash and I are totally over. Not only has that ship sailed, it sank and is sitting on the bottom of the ocean. And eighty-five years from now, somebody in Hollywood is going to make a movie about the wreckage."

"As long as there's no feelings. Especially of the tingly kind."

I didn't have the heart to tell her that the tingly feels were still in effect when I was around Bash. Even though I tried my hardest to ignore them.

Fortunately, she didn't push me and instead asked, "Do you need help with your makeup?"

"I'm good." Deja's makeover would consist of fake eyelashes and enough contouring to make me look about twenty pounds thinner, but I didn't feel like it. There was a time and place for serious killer makeup, and then there were times when you wanted to be able to blink and touch your own face if you felt like it.

I thanked her for the loan and was about to leave when she stopped me. "Are you sure you don't have an ulterior motive for tonight? Hanging out with Bash again?"

My heart started beating so hard. If I'd been strapped to a lie detector machine, I would have failed. And considering Deja was basically the human version of it, I settled on a facsimile of the truth. "I don't want there to be a reason other than we're trying to be friends."

She studied me carefully and then nodded once, as if dismissing me. Taking the win, I ran into our shared bathroom and started fixing my hair and my face.

But the silence was giving me too much time to consider what Deja had asked. Did I want something more from Bash than friendship? I'd have to be a real glutton for punishment to try and go down that road again. He'd made it pretty clear that he wasn't interested in me like that. Because touching my not-flat stomach and curvy hips had sent him running for the hills.

Or was it that I'd told him I'd loved him? When I thought about that night, it was always easier to assume that I'd repulsed him. Because that was conceivably something I could change. One of my resolutions this year had been to lose ten pounds. I only had sixteen more to go.

But if he didn't love me? If I'd scared him off? If he'd run away because he'd never felt that way about me?

There was nothing I could do about that.

It was a really depressing thought.

And it wasn't even like I could give it the old college try and flirt my way back into Bash's heart. Our relationship happened because he thought it was cute I was committing a felony. The last boy I tried to flirt with before him was back in kindergarten, and I peed on the jungle gym just to impress him.

My flirting skills had not improved much since then.

I considered canceling. Even pulled my phone out of my pocket. And I might have done it had our doorbell not rang.

Bash. Mr. Ten Minutes Early Is Late.

How had I forgotten his ridiculous punctuality? Deja let him in, and I heard their voices as they introduced themselves.

I hurried up and put on the last of my lip gloss. I tugged on a pair of black boots and zipped up the sides. In the living room I found Bash charming my two roommates. Molly had even paused the game, and they were both looking at him like he had multiple women's volleyball national championships in his pockets. I couldn't blame them. He was looking ridiculously hot.

I grabbed my coat. "Hey. You ready to go?"

"Yeah." Was it my imagination, or had his eyes lit up when he saw me?

I told my roommates I'd see them later, and on my way out I heard Deja say, "Girl, don't fall on any grenades tonight."

Bash gave me a confused look, but I got the gist of what she was saying.

"Grenades?" he repeated.

I just shook my head as if I hadn't understood her, either. I wasn't about to tell him what was going on.

It was weird to be walking alongside him but not able to touch him. Why did he have to smell so amazing and be so pretty?

Life was seriously unfair, and the universe was stupid.

"How's your healthy eating resolution going?" he asked.

Was he as uncomfortable as I was? That was a random question. "I've only had one piece of cake today, so I'd say it's going okay."

"One piece?" He said it like he didn't believe me.

He had good reason not to. "If you don't cut the cake, it's still technically just one piece, so I've only had one piece of cake today."

"I don't think you can count it as a resolution if you never actually keep it."

"No," I protested. "I'm resolved to do it. That doesn't mean that I will, just that I want to. I've decided that, like with gifts, the thought should count."

"I'm pretty sure that's not how that works."

"I don't need to be mocked for my culinary choices."

"Hey, no mocking from me!" He held both his hands up, like he was surrendering. "I, too, had one slice of pizza today and one brownie."

How could he always make me laugh even when I was ready to get all indignant on him?

We reached a four-door sedan I didn't recognize. "Did you borrow it?" I asked.

"Yeah. From one of my teammates."

"We can take my car, if you want." I regretted the words the moment I said them. I had way too many memories of driving around with Bash in that car.

Of making out with him in the back seat of that car.

The look on his face made me wonder if he was remembering the same thing. "No, it's okay. I'll drive."

I put my hand on the door, and Bash called out, "Wait!" He ran around to my side and opened the door for me, bowing as he did so. "My lady."

Shaking my head, I got in and let him close the door behind me. A few seconds later he got in on the driver's side. He started the car up and let the engine run to warm up the inside of the car. It was seriously cold outside.

He asked, "Are we still on for our post-game recap tomorrow night?"

I recalled him mentioning something about it, but I'd thought he'd been joking. Because, no. The word was *no*. It was such an easy word to say. *N. O.* No. I didn't even have to open my mouth all the way to make the correct sounds.

And I was trying to say it. It probably would have been good for his ego to be told no every once in a while. In a way, I was helping him prepare for real life if I refused him.

Then he had to go and add on, "You know, so we can compare notes and see which one of us did the best job of setting up the other."

Oh, it was so on. Bethany had to be better than whomever Bash had chosen. "Yeah. I'm totally going to win. Speaking of, you never did tell me who I'm going out with."

If he said it was Dalton Johnson, I was going to punch him in the throat.

"His name is Todd Woodby. He can be a little goofy, but he's basically a good guy. You might like him."

"I *might* like him?" I repeated. That sounded bad. Nobody knew me as well as Bash had. How could he not know whether or not I'd like a specific guy? "Is this where you tell me he's okay and/or average as a person? It's not really a ringing endorsement."

Bash put the car in reverse and backed out of the parking spot. "I don't know what kind of guys you like."

You. I like guys like you.

Even though I didn't speak, Bash apparently felt the need to keep defending himself as he pulled out onto the road that went toward the main campus. "For all you know, he might be the love of your life, and when you look back on tonight, you'll be like, 'I was the luckiest duck, and it's all thanks to my excellent friend Bash.'"

"Quack, quack," I told him, my eyebrows furrowed.

"I didn't know you could quack sarcastically."

"Have you not been paying attention?" I asked him. "I do everything sarcastically."

"That's not true. I've seen you do lots of things with a totally open and sincere heart. I used to love that about you."

I was so glad that his gaze was focused on the road and he couldn't see my reaction, because there was no way I could have hidden the tears that sprang up in my eyes, how I couldn't quite calm down my breathing. My throat felt thick and my heart too heavy for my body.

Bash always could see me. The real me.

Grenades. Exploding grenades everywhere.

CHAPTER NINE

BASH

We arrived at the movie theater not long after I picked Ember up. I'd told Bethany and Woodby to meet us there, and as we pulled into the parking lot, I realized that it had never occurred to me to tell Ember the same thing. I probably should have; it would have made the most sense and taken less time. But from the beginning I had planned on going over and picking her up.

Even though she wasn't my date.

And she had her own car and could have easily driven herself.

What kind of mixed-up signals was I sending out?

Crazy signals that Ember was obviously picking up on because she had started acting strangely. Things had seemed to be going good at first, and then, I don't know. Something shifted. I wanted to ask her what had happened but figured it was better not to.

For the sake of the friendship and all.

We parked the car and walked in silence to the front of the theater, where Woodby was waiting for us.

He came over to introduce himself. "Hi, I'm Todd. You must be Ember."

She nodded and smiled at him. "I am. Nice to meet you."

Then he held out his arms and hugged her hello. And in a moment of blinding jealousy, I almost decked him on the spot.

"Wow," Woodby said, finally stepping back. Which was good, because I was about to pry them apart. "Bash said you were beautiful. He obviously underpromised and overdelivered."

It was so smarmy and stupid. Was Ember going to fall for this line?

She wasn't looking at him. She was looking at me. And there was something in her expression, something so bewildered and vulnerable that it made me catch my breath.

Then she faced Woodby again. "That's so nice. Thank you. We should go in."

The snow had started to fall again, and he agreed. He ran over to open the door for both of us. As she brushed past me, making all of my nerve endings riot with sensation, she murmured, "Are you kidding me with this guy? I am so going to win."

I tried to hide my smirk. I should have known she wouldn't have been taken in by such a cheesy line.

She turned back to smile mischievously at me, and I almost tripped over my own feet. With the snow coming down, the light from the theater backlighting her, she looked stunning. I'd had the same reaction when I saw her in her apartment just a few minutes ago. I'd forgotten how to breathe.

And it wasn't because she was somehow more beautiful than normal. She did look nice, and I could tell she'd made an effort, but that wasn't it. It was the same reaction I had every time I saw her. Like being struck by lightning.

At first I thought it was the shock of being around her again or that in our time apart I'd somehow forgotten how gorgeous she was and how she made my heart feel like if it skipped any more beats I'd wind up in an emergency room. But since it kept happening, I was starting to accept that this was just how I was going to feel every time I saw her.

Like I'd been headbutted in the stomach.

I collected myself and followed them into the lobby. Bethany was waiting inside, and her face lit up when she saw us. Ember introduced her to Woodby, and then Bethany made her way over to me.

"Hey," I said. "You made it."

"I did! I had my roommate drop me off." Then she stood up on tiptoe and pressed a kiss to my cheek.

My gut reaction was to feel . . . guilt. Like I had done something wrong in front of Ember.

Who wasn't paying attention to me and was eyeing the concessions menu.

Then I felt bad that I wasn't more excited to see Bethany. She was cute and seemed sweet, but she was very dedicated to the color pink. Pink sweater, darker-pink pants, and a bright pink bow in her hair.

She reminded me of one of my little sister's Barbie dolls.

"How are you?" Bethany asked, and it was then that I realized I was being rude by staying quiet.

"Good. And you?"

"I'm doing amazing," she said with a toothy grin. "Do you have the tickets already?"

"Yes, I bought them online." I got my phone from my pocket and opened up my email that had the receipt.

Woodby handed me a twenty-dollar bill. "Thanks for buying those. That's to cover me and my date."

Ember thanked Woodby as Bethany took out her wallet from her purse.

"It's okay, I've got it," I told her.

"Thank you." She looked a little crestfallen, so I was about to suggest that she could buy us some popcorn if she wanted to split the cost that way.

As if she could read my mind, Ember said, "Should we get some snacks? My treat."

"I'm not hungry," Bethany said.

"Oh." Ember sounded confused. "Just some popcorn then?"

Bethany scrunched up her nose. "Do you know how much sodium and artificial flavoring there is in movie popcorn?"

Ember shot me a panicked look and mouthed, *What's happening?*

I offered, "We are going out afterward to a restaurant." She wouldn't starve before then. But I got where she was coming from. I never watched a movie without a buttload of popcorn and candy.

"Then it's settled," Woodby announced. "We'll get something to eat after the movie."

As a group we headed over to the ticket taker, and I gave him my phone so that he could scan the QR code. He told us our movie was in Auditorium 2, and as we walked to our theater, Ember snuck over next to me, her shoulder brushing against my bicep.

"Are we really going to do this without popcorn?"

"It's just one night. I'll feed you popcorn later, if you want."

I'd meant it as I'd buy her popcorn if she wanted, but the image of feeding it to her, one kernel at a time, her soft, pink lips brushing against my fingertips made my mind wander off into some places it shouldn't have, especially considering the fact that I was out on a date with another girl.

"Fine," she muttered.

We found our row, and I told them the seat numbers. I figured I'd sit next to Bethany and Woodby. Only Woodby stood aside, letting us go in ahead of him so that Bethany was on the end, followed by me, Ember, and then him.

The opening preview started right as we sat down.

"Just in time!" Bethany said with a smile. She'd left the armrest up. Ember, meanwhile, had lowered the armrest like a barrier between us. I felt slightly bad about it until I saw her do the same thing to Woodby.

Ember took her coat off, and her left arm got stuck in the sleeve. She struggled for a few seconds before I reached up to pull the sleeve away from her shoulder. Which turned out to be a mistake. I could feel the heat of her skin through her black shirt, and it took all the strength I possessed to move my hand away from that warmth.

"Thanks," she said, her voice sounding unusually breathy.

Had I had that effect on her? She turned to say something to Woodby, shattering my illusion.

I shifted in my seat, and my knee knocked into Ember's, sending a jolt of heat and awareness through me. "Sorry," I whispered.

She just shook her head, which made it so that the scent of her shampoo wafted over to me. It was the same one she'd used in high school. It smelled like coconuts, and it had always made me think of sunshine and suntan lotion and beautiful beaches, but mostly it reminded me of her.

When I first went to live with my grandparents, they'd kicked around the idea of taking a vacation to Hawaii over winter break, and I'd pushed hard for a ski trip instead. I couldn't stomach the idea of going to an entire state that would smell like Ember. It would have driven me insane.

Much as it was doing now.

Especially since the last time we'd sat next to each other in a darkened theater, there'd been no movie watching happening at all.

I forced myself to pay attention since I'd been the one who'd chosen the movie. It was a superheroine movie, one of the latest based on a comic-book character. I figured it was a popular movie that everyone could enjoy.

Or I would have enjoyed it more if I'd not been so in tune to every movement Ember made. All the times she changed her position in her seat, put her elbow on the armrest between us, or let her dark hair fall forward in a curtain of soft silkiness, I saw it. Felt it.

Then the movie ended, and we stayed through the credits to watch the stingers. As the house lights came up, I let out a sigh of relief that

I was no longer going to be confined to a dark space so close to Ember without the possibility of touching her.

When we got outside I told them the restaurant was just around the corner. It was a chain, family-oriented type place. I picked it because it was so close to the theater. I'd also figured it wouldn't be too loud on a school night.

Ember started talking about the lead actress, whose next film would be with Chase Covington and how it was based on one of her favorite YA fantasy novels. I listened, loving the cadence and tenor of her voice. I'd always found it soothing.

That is, when I wasn't finding it exciting.

Shaking my head to rid myself of those kind of thoughts—because nothing had changed in our situation—I held open the door to the restaurant to let everyone go in.

"Woodby's got this, dude." Woodby insisted on taking the door from me so that I could go in first. I couldn't figure out if he was just trying really hard to impress Ember, or if this was some kind of power play that was going over my head.

I let him take it because I wasn't interested in a pissing contest.

When the hostess asked us how many, I told her four. She grabbed four menus and asked me to follow her. She led us to one of those long benches that were built into a wall with several tables and chairs situated in front of them. Bethany and Woodby sat on the bench while Ember and I sat across from our respective dates. I immediately realized this was not an ideal situation for two reasons; the first being that the restaurant was noisier than I'd anticipated, and in order to talk to Bethany I had to lean over and speak loudly. The second was that I was again close to Ember, our arms brushing against each other, and every time she touched me, my stomach made a whooshing motion while heat and desire swirled inside me.

As we were looking over the menus, I asked Bethany, "What did you think of the movie?"

She gave me a polite smile and raised her eyebrows, as if she hadn't heard. I repeated my question a little louder.

"Oh. Um . . ." She reached up to grab some of her blonde hair and twirl it around her fingers. "To be honest, I don't really enjoy movies like that. Where it's all blowing stuff up and people have these powers that nobody in real life has."

"Agreed," Woodby said. "Also, Woodby doesn't like it when they depict women so unrealistically."

"Like how?" Ember asked, and I wondered if I was the only one who could hear the warning in her voice.

This was not how I thought this conversation would go. I probably should have asked everyone for movie suggestions before I chose one on my own, and I felt bad that I hadn't thought of it.

The hostess stopped by our table to give us wrapped-up silverware and glasses of water. We thanked her, and Ember leaned forward, expectantly. "I'm waiting."

"Come on, let's be honest. Even if a woman had that kind of power, when she came up against a male villain with similar abilities, he would take her out in a fistfight. That's just a fact."

I could almost see Ember's temperature rising, and I said, "We should look at the menus," before Ember dumped her glass of water on Woodby's head.

Ember picked her menu up and held it in front of her face. "I loved the movie," she told me.

I instantly felt relieved. "I'm glad you enjoyed it." And the fact that she'd liked it made it so I suddenly didn't feel bad anymore. Or care what anyone else thought.

Which wasn't great.

Her confession also led me to discover that there was actually a third problem—that Ember and I could easily talk to one another without our dates overhearing us. I started taking a drink of my water just as she murmured, "You know, I was so worried this restaurant wouldn't have any casual sexism on the menu. Good thing we brought our own."

I spewed water on the table because I couldn't stop from laughing.

Bethany let out a little cry of alarm while Woodby pointed at the spill and said, "Nice! Woodby approves!"

As I used my napkin to sop up the water the best that I could, Ember chose that moment to lean in and say, "Also, I don't think he knows how facts work."

Thankfully our waiter arrived just then, introduced himself as Simon, and asked what he could get us started with.

"Do you have any vegetarian options?" Woodby asked, and Simon went over to show him where those items were on the menu.

Ember's mouth dropped. "He's a vegetarian? Did you really set me up with some fern-fondling, seaweed-munching druid?"

I put my damp napkin over my mouth to conceal my smile and grit my teeth together so I wouldn't laugh. I would never be able to see Woodby again without thinking of the word *druid*.

Then she went and made everything worse by saying, "I mean, nothing against his choices. I know I'm biased against it because the last guy I went out with was vegan, and that was one of the three things he talked about. The other two were his dog he'd rescued and doing that Ironman competition. If your friend here tells us he's been to an animal shelter or training for any kind of marathon, I'm out."

I found myself torn between amusement and jealousy. I didn't like to think about her dating other men. Even though we were currently in a situation where she was on a date with another man.

"Let's get the house salad as our appetizer," Woodby said. Our waiter nodded and went off to put that into the computer.

I had been eyeing the fried mozzarella sticks and the ahi tuna and was disappointed that our waiter left so quickly.

"When did you become a vegetarian?" Bethany asked Woodby.

"I'm majoring in nutrition and thought it was hypocritical to not be eating cleanly if I was going to be telling other people to do it, so I made the switch last year. Best thing Woodby ever did. And I cut all carbs."

"Personally, I think the best way to cut carbs is by slicing a pizza." Ember said this one loud enough for the whole table to hear.

I laughed, Bethany smiled weakly, and Woodby frowned. Bethany asked him about the kind of classes he was taking.

Ember was again using the pretense of studying the menu to talk to me. "Why does Woodby talk about himself in the third person? He's mentioned his name more times than a rap star in one of his songs. It's weird."

"It's just Woodby. He doesn't do it all the time. But when he does, you get used to it," I told her. "It's why everybody calls him Woodby instead of Todd."

"Bash may be used to Woodby, but Ember is not and doesn't care for Woodby's style of talking."

Pressing my lips together so that I wouldn't smile, I turned my attention back to the menu, too.

Deciding on what I wanted, I looked up to see Bethany on her phone.

"There's no nutritional values listed on their website," she said.

Woodby came to her rescue. "Don't worry. I have an app for that." He handed her his phone.

And speaking of everybody being on their phones, I noticed Ember on hers, but she had it under the table and was texting someone. Before I had a chance to wonder who she was talking to, she turned her phone off. She saw me and smiled.

"Texting my mom. I like to check in on her," she said, and my heart twisted painfully.

This was one of the things I loved best about Ember. She cared deeply about her family and friends. She protected them. She was totally loyal. I hated that I'd destroyed those feelings between us and lost her.

Even if it had been necessary.

I didn't want to think about that. "You should be paying attention to my vastly superior candidate," I said.

"Ha. Mine sought you out. She's already attracted to you. Your date will be better based solely on the fact that she's never once called herself Bethany."

Simon returned with the big house salad for us to share and handed us individual plates. Everyone served themselves, except for Ember.

"You don't still claim to hate lettuce, do you?" I asked.

She rolled her eyes. "Lettuce tastes terrible!"

"Lettuce has no taste."

It was painfully familiar—an argument we'd had many times before.

"Besides," I continued, "this one is mostly spinach and quinoa."

"Is that supposed to make it better? Because I think you just made it worse."

"You should try it," Woodby piped up. "Come on, Bash told me you were adventurous."

I didn't remember saying that, but it had the intended effect. With a defiant look, Ember used the tongs to give herself a serving of it. Everybody dug in, and I couldn't help but watch as Ember pushed her food around the plate.

Bethany and Woodby were talking about how much they liked the salad and compared it to other salads they had tried. Ember finally worked up her courage and took a bite. The most interesting and hilarious expressions passed over her face, and I wished I had thought to record it. She grabbed her napkin and spit out her bite, something that only I noticed.

"Did you really just spit that out?" I asked.

"It tasted like a tree just threw up in my mouth," she said in disgust, grabbing her glass to get a drink of water. The drink didn't help, and she tried to wipe the taste off with a different part of her napkin. "How do I make it stop? Why is there an aftertaste?"

"There is no taste," I reminded her, just to see her get fired up.

She did not disappoint. "Just keep eating your sad food and be quiet."

I laughed for probably longer than what would be considered polite.

"What did you think of the salad?" Woodby asked Ember. "Wasn't it great? This is why it's good to try new things."

Suddenly I had perfect clarity as to how this evening was going to end up. Me paying Ember's bail after she stabbed Woodby with her butter knife.

I needed to do something, fast.

Time to defuse the situation.

CHAPTER TEN

BASH

Trying to take the focus off the food, I asked, "So, Bethany, what's your major?"

"Same as Ember! We're both majoring in nursing."

"Nursing?" I turned to Ember. How did I not know that? "You're studying to become a nurse?"

"Why do you say that with such a disheartening amount of surprise?"

Because I knew what she'd dreamed of being. A writer. "I just thought you might major in English or creative writing."

"Things change."

Things had changed. A lot. It was weird being around Ember. I knew these things about her that nobody else knew, but at the same time it felt like I was meeting her for the first time. Learning all this new stuff about her.

Which led me to other thoughts. What would it feel like if I kissed her again? Different but familiar? Would she react to my touch the same way she had before? Would she still sigh when I pressed my mouth against her neck? Whimper when I teased her lips?

"Bash. Bash."

It startled me to hear Ember calling my name, and I realized that Simon had returned to take our order. Woodby finished ordering something with eggplant, and the waiter turned to Ember.

"I've been having a hard time choosing between the two, so I'm going to go with the barbecue chicken and ribs combination platter."

"You do know vegetarian means I don't eat meat, right?" Woodby interjected. "Were you hoping to split that dinner with me?"

He wasn't asking in a flirtatious way. More like he thought it was too much food for one person. Before I could say something to him, Ember came to her own rescue. "I don't share food. And before you ask, yes, I'm sure I want the combo platter. And could you add two extra sides of fries to that? Thanks so much."

She handed her menu to Simon and then looked at me expectantly.

"I'll take two of those combo platters, because that sounds delicious," I said, winking at Ember.

"Two of them?" Simon verified, and I nodded, giving him my menu.

He left to go put our orders in, and Bethany leaned over to say to Ember, "What kind of diet are you on that lets you eat like that? Keto? Intermittent fasting?"

"Oh, I have a condition that prevents me from dieting," Ember said. "It's called hunger."

Apparently not seeing the humor, Bethany pressed on. "You're not on a diet, like, at all?"

"I mean, I might be at some point. I'm just worried about getting caught up in one of those eat-healthy-and-exercise-frequently dieting scams."

Thankfully, I wasn't drinking anything when she said this. I'd lost count of how many times she'd made me want to laugh out loud tonight.

Bethany looked stunned. "I don't think I've ever met a woman who wasn't on a diet."

"Today must be your lucky day," Ember responded. "You should buy a lottery ticket on your way home."

I was about to suggest that maybe she'd find a leprechaun and the accompanying pot of gold when Woodby announced, "You shouldn't think of it as a diet, but as a lifestyle change."

He was never this obnoxious on the field, and I wasn't sure what had happened tonight. It wasn't like I could ask him here at the table.

Bethany agreed with him while Ember muttered, "The only lifestyle change I'm going to make is one where Woodby is not in my life. Just so you know, I a thousand percent win this situation."

Unless Bethany confessed to harvesting black-market organs, I was afraid Ember was right. Sadly enough, some part of me was hoping Bethany might say something awful when she opened her mouth. Instead, all she said was, "What about you, Bash?"

"I'm not on a diet, either," I told her.

She let out a little laugh. "I'm sorry, I should have been more clear. What are you majoring in?"

"Business."

"That's interesting. And what do you hope to do with that?"

"After I finish playing professional football, I want to start some businesses with my name on it. Car dealerships, movie theaters, that kind of thing. I figured I better know what I'm doing when I get to that point."

Bethany frowned. "Professional football? That's your plan for your future?"

"Yep." Football was profoundly important in my life. When my mom left, it was the only place for me to take out all of my rage. And I was naturally athletic and willing to work hard to improve. When I was good at something I became heavily invested in it. "I know playing professional football is just a fantasy for most athletes, but I think I can make it."

"That's not really a life plan, though, is it? Don't you have a backup plan? A Plan B?"

"Not really."

Bethany shook her head disapprovingly. "Football is such a violent sport. I can't stand to even watch it. I mean, you could get seriously injured tomorrow, and then where would you be?"

If I hadn't figured it out already, there it was, in black and white. I could never be with someone who not only wasn't into football but wouldn't support me in chasing after my dreams.

"Bash doesn't need a Plan B. He'll swing for the fences, and somehow he'll make it all work out for him in the end," Ember said.

And of all the times recently when I'd wanted to kiss her, it was then that I wanted to kiss her the most.

I cleared my throat. "I don't know what's going to happen. But there are other leagues besides the NFL. Some of them are in other countries. I have options, and our coach has really good connections."

Simon arrived with our food then, and we took our plates as he passed them around. Bethany had ordered some kind of baked chicken breast with vegetables and was busy cutting it into tiny pieces while Ember dipped some of her fries into barbecue sauce.

"Enjoy!" our waiter said, and that was part of the difference between the two women. I'd always loved the way that Ember enjoyed life and all it had to offer.

If Woodby couldn't see how special she was, then he was a flicking mortar-feathering moron who didn't deserve her.

As Bethany cut up her chicken breast she said, "So why are you called Bash?"

My gaze flickered over to Ember, wondering if she was going to volunteer an answer, but she was busy attacking her french fries.

"It's a nickname from my last name, Sebastian. One of my coaches in fifth grade came up with it because of how much I love to tackle people."

"So what's your actual name?"

This was when Ember entered the conversation. "Ian. He doesn't like using it."

Worried that Bethany might ask why, I added, "Only my dad and his wife use it."

"Wife? Wouldn't that be your mom?"

"No," I said with a cough. "My dad remarried." Ember and I exchanged loaded glances, and I decided that was all I was going to say about that.

"Oh." Apparently recognizing that I considered the topic closed, Bethany paid attention to her plate. There was a lull in the dining room that allowed me to hear her humming. It was a tune I didn't recognize.

"Is that from *Hamilton*?" Woodby asked.

Her whole face lit up. "It is! I love musicals."

"My mom dragged me to see *Hamilton* last year and it surprised me how much Woodby liked it," he said. While they started chatting about their favorite scenes and songs, the noise in the restaurant picked back up again. I turned to see Ember giving me another one of those what-have-we-gotten-ourselves-into looks. Woodby sure seemed to like Bethany and to be bonding with her. Did he not understand who was supposed to be with who here?

Did he not realize he was guaranteeing Ember victory?

"So superhero movies are completely unrealistic, but people spontaneously breaking into choreographed dances and perfectly harmonized show tunes, that's real life?" Ember asked me.

I shook my head, hiding my smile. "Don't you think perhaps we should try and join in their conversation? Maybe you should get to know Woodby better."

"I don't know. I think making snarky comments about the things he says is way more fun."

"He's a good guy," I protested. A little gung ho on the whole nutrition thing, but usually decent.

"Probably. But he's not the guy for me, and I knew that within two minutes of meeting him." She bit into her ribs and let out a groan of appreciation that I felt deep in my gut. I was jealous that I hadn't been the cause of it.

While I was busy imagining what exactly I could do to her to recreate that sound, she continued talking. "What about Bethany? She's cute."

"She's not the girl for me, either."

The girl for me was the one I was currently talking to.

"I can see that." Ember nodded. "She probably thinks a Super Bowl party involves making really big pottery."

Amused and delighted, I again had to refrain from kissing her and focused instead on my food.

The conversation between the four of us continued to be awkward, only flowing when Bethany and Woodby loudly discovered something else they had in common, such as their love of detoxing, or when Ember and I enjoyed some private joke.

As soon as it seemed like everyone was done eating (I had to guess when it came to Bethany and Woodby because most of their food was still on their plates while Ember had literally just licked the barbecue sauce from her empty platter), I flagged down Simon and asked for the check.

"Did anyone save any room for dessert?" he asked.

I could only imagine how that conversation would go down. I guessed it would involve a lot of words like *refined sugar* and *carbohydrates*. "No dessert. Just the check, please."

He must have gotten that I was in a hurry for this evening to end as he came right back. Woodby reached for the check. "Woodby's got this."

We all protested, me the loudest. "I ate twice as much food as everyone else. At least let me pay for half of it."

He took out a credit card and handed the little leather folder back to Simon. "No, Woodby insists."

Bethany smiled. "That is very gallant of you."

"Huh. She didn't think it was so gallant when you wanted to pay for her ticket," Ember commented. And maybe it should have bothered me, but it didn't. Bethany's opinion of me had become entirely irrelevant.

Our waiter again returned quickly, and once Woodby had signed the check, everybody stood up at once. We all wanted to get out of there.

We went outside and walked back toward the movie theater parking lot. On the way I asked where Bethany lived so that I could drive both her and Ember home.

She named an apartment complex that was quite a bit south of campus.

"I'm going right by there. I can give you a lift," Woodby said. Which was totally untrue, since I knew he lived in the dorms.

"And Bash is taking me home, so I guess we say goodbye here," Ember declared. There were no hugs this time, just a bunch of nice-to-meet-yous and thanks-so-muches, and then, thankfully, it was over.

I opened Ember's door and looked over to see Woodby doing the same thing for Bethany. He waved to me, and despite still kind of wanting to punch him for making Ember unhappy, I waved back.

It was okay. I could take my frustrations out on him at practice tomorrow.

"Did we just both get dumped?" she asked when I got in the car.

"Not possible. We're awesome."

"Despite our awesomeness, that was awful," she responded. "I don't know if we can declare a winner since both our dates were terrible."

I pulled out of the parking lot, suddenly worried that she might try to back out of our post-game recap. I'd been looking forward to spending time with her. Alone. "So we're not picking a winner? Does this mean you're bailing on tomorrow night? Thus making it so I win by default?"

"Oh no. I think Ember has an open-and-shut case for why Bethany is better than Woodby."

That made me laugh, and it warmed my heart that she was laughing, too.

"Speaking of awkward things from tonight," I said, "what did you really think of the movie?"

"I did like it. I wasn't saying that just to spite the Unfun Police. Although that actor they had playing the villain? That's what he does in every movie. He's the bad guy who says sarcastic things. He's always the same. He's a one-trick pony."

"How many tricks would a pony have to know to impress you? One is pretty awesome."

That led us on a tangent about talented farm animals and actors who couldn't act that carried us all the way to her apartment building. I found a parking spot and turned off the car. When I did that, the entire atmosphere changed. It was no longer just two friends saying good night. There was something more there. I could see it in Ember's eyes, too.

"Okay. Well, Bash, tonight was awkward and confusing as always, so thanks for that." Before I could respond, she was already out of the car.

She couldn't just walk away after saying something like that. I needed to make things okay between us. I threw the door open and jogged a few steps to join her.

"What are you doing? I don't need your help to get back to my apartment."

"I always walk people to their door. And it's not a sexist thing. I'm not saying you can't handle yourself. It's actually a very selfish act on my part, if you must know."

"Selfish?" she repeated.

"Yeah. Because of how upset I'd be if somebody hurt you between here and there. I could never live with the guilt."

"Oh. Well, if I got attacked I wouldn't want to have your guilt on my conscience."

We made it all the way to her door where I expected her to breeze through it while saying goodbye. Instead she hesitated, and my heart started to thunder inside me.

My plan to make things better had not worked and instead was about to make everything more complicated.

She put her hand on my chest and looked up at me through her lashes. My normally strong thighs suddenly felt weak, as if they weren't capable of sustaining my body weight. She took a step closer, and all the air left my lungs.

"There's just one thing I wanted to say."

I held what little breath I had left as she stood on tiptoe, her sweet coconut scent invading my senses, the warmth of her body begging me to pull her closer.

"Tomorrow night?"

Her breath was hot on my ear, sending shudders down my spine.

I could almost feel her smile before she whispered, "Tomorrow, you owe me a dessert."

Ember stepped back, and I had to struggle not to reach for her, not to finish what she'd teasingly started.

She went inside sporting a gigantic smile and closed the door behind her.

I stayed out there for a minute or two, not able to feel the cold air or the snow but instead reliving the personal torture of having Ember so close but still totally untouchable.

Even if our date had been a bust, I'd still had the most amazing time. With her.

Which was a problem.

We shouldn't go out tomorrow, regardless of whether she thought I owed her dessert.

But even as I thought it, I knew I'd go through with it. With a smile and a whistle, I turned around and headed back down the stairs.

If I were a smart man, I'd stay away.

Unfortunately, nobody had ever accused me of being smart.

CHAPTER ELEVEN

EMBER

Bash sent me a text saying we were going to meet and debate who had set who up with the best date on hallowed ground. That meant one of two places. And I was guessing that, given the coldness outside, he didn't want to meet on a football field.

Which meant going to the Silver Trough, Bash's favorite buffet restaurant. He said the loser could treat the winner. I told him I was looking forward to my free meal.

We arranged to meet there at five thirty, before it got too crowded. I planned on going and enjoying my victory dinner. And pretending like nothing had happened between me and Bash last night.

Because nothing had happened. Even though I'd wanted it to. While Woodby had turned out to be a bust, I'd had a fantastic time with Bash.

Admittedly I spent a lot of my time around him imagining what it would be like to kiss him again, but those feelings had actually escalated. I blamed it on the talk I'd had with Jess. Reliving that story made me remember how badly I'd ached for his touch.

So much so that when he walked me to my front door, it felt so much like a date that I couldn't help but put my hand on him and realize that I did remember how to flirt. I didn't know if the flirting had gone well, given his lack of response, but I'd walked inside my apartment feeling pleased with myself that I hadn't peed on him.

Bash was waiting for me at the entrance to the restaurant, and my heart stumbled at the sight of him. He hadn't shaved today, and the stubble along his chin gave him this masculine, slightly dangerous yet sexy look that thrilled me.

It's not a date, I told my hormones. *Just a free dinner.*

They did not care and instead zoomed around inside me with excitement. He was so very handsome.

"Hi!" I said brightly, hoping to mask how pathetically I wanted him.

He smiled at me, and it seriously made everything worse. Then he had to up the ante by saying, "Hey," in this low, growly voice that made my pulse pound loud enough to block out all other sound.

So instead of behaving like a normal human being, I grabbed the door and went inside to the cashier to pay for my dinner. Bash stood right behind me, so close that if I moved slightly I could press my back to his front. And then he could have nuzzled the base of my neck in that way that drove me crazy. My hormones were now doing spinning cartwheels at that prospect.

I cleared my throat, hoping it would also clear my head, and handed the cashier my debit card.

"I'll get a table," I said while Bash paid for his meal. I needed to put some distance between us.

I found a booth and sat down, trying to catch my breath. I could do this. I could sit here with him and laugh and joke, and we could be friends.

Right?

Of course, Bash had to go and disprove that whole theory by sauntering over with that particular and well-deserved swagger of his, taking up all the space in the room so that he was the only thing I could pay attention to.

He sat across from me, taking off his coat while I hungrily watched the way the muscles under his shirt flexed and moved.

"Shall we?" he offered, and it took me a second to realize what he was offering.

"Yuh-huh." It was the best I could manage.

I still had my coat on, so I shrugged it off quickly, leaving it on my seat in the booth. He walked confidently over to the buffet line, knowing exactly what he wanted.

"In case you forgot, I have some tips," Bash said in a confidential tone, leaning in so that I could smell that fresh, clean scent of his that I loved so much. "Bypass the starches. They want you to fill up on those and not get down there to the end, where they keep the good stuff." He handed me a plate. "And remember that they use heavier plates, and the serving utensils are heavy so that your brain will think you have enough food already. Don't fall for it."

"Mr. Buffet Expert, I know how this works. I've been here with you before. We got thrown out, remember?"

Bash was still doing his recon, checking out what area he wanted to attack first. "If they say all you can eat, then they shouldn't be upset when I accept and defeat their challenge."

"You're just lucky they don't have your picture up on a wall of shame."

"Since it's been a few years, I figured there has probably been enough turnover of the management and staff so that I won't have to worry. Okay. Let's divide and conquer, and I'll meet you back at the table."

I nodded. I'd done enough perusing and decided to get myself some lobster and top sirloin. They were in small containers, probably to discourage people from taking too much. Even though Bash had moved to the opposite end of the bar, I could almost hear his voice reminding me they had plenty more in the back and I didn't need to accept tiny portions.

I grabbed some mashed potatoes and corn on the cob, throwing a couple of rolls on the top. They had some lo mein and orange chicken that I planned on coming back for after I finished this first round. I headed over to our table, and Bash was right behind me, carrying two plates with mountains of food on each. I was impressed at his balancing skills.

"I'm not sure Woodby would approve," I said, pointing to his food. "I overheard him saying something last night about moderation in all things." I mean, logically the things Woodby and Bethany had said were true. Most people would probably have agreed with their statements. Only Bash and I had never been moderation-type people.

It was one of the things that had made kissing him so very much fun.

"Bah," he muttered. "Moderation is for wusses. Speaking of Woodby, he sent me this lovely text today."

He pulled his phone out of his pocket, swiped a couple of times, and handed it to me. I tried carefully to avoid any contact with his hand as I didn't want to drop his phone into my pile of mashed potatoes.

There was a picture of Woodby with Bethany sitting on his lap. They were both smiling at the camera. The writing at the bottom said, "Thanks for the introduction!"

"I'm pretty sure you're not supposed to go on a blind double date and end up with the other girl. Who was not your date." I mean, I'd never been very good at math, especially the relationship kind, but this did not add up.

Bash looked concerned. "Does it bother you?"

"What? No! But I mean, does he know he wasn't there to meet Bethany?" I handed him back the phone, again being careful to avoid any sort of physicality.

"I'm not sure. I think so. Either way, I think he's attempting to warn me off Bethany. The picture is so I don't get any ideas. Which is unnecessary."

Why did I feel so relieved to hear that? "At least last night was good for something. For all we know we might have just introduced Todd and Bethany to their future spouses."

Bash swallowed a big bite, nodding. "Maybe we can hire ourselves out as reverse matchmakers. Can't find love? Come on a double date with us and find the man of your dreams! Hint, it won't be me."

As if. I nearly laughed out loud, but managed to refrain. Bash was the man of every woman's dreams. He had starred in mine quite frequently.

But of course, I couldn't say that.

So instead my brain decided to say something stupid. "We can only do it for a fee, of course. Bethany gave me her notes and some cookies to get me to convince you."

"She bribed you? With cookies?"

"Crap. I wasn't going to tell you that part. And don't think of them as a bribe. Think of them as motivating incentives." Chocolaty good ones that I was glad Bash never got to taste. Because if he had, I was pretty sure he would have been sitting here with Bethany instead of me.

"Huh." Bash rubbed his chin thoughtfully. "It sounds like you owe me some cookies."

Which, of course, brought me back to my not-so-subtle attempts to flirt with him last night, telling him he owed me a dessert and how he hadn't reacted to my moves at all, and so I didn't say anything in response.

I just ate instead. Eating in companionable silence was something Bash and I had always done really well.

"How's your steak?" he asked as he cut into his salmon. "It looks delicious."

I held my fork and knife protectively over my meat, and he laughed.

"Don't worry," he reassured me. "I'll go get some of my own. I'm not Woodby. I know better than to ask you to share."

He always made me laugh, and filled me up with so much delight that I couldn't help but ask, "Do you know what I love best about you?"

What? How had I just said that? I didn't say *loved*, past tense. I'd said *love*. As in right now. This very moment. I held my breath, wondering what he would say in response.

But he didn't seem to notice how I'd misspoken or that my cheeks were turning a bright red as he contemplated a response.

"My devastating good looks? My incredible strength? Or my amazing dexterity and ability to tackle anyone, anywhere, anytime? My killer sense of humor? My willingness to drive you to the airport or help you move into a new apartment? Or is it my ability to eat the contents of an entire McDonald's menu in one sitting?"

I laughed again, my stomach hurting from laughing so hard. Heaven help me, I loved all of those things about him.

When I could breathe again I said, "Actually, it's your humility." Now it was his turn to laugh, but I continued on before I lost my nerve. "You don't try to monitor my eating habits. I can't even tell you how many guys I've gone out with who acted like they were the food police and it was their personal responsibility to watch every bite that went in my mouth. Like I have some secret sign on my forehead that said, 'On a diet, please help and monitor my choices.'"

He actually stopped eating to stare at me, like he couldn't believe that what I'd just said was true. "Are you serious?"

I nodded. "I don't know where it comes from or why some guys do it, but I don't need their help. So thank you for not trying to correct me." Like Woodby had done last night.

"That would kind of make me a hypocrite, don't you think? Besides, I like the way you enjoy things." It was this kind of intimate remark that made my heart pound hard against my ribs, but then he waggled his eyebrows as if he meant it as a joke, and I didn't know how to respond.

Bash said, "I'll get some of that steak the next time I get up." Which was going to be soon, given his rate of consumption.

"Tsk-tsk. Were you not paying attention last night? Eating meat is killing our planet." It was one of the very fun things Woodby had shared while I was trying to enjoy my dinner. "But to be honest, I don't want to live on the planet without meat." Which I knew Bash got, because he would eat until the cows came home. And then he would eat them, too.

He agreed with me by saying, "You are preaching to the choir. And I'll be right back."

I trained my eyes on my food so that I would not watch him walk away, given that his perfectly sculpted rear end was right in my sightline. Okay, fine. I might have stolen a peek or two.

Or twenty.

When he returned, he put a bowl filled with chocolate soft-serve ice cream covered in Reese's Pieces in front of me. Just the way I liked it.

A light, fluttery feeling roosted in my chest. He had remembered. I was so touched by his thoughtfulness that I wasn't sure what to say. I couldn't read too much into this, could I? "I, um, wasn't done with dinner. I can't have dessert yet."

"That's the beauty of the buffet, E. You can have dessert whenever you want and still have more dinner. But as you've reminded me, I owed you a dessert."

My heart stuttered and came to a stop before bursting back to life. He'd called me E. Probably without even realizing it. *Just a slip of the tongue,* I told myself. It hadn't meant anything. An old nickname that had surfaced for absolutely no reason at all.

I also needed to ignore him mentioning owing me a dessert. Because that wasn't a reference to my sad attempt at flirting last night, was it?

Bash was a thoughtful guy who did nice things for people. That was it. I wasn't allowed to try and read more into it.

His phone buzzed loudly, and he picked it up to look at the screen. He frowned slightly. "Sorry. I hate when people do this. Let me turn it off."

As he shut it down, jealousy spiked through me as I wondered who had texted him and why.

"That was from Woodby," he said, without me having to ask for an explanation. Another thing I liked about Bash. He didn't try to hide things. What you saw was what you got. "He now apparently thinks he needs to thank me, and he plans on doing this by fixing my 'nutritional issues.' He's recommended a detox juicing cleanse that will, for a fact, clear out all my toxins."

"Again, I don't think this guy knows what facts are, and juice detoxes are not a real thing. You may temporarily lose some weight, but wheatgrass, acai, and guavas are not going to clean out anything except your wallet." I took a big bite of my ice cream, sighing as it made its delicious way down my throat. "Maybe I should do a retox. That's where I plan on introducing lots of bad toxins into my body and seeing what happens."

"Are you hoping for some kind of superhero outcome?"

"Mm-hmm. I'll be able to eat all the junk food I want, and I'll get the power to not gain weight. I'll call myself Super Caterpillar. Because those things eat constantly and still turn into butterflies."

"But you're already a butterfly." He said it with his trademark grin, and the combination of his words and that smile made my heart feel like it was an actual butterfly, light and fluttery and about to take flight.

I had to remind myself that Bash was a natural flirt. It was what he did. He couldn't help but be charming and adorable. It didn't mean anything. I needed to stop reading into this situation.

"Yeah, well, when it comes to eating, someday we're going to have to stop eating like this. When we're no longer practicing or training every day and our metabolisms are shot. Or else we're going to have some weight issues."

Bash lifted up his shirt and patted one of his hands against his washboard abs. "I think I'll be okay for a while."

My mouth went dry, my eyes practically bugged out of my head, and I wondered how rude it was to blatantly ogle him, considering he was the one showing off. I heard Deja warning me in my head about boys who worked for six-pack abs, but I did not care what the implications were. Only that Bash was seriously the hottest guy in the entire universe.

And also, that I had not made an appropriate response to his statement.

"Yep," was all I could manage by way of agreement that his perfectly sculpted stomach was A-okay. Why was it suddenly so hot in here? It was snowing outside, and I was eating ice cream. How could I be sweating?

When it became obvious that I currently lacked the ability to start up a conversation, Bash asked me about my major, what kind of classes it entailed, the requirements. "Like, do you still have to take a foreign-language class?"

"Yeah. It's called math."

His laughter was starting to help my too-thick tongue to shrink in size, but he was still doing the heavy lifting. "I have to say, I'm surprised that you're not planning on being a writer. I remember how I used to see you in the hallways at school, writing in a notebook. I always wondered what you were writing."

Um, mostly odes to how hot he was. "I did use to do that. I can't believe you remember that." But then another thought occurred to me, something that I couldn't make line up with our past timeline. "But I did that before you and I, you know . . ." I was ridiculous. I couldn't even say when we used to date.

He rolled some lo mein around his fork like spaghetti noodles. "I noticed you a long time before I worked up the courage to talk to you."

My heart butterfly mutated into one big enough to take down New York City, making it impossible for me to breathe. I was about to say something sappy and really embarrass myself. I would ignore those giddy, sighing feelings I was having that made me want to climb over this table and throw my arms around his neck. Because seriously, he had noticed me for a long time? He was afraid to talk to me? He might have had a crush on me for as long as I'd had one on him?

When and why had all of that changed?

Needing to keep things lighter and more platonic, I ignored my heart, which was currently begging me to ask him questions. What had we been talking about before? Right. My major. "I got into nursing after my mom's first round of chemo. The nurses in the oncology department were so amazing that I decided I wanted to do that for other people. Besides, it's really hard to make a living as a writer, and I enjoy things like having a place to live and stuff to eat. And because it was my dad's thing."

I hadn't meant to say the last part out loud. I'd never admitted that to anyone before. I loved reading, I had adored writing. But writing was what my father had been famous for, and the absolute last thing I wanted was to follow in his footsteps. Or for him to get any posthumous credit for how I turned out as an adult.

"That makes sense." Bash nodded. "But poetry's not the same thing as fiction. I know that because while I have loved many books, I can't think of a single poem that I love."

It proved nothing and was utter nonsense, but I appreciated him trying to make me feel better. "All poems? Even the ones that start with *there once was a girl from Nantucket*?"

"I will confess to a certain amount of admiration for limericks," he said with a wink.

"Well, I'll confess that I know it's stupid and I shouldn't care what anyone else thinks. But I don't want people to draw comparisons between me and him. I mean, if I was a good enough writer to even get published."

"That's silly. You're good at everything you do," he said, and I could hear the sincerity in his voice. Even if it wasn't true, he meant it. My mutant-butterfly heart started banging against my rib cage, trying to get free and go to him. "I get it, though. Coach has rules about not partying, and it's been surprisingly easy to keep. I never wanted to drink or do drugs because I didn't want to end up like my mom. And yet, that's why I got featured on ISEN when my last coach kicked me off the team. For listening to an idiot teammate who said it worked for him and thinking it was a good idea to use marijuana to try and fix my medication problems. It's now what I'm known for."

Without thinking I reached across the table and put my hand on top of his. "That is not what you're known for. You're one of the best inside linebackers in the entire country. You're a good person with a big heart. You are kind and sweet and a good son and a good brother. And a good friend."

He turned his hand over so that we could hold hands for a moment. He squeezed gently, and I was filled with so much warmth and love for him that I had to pull away before I did something idiotic.

"Thank you." He stared at the plate in front of him for a minute. "Did you know that my mom contacted me?"

"What?" I did not know that. I remembered all of the pain he'd carried around with him as a teenager over his mom leaving their family. It had been something we'd bonded over, how we'd felt betrayed by two of the most important people in our lives.

"Yeah. Basically she apologized, like it wasn't too little too late. And then she said that she wanted to see me and Marley and that she's gotten her life together and remarried. And I have a half brother and sister she wants us to meet."

I was stunned. While my father had left and died not long after, I knew that some secret part of Bash had always hoped his mother would return. I had sometimes wondered if that was why he had moved out after our parents had married. Because a sad little boy inside him still wanted his mom to come home.

"Wow. I don't even know what to say." He had left his hand on the table, palm still up, and I wanted so badly to put my hand back on his. To share what strength and compassion I had for him and his situation.

Bash cleared his throat. "Nobody here knows about her. Not even my roommate. I talk about her like she's still in my life. Stuff like, 'my mom always says.' As if she's around and giving me any kind of advice."

"Why do you think you do that?"

"I don't know. Shame? Embarrassment that my own mom doesn't want to be around me?"

His voice caught, and it shattered whatever reserves I had about not comforting him. I took his hand again, and this time he gripped it, like I was his lifeline.

"She does want to be around you," I reminded him. "Maybe you should hear her out. See what she has to say about why she did what she did." Maybe, if she was an actual human being with any sense of decency, she could give Bash some peace of mind. I knew he had often blamed himself for her leaving, as little kids do even when they rationally understand as adults that it wasn't their fault.

Maybe she could heal that piece of his heart that she had broken by leaving.

He still squeezed my hand tightly, as if he'd forgotten how big and strong his hands were. "I've been thinking about it."

"I'll go with you." I should have regretted the words, but I didn't. I knew how much she'd hurt him and how much he needed to heal. I would be happy to stand by him as he talked to her.

So much for me keeping things light and platonic. I might as well have just told him I was still in love with him and always would be just to pile on to his emotional trauma.

"Thanks." The word was soft and heartfelt. Then he finally let my hand go, and I saw the change in his eyes, heard it in his voice, as he threw up his defense mechanisms and shifted from being sad to upbeat. "Tell me more about what's been going on with you. Any shows you've binged recently that you'd recommend?"

In between getting up to go grab more food, Bash and I talked. Really talked, in a way that we hadn't in years. It made me feel like I was seventeen years old again, crazy in love, and wanting to know everything I possibly could about the person sitting across the table from me. We talked about TV shows and movies, his favorite football teams (go Seahawks and Jacks!), caught each other up on some of the things that had been going on in our lives the last few years, our classes at school, my part-time job at the library, Bash's declaration that bacon was the greatest food achievement of mankind (while I argued that it was actually cake), the kind of training we were doing for our teams, how I'd dealt with my mom's cancer, which then led us into some dangerous territory. How things were going with our respective parents and our siblings.

"Speaking of family," he said, "my dad invited us up next week to take part in the Sebastian Thanksgiving football bowl."

"Shouldn't that be at Thanksgiving?"

"Since we didn't have it last year, they wanted to get together and do one now. You should come and play with us."

I knew about the game because I'd celebrated the holiday with Bash's family before (even though he wasn't there). But I'd never participated in the game. I glanced at the windows behind us. "They do know it's snowing, right?"

"Sometimes it snows at Thanksgiving, too, and we still play. Maybe it'll clear up in time for next week."

That was entirely possible. The weather in Washington State was often bipolar.

But given all the feelings I was currently catching, I wasn't sure that returning to my childhood home, a.k.a. the scene of our relationship's biggest crime, was in the best interest of my emotional health. "I have a lot of work to do."

"My apologies," he said with a flourish of his hand.

"Apologies?" I repeated.

"I didn't realize you were a chicken. Afraid to play with the big boys."

While I knew what he was doing, I still responded. "I'm no chicken. And I am coming, and I am going to play, and I'm going to tackle you so hard your teeth will rattle."

"Ha. The last thing you tackled was a bag of Doritos."

Now I was definitely going. I was going to play opposite Bash's team, and I was going to win just so that he would have to eat his words.

Judging by his laughter from my expression, he knew what I was thinking.

"At some point this tricking me into doing stuff by using my competitive nature against me is going to stop working," I told him.

"Don't think of it as tricking you. Think of it as a motivating incentive!"

I reached over to smack him while he laughed at his own joke. His biceps were so nice and big and strong. I considered leaving my hand where it was but regained my sanity.

He doesn't like you that way, I reminded myself.

There was this awkward moment when I took my hand away, hoping he hadn't noticed my attempt to feel up his arm and then he said, "We should go. I think I'm full."

That couldn't have been possible, given that I'd never known Bash to ever be full, but I did need to get home. I had a paper I had to finish up before class tomorrow, and I'd reached my daily quota of personal humiliation. "Okay."

As we both put our coats on, he asked, "Can I catch a ride home with you? I had one of my teammates drop me off."

"You should have called me to come pick you up. I could have done that."

We walked past the cashier's station and got out front. I pointed to where I'd parked, and we headed in that direction.

"I know I could have. I mean, I would have, except then it would have felt too much like . . ." His voice trailed off, as if he'd said more than he'd intended.

I pushed the button to unlock my car, and while Bash climbed in on the passenger side, I stood outside, my limbs shaking. What had he almost said? There was only one way to finish that sentence, right?

Too much like what? Too much like a date?

And he didn't want it to feel like a date?

At first there was this glimmer of hope, that he thought maybe we had the potential to be something more. Something date-like.

But then I realized that he didn't want it to be like a date because he didn't want to date me. And he didn't want me to get the wrong idea about his intentions.

I was the dumbest person alive. When was I going to get it through my extraordinarily thick skull that Bash was not into me? That no matter how much I wanted him, no matter how gorgeous I thought he was, he did not feel the same.

He kept making that pretty clear, and I was the one who kept choosing to hope for more.

Resigned, I got in the car and started it up. I asked him which dorm he lived in so that I would know where to drop him off. Because I would not be walking him to the door, and like he claimed last night, my motivations were entirely selfish. Despite what an amazing time we'd been having, now I just wanted this night to be over so that I could go home and eat a pint of ice cream and pity myself for my poor taste in men.

I blamed my mother. It was probably genetic.

While I drove, Bash messed with my radio stations. "These are the same ones you listened to in high school."

"Yep." A lot of things were like they'd been back in high school. Including the fact that I was still in love with him.

Bash asked me who my favorite singer/band was, and we discussed the current state of pop music on our drive back to his dorm.

Then we arrived, and I was ready for him to go. I put the car in park but did not turn it off. "Okay. Thanks. See you later."

"Wait. We didn't decide who won the bet and had to pay for dinner."

"Then we probably shouldn't have gone to a place where you pay before you eat and make decisions."

He smiled. "Probably. But I'm thinking . . . we call it a draw?"

117

"That's a good idea, given that I think we made Bethany and Todd fall in love by being terrible dates."

That earned me one of his toe-tingling grins, and I forced my hands to stay on the steering wheel. "We are," he agreed.

He sat there smiling at me, and it made the back of my knees feel faint, and I was in serious danger of embarrassing both of us. "Okay. Bye now."

Then he finally took the hint and opened his door, nearly hitting the red car parked next to us. A car with extremely fogged-up windows.

He made a sound of disgust, and I couldn't help but ask, "Who is that?"

"It is my roommate and his girlfriend." He turned his head to yell the next part. "They forget that their windows are see-through!" Then his smile was back, and he was looking at me again. "Anyway, this was fun. We should do it again sometime."

He closed the car door, leaving me even more confused. We should do what again sometime?

As I put my car in reverse, I listened to all of his words running through my head, and there was one thing he'd said that wasn't true.

He'd agreed with me that we were terrible dates. But after last night and tonight, Bash might have been a lot of things, but a terrible date was not one of them. At the edge of the parking lot, I checked my rearview mirror and movement had me glancing back. Jess and Logan climbed out of her car, laughing and holding hands.

I remembered making out in a parked car with Bash. And I wanted to do it again.

I was so super pathetic.

This friend thing was not going to work out. I didn't think I could keep myself in check for much longer. I would probably have to tell him how I really felt and see what happened next.

Why did that idea fill me with so much dread?

CHAPTER TWELVE

BASH

I saw Ember in our algebra class, and things seemed to be okay. We were friendly, but right as class let out on the day before the family football game was scheduled, she said, "I don't think I'll be able to make it. I've got too much to do. But have fun!"

"Are you sure?"

"So sure. I'm just . . . busy, busy. You know how it goes."

I considered goading her into coming but stopped myself. The last week had been about proving that I could be around her and that we could chat like friends. Thing was, it wasn't like it had been at the buffet. Where we'd shared personal things and talked about our likes and dislikes and spent time getting to know each other. There was a distance between us again.

Part of me wanted to accept it as our new normal. This was what needed to happen.

But I'd loved spending time with her. The real her. Not this polite facade she put on.

Compartmentalizing my life was kind of my go-to. It was easy for me to put stuff in mental boxes. Food I Could Eat. Places I Could Go. Girls I Could Date. Girls Who Could Only Be Friends.

But no matter how hard I tried, Ember would not stay put in that last box.

So maybe it was a good thing I was going up to my dad's alone. I had planned on driving with her, but I could catch a bus. Even if it would take a little bit longer, it was time I didn't have to spend in Ember's company acting like I just wanted to be her buddy.

Because nothing could be further from the truth.

It would also be good for me to go back home to remind myself why I was playing the martyr here. Why I was giving up something that could be amazing so that everybody else could be happy.

When I arrived home, the entire place was in an uproar. Aunts and uncles, cousins and grandparents were coming in and out of rooms, talking and laughing, hugging me hello. The kitchen smelled amazing, and I greeted everyone, including the little kids who attached themselves to my legs and hugged me.

Roscoe danced in circles around my legs, and I scratched him in between his ears, which seemed to make him supremely happy. If only life were that easy where people were concerned.

"Come on, you monsters. I have to go start some laundry. Go play in the other room." I tousled my cousins' hair, and they ran off to find somebody else to torture. Roscoe raced after them, apparently having appointed himself their guardian for the afternoon.

I hefted my duffel bag on my shoulder. I figured as long as I was here, I might as well get some free laundry done.

"What's in the bag? Are you smuggling in some contraband? Are you sneaking in reefer? Mary Jane? Moocah?"

My sister, Marley, had called out to me from her room, and I went in to see what she was talking about. "What?"

She closed the textbook she'd been highlighting. "I'm just making sure you're not trying to bring your marijuana into this house."

I dropped my bag on the floor and went to sit on the foot of her bed. If there was one thing my sweet, bubbly little sister enjoyed more than anything else, it was teasing me for why I'd been kicked out of college. "Maybe I would have understood you better if you'd bothered to use some terms that are actually from this century."

"Sorry I'm not up on all your hip lingo for your illegal substances," she said with a grin. "But since I know both our parents are addicts, I never mess with the stuff."

"Yes, you're superior to me in every way," I said. "But in my defense, I wasn't thinking clearly at the time. My depression meds weren't working."

Her demeanor shifted quickly from mocking to concerned. "I know. Nobody blames you."

"I blame me."

"Well, you shouldn't," she said decisively. "And look at how good it all turned out. If you were still in Pennsylvania, you couldn't stop by and see me. You're my brother, but you're also one of my best friends, and I'm so glad I can see your ugly face in person."

Her words made me feel guilty. I hadn't been great about coming by as often as I should have. "I'm sorry I haven't been around more."

She made a dismissive gesture. "I kind of got used to it. It was like you left for college a year earlier than we'd expected. I missed you, but I didn't *miss you* miss you. You know? Plus, we talked all the time."

That at least I could feel good about. I had made a serious effort to stay in touch with her and my dad. I had been willing to sacrifice my home, but not my relationships with them.

"What do you have going on today?" I asked. "Are you going to play in the game?"

She let out a giggle at my suggestion and rolled onto her back. "Um, no. Lauren and I have decided to watch and eat a bite of pumpkin

121

pie every time somebody does something stupid while they're playing. I figure I'll probably gain five pounds today."

I laughed at the mental image she painted, and was very grateful that Lauren had stepped in to help fill the hole created by my absence. It was one of the reasons why I'd removed myself from this situation. The bond between Lauren and Marley had been instant, despite how different they were in appearance and temperament. They were sisters from the moment they'd met, and they adored one another. I wouldn't have wanted to put that in jeopardy.

"That sounds like a plan. I hope you guys enjoy yourselves." I stood up and grabbed my duffel bag. "Hey, is there anything else you want to talk about?"

"No." She shot me a confused look. "Is there something I should want to talk about?"

"Nope. Just, I'm around if you need me."

I left her room and dropped my bag off next to the washing machine. I needed to find my dad. He hadn't told Marley about our mom's letter. Because if he had, she would have called me. I'd actually spent the last week and a half expecting her call. Why hadn't he? When he was the one who said he wasn't going to keep anything from her?

It was just another stressor to throw on the pile of things that were currently stressing me out. I used one of my breathing/calming exercises a long-ago therapist had taught me and told myself that I was in control of my reactions to the things that were happening around me.

Honestly, I'd kind of hoped to be able to take out some of my frustrations on Woodby, but he had skipped practice for the whole week. It wasn't mandatory, so he could get away with it, but it was something the coaches were sure to notice. From wherever they hid and watched while we played.

There was a reason they called EOL End of the Line. For most of the football team, this was our last chance to either get back to a

Division 1 school or get noticed by the NFL. I didn't understand how anyone could skip practices or training, mandatory or not. I was determined to make the most of the second chance I'd been given by being here. I wouldn't take it for granted.

I began searching for my father. When I checked in the family room, I saw that there was a football game on, and it looked like something that had been previously recorded. I forced myself not to watch, because football had a way of drawing me in and blocking out the rest of the world. I didn't need the distraction.

After looking around the rest of the house and asking some questions as to Dad's whereabouts, I was told to look in the garage. That should have been the first place I'd gone.

My dad loved his extended family, but he was a big introvert who needed to decompress from this many people. Sure enough, he was in the garage working on his old Ford truck. The space heater was on, and I took off my coat when I got inside. "Hey, Dad."

He looked up from the engine he'd been bending over. "Hey, son. Come help me. Tricia's going to kill me if I stay out here much longer. You can change the oil. This beauty's nearly ready to pass her emissions test."

"Wow. You got it roadworthy." He and I had been working on this since I was about twelve. I couldn't believe he was almost done. It felt a little sad closing this chapter of my life, and that he'd finished it without me.

"Something on your mind?"

"Yes. Why haven't you talked to Marley?"

He used an oilcloth to clean off the screwdriver in his hand. "Just hasn't seemed like the right time yet."

"What are you waiting for?"

Hanging the screwdriver back on his pegboard where he kept his tools, he said, "Actually, I was waiting for you."

"For me?"

He was quiet, studying me. "I needed to know where your head was at. If you decided against reaching out to your mom, I had to know that. To let Marley know that you wouldn't be there."

"Of course I'd be there for Marley."

"I mean physically there, sitting next to her on the couch. Not emotionally supporting her from a distance."

I ran my fingers through my hair. "And if I decide to see Mom?"

He leaned against his workbench. "If you do, and it's probably unfair of me, but I wanted you to get the lay of the land. What is she expecting? What are her explanations? What will she say? I've been hoping you'd decide to get in touch just so that we can get the full story. But it's your choice. If you're not going to see her, I have to prepare Marley. And if you are, well, I need to know what she's walking into. She's only sixteen. It's my job to protect her."

It was something I understood all too well. Protecting people was part of my nature. Probably something I'd inherited.

But having to talk to my mother? Feeling like I didn't have a choice in the matter? That I was not okay with.

It was getting hot in here. I pulled my sweater off, leaving just my white T-shirt. I folded my arms because my desire was to go outside, find an unsuspecting cousin, and just tackle him into the ground for some relief.

"This is total bull shirt," I muttered.

"Ian! Language."

"I said *shirt*. With an *r*. Coach doesn't want us to swear." I watched as he started gathering up all the supplies I'd need to change the oil. "Maybe Marley and I should go see her together."

Even without my dad's expression, as soon as I said it, I knew it was a terrible idea. There was no way I could just toss my sister into the deep end and hope she could swim. I was going to shelter her from as much pain as I could in this situation. I would sacrifice myself for her sake. It was what I did. In football and in the rest of my life.

"Forget I said that," I told him. "I'll think about talking to Mom and let you know what I decide."

He nodded. "You know where everything is. I'll see you inside once you're done."

While I understood his reasoning, it still seemed strange that my father would be encouraging me to talk to my mother. Especially given the way that her leaving had nearly destroyed him. But I didn't like thinking about that time in my life.

In fact, ever since he'd come to see me at school, I'd pretty much put her out of my mind. Other than telling Ember about the letter, my brain had been blissfully Mom-free. Delaying and avoidance had always been my go-to moves when faced with something I didn't want to face. I knew they weren't healthy coping mechanisms, but they were my factory-set defaults.

But regardless of me avoiding my problems, there were questions that I'd been carrying around with me for years. Not knowing why she'd left still really bothered me. Where did she go? What did she do? Had she been in prison? On the streets? Holed up in some random guy's house getting high?

I knew my maternal grandparents had tortured themselves with the same kind of questions. I wondered if she'd gotten back in touch with them, but I was afraid to reach out and ask. If she hadn't, it would absolutely kill them. They had always blamed themselves for not recognizing the signs of her addiction earlier and getting her the help she'd needed.

I picked up the socket wrench to loosen the nut on the oil drain plug, confident my father had already chosen the right size. I double-checked the jacks, knowing it was unnecessary. My dad didn't make mistakes when it came to cars.

I grabbed my dad's creeper and laid it flat on the ground. I knelt down and turned over, placing my back squarely on it. I used my feet to scoot under the car.

I looked up at the light filtering through the engine and tried to figure out the right thing to do. What would Marley want? Maybe she wouldn't be interested in talking to my mom. Or maybe she would. She'd been a lot younger than me when Mom had left. Her normal had been growing up without a mother. Would she have questions? Or would she just . . . not care?

The problem was, Marley and I had never discussed this possibility. I didn't know how she would feel or react. Mom was basically a non-subject in our household. Dad had been both parents for us.

Of course, my mom and that whole situation wasn't the only thing I'd been avoiding. I was also avoiding my feelings for Ember. Trying to put us in the friend zone and make it all nice and platonic so that I could still have her in my life. I'd missed her. And hadn't realized how much until I'd seen her again.

And now it was like I missed her even when she was sitting next to me in class.

Not to mention how hard it was to pretend like I didn't want her so badly that I felt like I was drowning with my need for her.

I lifted the socket wrench, glad that I had something to do with my hands, a way to turn my mind off and just focus on the task in front of me.

Instead, I saw Ember's face. She still wouldn't stay in her box.

I felt like I'd been living my life for other people. To keep them safe and to make sure they weren't hurt.

When was that going to happen for me?

Or was it my responsibility to make it happen? To find Ember and tell her everything that was still in my heart?

I let the wrench lower to the ground as I considered that it might not even do me any good. She hadn't seemed to indicate a whole lot of interest in me. I mean, I got the distinct feeling that she was still attracted to me, but nothing much beyond that. Maybe she'd met someone recently. I only had to look at how fast Woodby and Bethany had become serious. Ember could have met someone new, and I didn't figure into her plans at all.

Or there wasn't a guy involved, and the past was the past for her and she no longer had those feelings for me.

I only had to close my eyes, and I was back in the moment where I hovered over her in her bed, with her telling me that she wanted me. The way her dark hair had spread out all over her pillow, how her eyes had darkened with desire, her lips swollen from my kisses. She'd said, "I love you," and it was both the best and worst thing I'd ever heard.

I didn't know if I was ready to let go of the possibility of her. If I told her my true feelings, that I'd never stopped loving her, she might rip my still-beating heart out of my chest and stomp on it in response. And what if she said there could never, would never, should never be anything between us? It would be the right thing, what was best for our loved ones, but I didn't know how I was supposed to move on from her.

I suspected it would involve another cross-country trip. Although putting miles in between us last time hadn't changed anything.

I worried it had only delayed the inevitable.

What was I supposed to do, then? It was better that Ember wasn't coming here today. I needed the reprieve to figure out what I should do next. Because with both my mom and Ember, delaying wasn't a long-term solution.

Time for me to figure out my next move.

CHAPTER THIRTEEN

EMBER

"I really do need to get laundry done," I told Deja.

She wasn't buying it. "I thought you were going to stay away. No more Bash. For someone you don't want to spend time with, you seem to spend a lot of time with him."

"It's not my fault I keep seeing him everywhere."

"That probably happens because you're stalking him."

Throwing the last of my stuff into my laundry bag, I swung it over my shoulder. "My mom also texted me this morning and asked me to come. You know I can't tell her no."

"If that's the lie you have to tell yourself." She followed behind me as I made my way to the living room. "And what other plans do you have for today?"

"My laundry, checking in on my mom, saying hi to my sister. And there will be Thanksgiving food and a game of touch football." I opened the door, ready to escape this conversation.

She wagged her finger at me as she said, "Touch football doesn't mean that you should be touching football players."

"I second that!" Molly called out from her room. I shook my head at both of them and said I'd see them later.

On the drive to my mom's, I admitted the truth to myself. I'd done my best to be strong this past week. I'd seen Bash three times when we had algebra together. Of course he'd been funny and bantered with me and Sabrina. He drew little pictures on the margins of my paper, and it was as cute and adorable as it sounded. He kept making me forget that he wasn't attracted to me and didn't love me and most certainly did not want me to be his girlfriend.

That was the problem with Bash. He made it too easy to get caught up in him.

Just yesterday I'd told him I wouldn't be going to the Sebastian family event. That I was too busy. Which was true. I was always busy. There were always more things to do than hours in the day to get them all done. But somehow, like every other college student in the country, I managed while still finding time to have a social life. Usually this meant a massive lack of sleep. I was willing to lose sleep for Bash's sake. I'd certainly done enough of that in the past since he'd been the cause of many a sleepless night.

I considered turning around multiple times. I knew that I should have. But instead I just kept driving. I was pathetic. A Bash addict. I wanted just one more little hit. In a room full of people related to him, which would hopefully deter me from doing anything unseemly or sad. I could just watch him, drink him in, and then come back and beat myself up for my weakness later. And probably eat cake while I was doing it.

I arrived quickly and had to park several houses down as there was no room anywhere else in the driveway or in front of the house. The noise hit me when I reached the front yard, but once I was inside it was nearly deafening. A total madhouse. With all the different people and blended families, I'd given up remembering who belonged to who and what branch of the Sebastians they came from a long time ago. Roscoe bounded over to me, his tongue out, happy to see me. I crouched down to give him a quick rubdown. As soon as I finished he ran back to some small kids who he kept nudging with his head.

"Mom?" I called out, and several adult women turned to look at me. My mother stuck her head out of the kitchen.

"In here, sweetheart."

What had she done to her head? I set my bag down on the staircase and went into the kitchen. It smelled divine, all turkey and pumpkin-y. But I couldn't stop staring at her hair.

She noticed. "Like it?"

After chemo, her once dark, thick, and straight hair that had hung down to her waist grew back in gray, curly and coarse. She was never quite sure how to style it since it was so different from what she'd been used to.

But right now it was bright pink. I mean, shocking pink. It looked like her head had blown a giant Bubble Yum bubble.

"It's in honor of breast cancer research," she said, and I realized that I hadn't spoken in a while and was probably making her uncomfortable.

"If you like it that's all that matters," I told her.

"That's awfully polite of you." She said it with a knowing smile.

"So what can I do? How can I help?" I clapped my hands together, ready to get to work. There were probably a million things she needed done.

I saw the irritation that flashed briefly through her eyes. "Everything's almost ready, actually. You can go join the others."

"Come on, let me help."

"I'm not an invalid anymore," she said, her shoulders squaring off like she was getting ready for a fight.

I threw up both of my hands, like I was surrendering. "Whoa, I'm not saying you are. Only that you have a house full of Sebastian men who can eat more than a killer whale at a sea-lion buffet."

Before she could presumably protest, Marley stuck her head in the kitchen. "Hey, Ember! Tricia, my dad can't find the serving platter."

Mom closed her eyes for a moment. "Tell him, for the third time, that it's in the garage. On the right side, fourth shelf from the bottom. He needs to get it and clean it so we can use it for the turkey."

"Dad!" Marley yelled as she ran off, presumably to share this information.

"I swear, marriage vows should include that you'll have to promise to help your husband find stuff that is right in front of him. Things you've given him explicit instructions for. Because sometimes I feel like that's all I ever do."

"You're giving me so much hope for marriage," I told her, trying to keep the snark to a minimum but unable to help myself. "To be fair, he did really step it up with that whole in-sickness-or-in-health part."

She reached up to touch her flamingo hair. "Yes, he did."

I grabbed some baby carrots. "I think your marriage vows should have included something about how you'd love him completely even though he chews his food so loudly. You should probably get an award for putting up with that nonsense."

"Are you being sarcastic? I can never tell."

"You can't tell? Here's a hint: I'm always sarcastic."

Mom's phone buzzed, and she picked it up. "It's Doug. He still can't find the platter. That's how you can help me. In the garage, right wall, fourth shelf. This isn't rocket science."

"Sure." I felt like I was being Mom-nipulated. More of her trying to throw me and Doug together. Like she believed that if we just spent a few more minutes together, everything would click into place, and he'd be my new dad, and we'd be one big happy family.

Don't get me wrong, Doug was a great guy. He just wasn't a father to me. Things might have been different if they'd gotten married when I was, like, eight. If I'd grown up with him as the only father figure in my life. But that didn't happen.

I lived in the same house with him for one year, and during that time we were both focused on my mom and her treatment and recovery. Plus, I didn't know what to say to him because I hadn't known what Bash might have told him. So I just kept to myself, and then I went away to college. Not very far away to college, but I was living on my own.

It was different for Lauren, and that was good. I think my mom wanted me to have the same sort of relationship that Lauren and Doug had, but she didn't realize that was never going to happen.

I made my way out to the freestanding garage and was immediately hit with a blast of heat. Doug was nowhere to be found. Jeez, he wasn't even in the right part of the house to find the platter. I started over to the far wall, already spotting the platter when I noticed a pair of legs sticking out from underneath the front of the truck. The jeans molded nicely to the strong legs, and I didn't remember any of Doug's relatives being this hot.

The legs moved, wheels rolled, and next thing I knew, I was looking at freaking Bash. He had a drop of oil on his cheek. How was that sexy?

Suddenly I understood why my mother had cut her own fan belt.

"You're here?" he asked in a way that made me think he wished I wasn't. He stood up and I took a step back.

"I'm here. Unless I've died and turned into a ghost without my knowledge, in which case, it would make total sense that I would haunt you. You totally deserve it."

He grinned at me as I grabbed an oilcloth. I reached up to clean the drip from his face, and I was so shaken by standing so close to him that the rag slipped, leaving my fingers on his skin. How could he be so soft and so strong all at the same time?

I yanked my hand back as if I'd been scalded, because that was exactly what it had felt like.

We stood there for . . . I don't know how long . . . close enough to kiss, his breath washing over my face in waves, his Adam's apple bobbing as he gulped. My heart started somersaulting as flames roared to life inside me, rendering my limbs weak and shaky.

I somehow managed to move closer, swallowing as I did so. Was I ever going to be able to breathe normally around him?

He broke the spell first by walking over to his dad's workbench and put the tool thingy in his hand back on the wall. "I thought you were too 'busy, busy' to be here."

I leaned against the truck for support. How was he fine and talking when I felt like this truck had just run me over? "I . . . um . . ." I couldn't exactly tell him that I'd come here just to look at him because I'd missed him. "It was just . . . laundry!" My brain finally seized on something I could use. "I had laundry to do."

He grinned like he was thinking about a private joke. "I brought my laundry, too."

I wanted to groan. I couldn't even come up with an original excuse. He had beat me to it. "Yeah, well, speaking of, I better go get it started. So we can both, you know, do laundry."

"Sure thing. Hey, are you sticking around for the game? I seem to remember that you said something about how you were going to tackle me."

Tackling him sounded really good, so I knew it was time for me to go. "We'll see."

Rushing out of the side door, I hurried back inside, grabbed my bag from the stairs and got up to the laundry room. I opened up the bag and threw a bunch of clothes into the washing machine, added the detergent and fabric softener, and started a load. I let out a sigh and leaned against the wall. Now I was officially telling the truth. I had come to do laundry.

A large bag that I assumed was Bash's sat propped next to the machine. A green T-shirt that matched the color of his eyes lay on top, and without thinking, I grabbed it and smelled it. A little sweaty, but it still had that magic Bash scent.

"You're ovulating," my sister said as she walked past the open door.

Mortified that someone had witnessed me doing something that was so humiliating, I dropped the shirt and followed after to find out why she would say something like that. "What?"

She headed into her bedroom and flopped on her bed. "We just learned about this in chemistry. Women like the smell of men's sweat more when they're ovulating. It's the only way to explain the kind of gross thing you just did."

I ran through a series of possible excuses. I had mistaken his shirt for one of mine. I thought Roscoe had peed on something and was double-checking. Lauren was high and didn't see what she thought she saw.

None of them would work. My sister was too smart for that.

I looked back into the laundry room, where apparently I'd knocked over Bash's bag in my attempt to follow after Lauren.

And the irony of my and Bash's dirty laundry comingling was not lost on me.

"That must be it. Science," was the great explanation I came up with.

She nodded, going over to her nightstand, rummaging through the top drawer. "That, or you're completely in love with him."

My brain sputtered at her assessment. That she was right was irrelevant. I couldn't let her know. "What?" Had I feigned enough outrage and shock? "Why would you say that? There's nothing going on between me and Bash."

Technically true, even if I didn't want it to be.

Lauren straightened up to give me a look like she thought I was the dumbest person ever. "Please. I saw you guys together at the beginning of the summer. There was so much chemistry between you two that I was afraid I was going to get pregnant just by being in the same room with you."

And since this was my life, of course my mother chose that moment to be walking through the upstairs hallway, and she immediately said,

"Who's pregnant?" in a panicked tone that only a mother of two daughters could use.

"Ember. If she keeps hanging around Bash," my soon-to-be-disowned little sister said with a smirk.

That high level of alarm stayed in my mom's voice. "Is something going on with you two?"

"What? No." While I couldn't lie to my roommate Deja, I'd been lying to my mom about Bash for years, and it was basically like breathing at this point.

Not because I was a dishonest person, but because I knew how much it would hurt and upset her, and at this point I was all about protecting her from unnecessary stress. And there really was nothing going on between me and Bash, even if I did want to throw myself at him every time I saw him and beg him to whisk me away to some cabin in the woods where we could be all alone and he'd carry me across the threshold and then upstairs, where he'd slowly start to unbutton his shirt, his gaze never leaving mine, and then he'd reach for me and say I was wearing too many clothes, and . . .

"Ember?"

"Huh?"

"Are you okay?" My mom peered closely at me, like she did when I was little and she was worried I had a fever.

"I'm fine." Totally fine. Fantasizing about Bash while other people were in the room staring at me, but otherwise, totally fine.

"That's . . . good," she said, her disbelief evident. "Since I have you here, there is something I wanted to ask. It's a big favor, so you can say no." But even as she said the words, I knew that wouldn't be my answer. I couldn't disappoint her.

Her face lit up when I nodded. "So I'm helping host a fancy ball where we're raising money for breast cancer research. And they'll be having a little mini-ballroom-dance competition. Each board member has been asked to get three entries. I have the other two, and so I'd like you to be the third."

"I don't know how to dance like that. And good luck finding somebody tall enough for me."

"Ian can be your partner!"

Ian? Who was Ian? It literally took me a second before I realized she meant Bash. And okay, he was certainly tall enough, even when I wore heels. But seriously? Bash? "That's not going to work if neither one of us knows how to dance like that."

"That's the best part! It's just a waltz, which is actually easy to learn. And Ian already knows how to do it."

What? My mouth hung open. Bash knew how to dance a waltz? I could make all my dance-movie rom-com dreams come true?

Not all of them. There was no way I was going to do a tango with Bash in front of a bunch of strangers.

"Oh, say yes, Ember. It would be so great for Doug to have Ian around more."

Guilt crushed my chest. I didn't want to say no, and I didn't want to hurt anybody. "I don't know."

"You only have that one exhibition game left next weekend."

How did this woman have my schedule memorized better than I did? "Right, but I have school and training and my job and other stuff. I'm busy, you know."

"Please? It would mean so much to me."

My mother didn't ask very much of me, even when I'd offered my help to her. What else could I do but accept? "Okay. If Bash is in, I'll do it."

"Would you mind asking him? We've got so much going on today I don't want to forget. You know how my chemo-brain works. And it's time for dinner. Did you find that platter?"

The platter. In my hurry to escape Bash, I had totally forgotten it. And there was no way I was going back to get it. "Didn't see it. Sorry."

Letting out an exasperated sigh, Mom left.

Lauren grinned maniacally at me from across the room. I had forgotten she was even there.

"What are you smiling about?"

"This is going to be so good," she said. "I can't wait for all the drama."

"Okay, that's enough from the peanut gallery. I already told you that there's nothing going on with me and Bash. This dance thing doesn't change that."

"If you say so." Lauren smirked again. "But if you do get pregnant, I think you should name your first daughter after me, the sister who called it and saw it all coming."

CHAPTER FOURTEEN

EMBER

My mother reluctantly tasked me with rounding up the Sebastian clan and directing them into the dining room to the table of food they'd set up buffet-style. People were going to have to sit wherever they could find room. There wasn't enough table space.

I came across Bash in the family room, where he was being tackled by a bunch of tiny people. They were all laughing, and Roscoe was busy licking Bash's face, since he was on the floor.

My hand went over my heart, as if I could keep it in my chest. This strange surge of energy started in my feet and head simultaneously and then melded together dangerously close to my heart. I didn't stop to examine what the feeling was because, seriously, how were my ovaries supposed to stand the sight of him wrestling with a bunch of giggling toddlers while my puppy licked his face? It was too much.

Another thing I loved about him. He was capable of such gentleness and tenderness, which was sometimes at odds with his appearance. He was ferocious on the field. Nobody hit as hard or as often as he did. But then those same large hands that would pull a wide receiver to the ground could also hold a toddler above his head so softly and carefully.

It did make me momentarily sad that Bash might not get to meet his new siblings. They would adore him.

I cleared my throat when my powers of speech returned. "Time for dinner!"

Bash got up off the floor, shooing the children toward the direction of the dining room. They happily scampered off, Roscoe in tow.

"Hey, after you grab some food, I need to talk to you," he said.

"Well, that's good. Because I need to talk to you, too." His eyebrows rose in surprise at the anger in my voice. And I didn't know what I was most mad about—that he was adorable and children loved him, that he knew how to ballroom dance and hadn't mentioned it, or that I had been talked into dancing with him and was equal parts dreading it / looking forward to it with so much anticipation that it felt a little like Christmas.

I stomped off toward the dining room, waiting for my turn in line. Bash stayed at the back, which was probably a good thing so that the rest of us would have a chance to eat.

The kitchen, dining room, family room, and formal living room filled up really quickly. So I took a spot on the stairs. I probably would have risked sneaking off to my room if I thought my mother wouldn't notice.

Bash found me. Because of course. "Is that seat taken?"

I scooted over as close to the wall as I could, but it made no difference. As soon as he sat next to me on the step, the side of his body was flush against mine, and everything inside me melted at his touch. I tried to ignore it, but couldn't.

He asked, "Have you said anything to Lauren about my mom? And the letter?"

I was so fixated on the points of contact between us and how good it felt to be touching him that I had to concentrate in order to comprehend what he was saying. "No. Why would I say anything to Lauren?"

It wouldn't have been any of her business. Not to mention that I was currently annoyed with her.

"Please don't say anything. My dad hasn't given Marley her letter yet. He's waiting to see whether or not I want to get in contact first, and then he'll go from there."

"Oh. What do you think you'll do?"

"There are a lot of things I have to figure out," he said, and his words sounded heavy and dramatic. "But I haven't decided yet. I need to. Decide. And deal with the fallout from there."

His words pierced my heart, and I wasn't sure why. For some reason it felt like he was talking about me, even though he'd given me no indication that he was.

"Deciding's not really one of my strengths," he said conspiratorially. "I'm much better with avoiding things."

That one stung. "Yeah, I noticed."

He seemed to realize his mistake as I stood up. "E, wait."

"I have to go put some more laundry in." Now I was the one avoiding him. I had so little dignity left that I needed to fight hard for the bits I still possessed. I moved my wet clothes to the dryer and started another load of my delicates.

By the time I'd regained enough of my composure to go back downstairs, it seemed the family football game was about to start. As Bash had predicted, the weather had cleared up. The snow had mostly melted, but it was still cold. Mom had set up a hot-chocolate station on a table in the backyard. Some of the younger kids were busy filling their Styrofoam cups with more marshmallows than liquid.

Lauren and Marley had set up a couple of foldable outdoor chairs, and Marley had an entire pumpkin pie on her lap. "I read somewhere that guys don't like smart girls," she said.

"Then I must be a genius," Lauren responded.

"What kind of patriarchy nonsense is this?" I felt compelled to intervene. "If a guy thinks you're too smart, then he's a loser, and you deserve someone a thousand times better. If they don't appreciate what amazing women you are, then screw them."

"Oh, we know," Marley assured me. "There's a Valentine's Day dance a couple of weeks from now, and we're commiserating over the fact that we haven't been asked."

"How is that possible?" Was every guy at their school blind? Okay, Lauren I kind of got. Even if she was beautiful and funny, she could be scary when she wanted to be and would easily swallow a man whole. But Marley was outgoing and bubbly and gorgeous. Teenage boys were the worst.

Especially the one I'd been in love with.

They didn't have a chance to respond to my question before I continued on. "Plus, you guys are only sixteen. You have all the time in the world." To find a man who would make them constantly question themselves and whether or not they were good enough.

I should have taken my own advice. I should have forgotten about Bash and moved on. I had tried, honestly. It was just so much harder with him here.

In my mom's backyard.

He stood in the midst of a group of men and some women. My eyes were drawn to him automatically, like he was a flashing neon sign that I couldn't ignore.

There seemed to be two camps of players—ones who were taking this seriously and wanted to win, and the other group, who just wanted to have a good time. No one could agree on how to choose teams, leaving them at a loud standstill.

"Did you have a boyfriend at sixteen?" Marley asked me.

"No, I didn't. I was focused on volleyball and school."

"You're saying you didn't have a boyfriend, at all, when you were in high school?" Lauren gave me a pointed look, as if she already knew the answer.

Little minx. Did she know something? Or was she just guessing? Either way, it felt like we were bordering on dangerous territory.

I was saved by a mom interruption. She handed me a hot chocolate. "Would you go take this to Ian?"

"Bash can get his own hot chocolate." I took a sip of it. Delicious.

"Ember, stop. I really want to make a concerted effort to make Ian feel welcome. To remind him that this is his home. You especially need to make that effort."

Me especially? When had it become my job to make Bash feel welcome in his own house? Sighing, I headed out into the throng of people. I wondered why my mother was suddenly so gung ho about Bash. Did she suspect something? Or did she just think it was somehow my fault that he didn't want to come home?

I wondered if Doug had had a similar conversation with Bash. Was this why he was suddenly trying to be my friend? To make his dad happy?

Now I really wanted to tackle him.

I handed the cup to Bash. "This is from my mom. So you'll stop being a baby and come home more often." I paused. "That last part was from me."

"Yeah, I saw you enjoying my drink over there." He smiled and took a big gulp, and I wondered how it didn't burn the inside of his mouth. "I'm glad you're here. We're choosing teams. You should be on mine."

"No way. If I'm playing, I'm on the other team, whoever that is."

This somehow made his smile even bigger. "That works for me."

I didn't need his permission to choose the team I'd be on. I got on the serious player team, which I figured didn't bode well for me since I'd never actually played football before.

My team had the ball first and conferred for a few minutes about who would be doing what. My job was to block or to try to get to the quarterback, depending on whether we were offense or defense. After the roles were handed out, we lined up, and members of the fun team called out who they had.

"I've got Ember!" Bash said, lining up in front of me.

"That's hardly what I'd call a fair fight," I said.

"All's fair in love and football."

Then the game started, and while the defense counted before rushing the quarterback, I quickly discovered just how unfair it was. Despite me using all of my considerable height and strength, Bash easily bypassed me on each play and got to the quarterback.

When his team went on the offense, it only got worse. When I tried to get around him, he wrapped his arms around me, making it so I couldn't move.

"Hey!" I protested, but I couldn't help but laugh at how ridiculous he was. I'd gone into this game annoyed at him, but his teasing playfulness lightened my spirits.

"Is something wrong?" he wondered aloud. "Why aren't you getting the ball?"

Then during the next play, he grabbed me by the waist and threw me over his shoulder. I couldn't stop laughing and kept trying to call for fouls, but nobody seemed to be paying any attention to us. I was so tall that I'd often loomed over other guys, and I loved the way Bash felt so much bigger and stronger. How he made me feel delicate and feminine.

So while everybody else played, Bash and I messed around. I hadn't had this much fun in a long time.

Until it was the last play of the game. My team huddled up because we had the ball, and if we scored, we would win. Which was *very important* to the serious players.

Our captain, whose name was Chad or Brett or something like that, leaned in. "Bash is our biggest problem. We've got to keep him away from our QB so we can score. We need to distract him."

One of the teenage boys said, "Maybe Ember can flash him or something. But then everybody on the field would be distracted."

He said it matter-of-factly, as if this were a viable option, and while I was saying, "Hi, I don't need my boobs to play football," all of the older men around him were correcting him and directing him to apologize to me. He did so sheepishly.

"Awful suggestion aside, I think Ember could successfully distract Bash. What do you think?" one of the older guys on the team asked.

Chad/Brett directed his response to me. "You could tackle him if you catch him off guard. Just go low, aim for his midsection. Hit with your shoulder, and just drive."

"Tackling's against the rules," someone else said.

"In case you haven't noticed, Bash hasn't really been following the rules."

"That's true. I vote tackling him, then."

No, Bash hadn't been following the rules. Instead he'd been driving my internal temperature up to volcanic levels by grabbing and holding me close. Even if it had been done playfully.

Maybe flashing him wasn't too bad of an idea, after all. He deserved a little payback.

But I had promised him earlier that I would tackle him. And I liked being a woman of my word, so . . .

"I'll give it a try," I told them.

We lined up, and Bash waited once the ball was snapped, counting until he could run at the quarterback. He wasn't even looking at me.

I knew I had little chance of success but decided to try it anyway. I'd spent most of my time attempting to bypass him so that when I did decide to run straight at him, he wasn't prepared for it. I forgot to aim low like my teammates had advised me, and I crashed straight into his chest, wrapping my arms around him and throwing all my weight against him. I totally knocked him over!

And then we were falling together. I felt Bash's arms go around me as he landed flat on his back. He made a sound on impact, but his arms stayed tight, locking me in place.

Keeping me from getting hurt. My face hovered over his, and his eyes were closed. Wow. Had I hurt him?

"Is tackling fair game now?" he asked, his expression amused as his eyes reopened.

"I was supposed to distract you." It was the only thing I could think to say being pressed against him like this. Bash was everywhere, enclosing me completely, and I couldn't get enough. I loved the feeling of his hard strength against my curves. My heart was beating erratically. I'd thought it was from the running, but I knew it was all due to his nearness.

"Good job," he murmured.

"Told you I'd tackle you."

He had a lazy grin. "Yes, you did."

We had been lying together for longer than what would have been normal or comfortable. But one of his cousins had scored a touchdown, giving my team the victory, and everybody else was either cheering or booing said cousin as he did a victory dance in the makeshift end zone.

"You guys lost."

"I don't know." His voice came from deep inside his chest, making my insides tingle. "Right now it feels like I won."

My stomach tightened, and my breaths came out shaky and uneven. Won what?

"Just think. Someday," Bash said, "when I'm playing on an NFL team, you'll be able to tell people that you tackled the leader in that season's tackles."

Someday, when our lives were totally separate again. Because we didn't have a future together. Suddenly I realized how this would look if anybody was paying attention to us.

"We should, um, probably get up now." I was happy where I was, but other people might get the wrong idea.

"Right." He reached up, and I felt his fingers against the side of my face as he brushed some hair out of the way, tucking it behind my ear. I wanted so badly to turn my head and press my cheek against his hand, or leave a kiss on his palm.

I loved the feeling of him underneath me, the raw power that ran through his muscles, his heartbeat thundering beneath mine. Knowing that he could pick me up and carry me off without even straining himself was a really heady feeling.

I was quickly losing control and was about to do something stupid. In front of everyone.

"You can let go of me now." I whispered the words, but it seemed to finally get through his head.

"Oh. Yes." His arms went slack, and he rolled to the side so that we could both get up. He stood up first and offered me his hand, but I ignored it. I brushed off my jeans when I stood and headed back toward the house. Bash got caught in the tide of people celebrating the win or lamenting the loss, and I could feel his eyes on me as I walked away.

Lauren was sitting alone with an empty pie pan and said, "Just so you know, you and Bash are solely responsible for half of this pie being gone."

"What does that even mean?"

"How long has this thing been going on for?"

"What thing?" I asked in exasperation. Why was she being so weird and cryptic?

"This thing with Bash. Recently? Since you were in high school?"

"There is no thing with Bash. You're like Roscoe with a bone, and you're kind of driving me crazy."

She had on her best "wise woman" face. "You should never let anyone drive you crazy. Because crazy is always much closer than you think, and the walk's good for you. And I am officially shipping you guys harder than FedEx."

My nerves were still trying to settle after the Bash encounter, and I didn't have time for Lauren's nonsense. Plus, thanks to the empty pan in her lap, now I wanted pie.

I left without saying anything else. It didn't matter if Lauren was suspicious or not. She might have loved drama, but I couldn't see her causing any for no reason. She didn't want to hurt or upset our mom, either.

I found an untouched chocolate silk pie in the fridge and helped myself to it. I also grabbed a can of whipped cream. I planned on cutting myself a piece to be more hygienic, but literally every plate in this house was being used or dirty or in the running dishwasher. Same thing with the forks, so I found salad tongs in the drawer and used those.

What other choice did I have but to dig in?

"So you're not even pretending to keep your healthy eating resolutions now?"

I sighed, closing my eyes. I couldn't escape him. "Nope. Today's forecast called for a hundred percent chance of chocolate. You might as well know that I had Eggo cinnamon waffles with icing on them for breakfast this morning, but that's because I think it's important to support American businesses."

Basically, I was failing at all of my resolutions, especially the ones that included steering clear of him. It was like fate had decided we should hang out again and gave me zero say in the matter.

Bash grabbed the spoon side of the salad tongs and said, "May I?"

I hated sharing, but I was too worn out to fight him. Plus, I probably shouldn't eat an entire pie by myself. Obviously it wouldn't have been the first time, but it wasn't good for me. "Whatever."

He took a big bite and sighed happily, just like I had. "You said earlier you needed to talk to me."

I shook my head, as if to clear it. "You know how to waltz?"

"That's random. But yes."

"How?"

He took another bite. "My grandma used to be a professional dancer. She and my grandpa go dancing every Friday night. When he broke his hip a couple of years ago, he asked me to step in and take his place while he was recuperating and had physical therapy. I did, and she taught me the basics. Why?"

Gah, my ovaries were aching again with how adorably sweet that was. "My mom's helping to organize this ball-fundraiser-waltzing-competition thing to support breast cancer research, and she needs you and me to be one of the couples that enter. And I don't know how to waltz, and you do."

Then I held my breath in anticipation. I both wanted him to say yes and to say no. Either way had its own set of potential disappointments and heartache. I just didn't know yet which one would be easier.

"So . . . what you're saying is you need me. To help teach you the waltz."

"Am I not enunciating today? Yes."

He was in the middle of taking a bite when I said that and due to his laughter struggled to swallow. "Since you asked so nicely, how can I resist? I'll find us a room to practice in. Do you want to meet up Monday?"

"Okay."

He took one more bite before putting the spoon in the sink. "It's a plan. I'll text you the details. Get ready to be swept off your feet!" He left.

Suddenly I didn't want any more pie. I'd come up today hoping to get a tiny Bash fix. Just something to tide me over.

But this had turned out to be more than a little hit. I was dangerously close to a full-blown overdose.

CHAPTER FIFTEEN

BASH

It was a no-pads practice since this was our final week before we headed into training. Sabrina was down at the opposite end of the field practicing her kicks. She kept moving back five yards at a time to test her limits.

"Man, can that girl kick. I bet it's not the only thing she does well."

I rolled my eyes at Dalton Johnson salivating over Sabrina. "Not gonna happen," I told him.

"Why do you think that is?"

"Because she has good taste?" I offered. "Also, you're kind of a douchebag."

"Right." He nodded, very serious. "But I used to slay in high school. I don't understand what it is women in college want."

"I can't help you there." Mostly because I didn't want to. Leaving Johnson to ponder life's great mysteries, I headed over to the main group, where Logan indicated that he wanted to do a couple of practice throws with full offense and defense.

It was then that Woodby decided to finally grace us with his presence.

"Nice of you to show up!" Logan called out.

Without responding to our captain's sarcastic remark, Woodby went to line up. Where he made the very big mistake of pissing me off by not paying attention. First he was rude to Ember, then he blew off his team, and now he couldn't be bothered to listen to the play and respond correctly? I grabbed him by his jersey, pulling him close.

"What's your problem?" I yelled.

"What's your problem?" he responded, wrenching his shirt away from my grasp. "You're being a real jack—donkey's butt today."

I wished desperately that Coach hadn't instituted a no-swearing rule. There were so many that I wanted to use in that moment. "My problem is what a frelling jerk you were at dinner!"

He blinked at me, as if not understanding. "Dinner? You mean that double date? How was I a jerk?"

"You totally ignored Ember the entire night, and when you did talk to her, it was to belittle or tell her all the ways she was wrong."

A smug look settled on his face and it took all my willpower not to bash it in. "She was fine. She had you there to protect and entertain her. It doesn't seem to upset you that you ignored Bethany that whole time."

That knocked some of the wind out of my sails. Was he right? I hadn't meant to. I had wanted to be a good date. But it was hard to remember that there were other women in the world when Ember was in the room.

"I got the girl I was supposed to end up with," he said. "So you can calm down. It's not like Ember was so great, anyways."

I literally saw red. I was going to kill him. Rage roared to life inside me and I reacted. Since we weren't wearing pads, it was so much more satisfying to shove Woodby on his unprotected shoulders. He nearly fell down but regained his balance. Then he shoved me back, and several players intervened, pulling us apart.

Logan got in the middle of us and grabbed me by my shirtfront. "Let's take a walk."

Most of me wanted to shake him off and go finish what I'd started, but I knew he was right. Fighting was not allowed and would get me kicked off the team, ruining any hopes I had for the future. Woodby wasn't worth it.

When we'd gotten far enough away that I'd mostly calmed down, Logan asked, "You want to tell me what's going on?"

"That flicking piece of crud may be out here acting all normal and like he's everybody's good buddy, but he treats women like garbage."

"Didn't he just get a girlfriend?"

"Yeah, miraculously. And I think I get too little credit for the part I played in that. But you should have seen him with Ember. And did you hear what that son of a biscuit eater just said? That she isn't that great? Ember is fan-freaking-tastic, and if he's too stupid to see that, he shouldn't even be allowed to breathe the same air as her."

Logan crossed his arms. "You're awfully defensive of a girl who is not your girlfriend."

What was I supposed to say to that?

Especially since I couldn't deny it?

He rubbed the back of his neck. "Okay, look. I promised Jess that I wouldn't say anything to you, but I think this is worth risking her wrath over. You need to talk to Ember. She has what I figure are probably misconceptions about why you left. You know, that last night you guys were together before you moved out of your house."

Whoa. It felt like my best friend had just sucker punched me. How did he, or more specifically Jess, know any of that?

"Ember told Jess about that night?"

Logan just nodded.

"If you promised Jess, then why are you telling me this now?"

"Because lately on the field you've seemed . . . touchy. And I remember when I was the same way. And why."

"What are you trying to say, dude?"

"That I recognize this particular kind of frustration. Go work things out with your girl."

He just did not get it, and I was going to explain to him all the reasons why it wasn't a possibility, but he walked off, back to join the rest of the team.

Ember wasn't "my girl." She might have been a long time ago, but never would be again. She couldn't be.

As I headed back to the locker room to change and shower, I was struck with all these images from the Sebastian family get-together. How close together she and I had stood in the garage, with her hand on my cheek, burning my skin with the barest of touches. When she'd tackled me, lying on top of me, her delicious softness and warmth pressed into me. Her face when she'd taken a bite of that chocolate pie and how my knees had nearly buckled when she licked the fork side of the salad tong.

It was a constant torment to be so close to her and not able to act on it. Because just when I was about to give in, I'd always hear my dad's voice in my head. "Next thirty Christmases."

I'd sent her a text asking her to meet me outside of the locker room after practice. She'd responded with a short "okay." I had been looking forward to our first dance lesson ever since she'd asked me to help her.

Now I was dreading that I was going to have to hold her in my arms for the next hour or so. How was I supposed to do that and retain my sanity?

And despite Logan's urging me to talk to Ember, I knew that would only lead one way. Into total madness. When I first got home, it was all I'd wanted. To tell Ember the truth about everything so that she would understand. So that I wouldn't have to walk around with this guilt and regret. But had that been more about me trying to absolve myself than what was best for her? For us?

Now that we had this tentative and fragile . . . friendship or what-ever it was, I didn't want to ruin it. It was torture, but it was a torture I was willing to endure just to be close to her. I needed to hear her laugh. To smell her coconut-scented shampoo. Feel how my heart would race just because she stood next to me.

But talking things out? Laying all our cards on the table? It would mean I would lose everything. And it would make everything awkward and horrible again. Again, my dad's warning echoed in my ears. I didn't want the next thirty holidays to be awful. To have to stay away because I was in love with Ember and couldn't bear to see her with anyone else.

I'd already done this once. I wasn't sure I was strong enough to go through all that again.

I was just going to have to harden my heart. Put up some defensive walls and barriers to keep things right where they were now.

When I exited the locker room, I was surprised to see Ember standing there, waiting. I'd finished early, and I'd expected to have to wait for her.

"You're out sooner than I thought you'd be," she said with a smile, and all those walls came crashing down.

I should have refused the invitation. Said no to dancing. I could still say it. Tell her I'd made a mistake and I was too busy.

The words wouldn't come.

Instead I said, "I was having some disagreements with some teammates, and we all thought it was better for me to leave."

"Yeah, I remember your very colorful disagreements from when you played football in high school."

She'd come to the games? I'd never known that. My heart squeezed at the time we'd wasted before I'd approached her, and all the time we'd spent apart since then. "Coach Oakley has a strict no-swearing policy."

"Wow. Was that like losing a limb for you?" she asked, laughter tingeing her question. "Because you have enjoyed many a fine curse word."

Losing a limb? No. The transition to faux swear words had been easier than I'd expected. A minor adjustment.

The only time I'd ever felt like I'd lost a limb was when I lost her.

"Should we go? I found a place for us to practice." I led her farther into the athletic building, past the dance studios and down a back set of stairs.

"Where are we going?" she asked. "Is there a lair involved, and should I be worried?"

"Nothing like that." I opened a door and flipped on the lights. "This is where we store the old weight machines when we get new ones." The room was only half-filled, and every wall had floor-to-ceiling mirrors. "I tried grabbing one of the dance studios, but apparently the dance majors reserve them weeks in advance. I figured this would work. We have plenty of room and mirrors so that we can watch what we're doing."

Ember ran her hand along one of the machines. "This is your used stuff? I think it's nicer than what we have. Football players, taking all the good equipment."

"To be fair we bring in the most money from alumni," I said as I dropped my backpack on the floor.

She walked over to the empty half of the room and left her backpack against a wall. "Yeah, and you guys also get the most concussions, so I guess it evens out."

I stood in position and gestured her over. My anticipation built with each step she took toward me until she came to stand right in front of me. She reached up to touch the back of my neck. Was I sweating? The room was cold, and we hadn't even started. I swallowed, hard. I could do this. I could.

"I'm not a professional or anything," I reminded her. "I did have some dance training when I was little, but that was a long time ago."

"That's right!" Her eyes danced with that mischievous glint that I loved. "You used to be in ballet. How could I have forgotten that?"

"It's not that exciting."

"Are you kidding me? I used to love picturing you dancing in a tutu."

I shook my head. "I didn't wear a tutu."

"You did. And nothing you can say will ever convince me otherwise. Why did you take ballet? It seems very un-Bash-like."

"My grandma put my mom in ballet her whole life, and she loved it and wanted me to do it. My dad was fine with it because so many great football players had taken ballet first. To help with flexibility, strength, speed, finesse, balance, stuff like that. Even after she left, I stayed in those classes, waiting for her to return. I remember our first recital after she'd gone, thinking that if I did a good enough job at something she loved, maybe she would come back."

Ember's whole body changed. Her face fell, her shoulders drooped. "Now I feel mean for mocking you about the tutu. I'm so sorry." She put one hand on my upper arm. "I wish I could make it better for you."

My heart lurched painfully, and I had to nod. What was it about her that made it so easy to confess my deepest, darkest secrets? Things I hadn't shared with anyone else?

"We should get started. Okay. Your left hand goes on my shoulder." Without thinking, I took her wrist and placed her hand. I left my hand on her forearm for a beat longer than I should have, loving the waves of heat her touch sent through me. "Then I hold your right hand in my left hand, and my other hand goes on your waist."

As if it had just occurred to her that this much touching would happen, her eyes widened. She tentatively held up her right hand, and I took hold of it. I put my other hand in position, and my whole body sighed with relief that I was holding her again. Even if it was just so we could dance.

Then I explained the box step to her, how her foot would go back, then the other, bringing them together and then returning to the front. "Your torso should stay up straight but not locked into place."

After I'd showed her the steps a few times, she nodded. "I think I've got this."

"Let's try it then. Doing it is the best way to learn. I'll count us down."

"Wait, aren't we going to have music?"

"We'll get the steps down first, and then add the music after you're a bit more comfortable."

"Okay."

I quickly forgot about the thrill of having her in my arms as we just did not seem to be in sync. She kept stepping forward instead of back, didn't respond to the pressure I put on her waist or how I tugged her hand to show her where I wanted us to go next. She kept fighting me.

"Ember, only one of us can lead, and I think it should probably be the person who knows what he's doing."

"I can't help it! I don't mean to do it."

"I know. You have a control thing."

She arched her eyebrows at me. "A control thing?"

"I'm not saying you're a control freak or anything. But we learned about this in my psych class last semester. It's pretty normal for people who have lost a parent. I have my own control issues, too. Especially out on the football field. But you don't have to be in control of this."

Tears welled up in her eyes, and it was like something had slammed into my chest, hard.

"What did I say?"

She shook her head, trying to speak but not able to. I led her over to one of the mirrored walls so that we could sit down and take a break.

"I'm sorry I'm such an idiot," I said, which made her smile and let out a little laugh.

"It's not that. It's just . . . I came so close to losing my mom, and she's the only parent I have left. I don't know what I'd do if she died. I wouldn't have anyone."

"You'd have Lauren. And you'd have me. You already said I was a really good friend, so you know I'd be there for you. No matter what."

"I know. Thank you." Something caught her eye, and I saw a small spider next to her foot. She reached for her backpack and took out a note card. She coaxed the spider onto the card and went out of the room, across the hall, and opened an exit door to let the spider go free.

This was why I loved her. She was the kind of person who tried to rescue abandoned-weight-room spiders.

When she came back I asked, "Did you ever think that by releasing it during winter that you were actually condemning it to a worse fate? That it's survived this long because of this climate-controlled room?"

"I gave him a chance. If he stays in here somebody's bound to squish him. This is his best chance at survival. That little guy should be thanking me."

"Like in *Charlotte's Web*?" I asked, not able to help my amusement.

"Yes. I expect a spiderweb with the words *Ember is the best* written on it."

"You know, I don't know what freaked me out more about that story. That the spider could talk or that the spider could read and write." Another thing I loved about her. We could be discussing something as inane as a children's book, but I enjoyed talking about it because I was with her.

"The talking is definitely creepier. Though, to be fair, she only talked to the pig. Let's go again."

I stood up, and we went into the correct stance. I counted, and she immediately stepped forward instead of back, and cracked up at her mistake. "Sorry. It's good we're not trying to win this competition."

"Nope, just going for the participation trophy here."

"Hopefully, we'll get that at least. Dancing movies lied to me, by the way. One quick montage, and the girl who couldn't dance is suddenly an expert. Which is not happening here." She paused, looking at me with such intensity in her eyes that I felt it in my gut. "Just promise me I won't look stupid."

My first inclination was to tease her, but there was something so serious in her tone. "I promise, E."

That made her smile. "You know, I used to love it when you called me E."

"Why?"

"Because it was our private in joke. But also because back then I hated my name."

"Really?" She'd never told me that.

"Oh, yeah. I was teased mercilessly for years about it."

"Do you still hate it?"

"No. Now it's mine. And it stopped being about my dad's poem about how his love for my mom had turned to embers, a flame dying out. Which always seemed sad to me."

I couldn't help but grip her waist a little tighter. "I've never thought of embers as a dying fire. I see them as a fire still contained, waiting for the right person to come along and breathe life back into it. Plus, I've always loved your name. It's so uniquely you. And beautiful. Just like you."

Crud, crud, *crud*. I hadn't meant to say any of that. From the expression on her face, I had definitely said too much.

"Should we take it from the top?" I asked, my voice sounding rougher with emotion than I'd intended.

She nodded, no longer making eye contact with me.

I was such an idiot, and I was going to screw everything up.

Maybe this was happening because Ember was my first love. And first loves were hard to forget. Especially when you hadn't really moved on from the relationship.

Not to mention that she was basically forbidden fruit at this point. Maybe the feelings wouldn't have stuck around if our relationship would have been allowed to run its course. But even as I thought it, I knew it wasn't true.

She was still the only girl for me. The one person I couldn't be with. I was on a campus filled with beautiful and available women. And I'd looked.

There wasn't anyone else that I wanted.

Only her.

CHAPTER SIXTEEN

EMBER

Bash had called me beautiful, and it was like my entire world no longer made rational sense. We'd had two more practices since then, and I was slowly improving and stepping on his feet a lot less. (Where were those dance movies?) I'd wanted to ask him what he'd meant when he'd said I was beautiful. Like, it was all I could think about.

Why? Why had he said it? Did he really think that? Or was it just a nice thing he'd thrown out there? Like something he said to every girl he met? The only way to know for sure was to ask him, and that wasn't happening. I wasn't about to reopen old wounds that I was still trying to heal just because I was curious. Okay, I was obsessively curious about it, especially since there was a seventeen-year-old inside of me who was tossing handfuls of rose petals into the air and singing, "Beautiful! Beautiful! Bash thinks I'm beautiful!"

Instead I focused on the task ahead of us and tried to ignore that his hand on my waist felt like a gateway to other things. I tried hard to keep our dancing sessions PG despite the fact that one of us kept moving closer to the other so that when we finished our chests were usually touching, despite the fact that we started the dance with enough space between us to let a freight train through.

I suspected that I was to blame.

When Bash had declared me good enough to add music, my mom sent me a link to the song that would be playing during the competition. It was pretty and by some guy named Sting, a musician my mom liked. After listening to it approximately five million times in a row as we practiced, we both picked up the words.

Yesterday during our session Bash had been softly singing along, and he was actually pretty good.

"You can sing, too?" I asked. Did he have to be good at everything?

He laughed. "Not so much. I usually only sing in the shower."

That brought up a lot of unbidden soapy and wet images that I decided would not be safe to dwell on.

The next day I had my clinicals where we had to show off our injection skills. Since nobody liked to be a human pincushion, it forced the nursing students to practice on one another. But because I was already pretty decent at it, I got banned and told I didn't need to keep practicing.

But I wanted to be perfect. The best.

I tried talking Deja and Molly into it, but they refused.

"We've put our time in," Molly said. "There's no point in trying for an A plus when you already have an A."

Out of desperation I texted Jess, asking if I could stick her. With injection needles.

I half expected her not to respond; after she caught me up in math class we'd only randomly texted each other since neither one of us had much time to hang out. But to my surprise she answered immediately and said she was busy, but she'd see what she could do. She said to give her half an hour.

I sat at our little peninsula counter in the kitchen and laid out all of my equipment so that I'd be ready when she showed up. I reached for my notebook, which was empty. Flipping the cover open and seeing those blank lines filled me with an overwhelming sense of nostalgia for the girl I used to be, the one who dreamed about writing.

As I thought about how much I'd loved creating stories, my mind went off on its own tangent to its favorite topic—straight to Bash. I thought of his surprise when he found out I was studying to become a nurse and not a writer. I never had enough time these days to read the YA fantasy books I adored and even less time to write them.

I wondered if I was still capable of writing a story. I grabbed a pen and again saw Bash in my mind's eye. Only I saw him differently. In Viking armor, a beard, his blond hair long and in braids. He was carrying a sword and a shield, off to slay a dragon to protect his village.

I began writing down the details as I saw them in my head. Then there was a woman. Dark haired, dark eyed. A bit like me. But she was the commander of a Roman legion. She ordered the Viking to be caught and brought to Rome to fight as a gladiator. And in the midst of grabbing him, the entire group was attacked by the dragon.

My pen flew across the paper, and it was all I could do to capture everything that I imagined. Words just flowed out of me, like somebody else had put them there and I was trying to transcribe actual conversations.

I had forgotten this part of myself. I had always loved writing; it was my escape. Or it had been before my mom got sick.

I was so caught up in what I was doing that I hadn't noticed Deja reading over my shoulder until she said, "Are you writing about you and Bash?"

It was like my heart had dropped into my stomach. I slammed the notebook shut, but from the sly look on my roommate's face, the damage had already been done. "N-no. It's not about me and Bash."

"You are such a terrible liar." She grabbed the notebook despite my attempt to stop her. "So, let me get this straight. Sven the Viking here is tall and blond and muscular. And Julia has dark hair and dark eyes. Yeah, I'm searching for the hidden subtext here and how it's not about you and your massive crush on your ex. You know how I feel about exes. And football players. But I couldn't blame you for wandering into that territory again. Because let's be real, Bash is fine. I could totally see him as a hot Viking conqueror."

"Yep," Molly said from the couch. "I'd hit that."

"You have a boyfriend!" I reminded her as I snatched my notebook back from Deja.

"I know. But if I didn't, I'd let Bash pillage my village every day of the week."

Deja cackled at that while I set my notebook back down on the counter. Now that it was safely away from her prying eyes, I flipped to the page she'd been reading, wondering if it was badly written or if she just enjoyed teasing me.

When Deja finally stopped laughing at Molly's joke, she said, "I bet you Bash is a real holds-your-face-while-he's-kissing-you kind of guy."

"I love when guys do that," Molly sighed.

There was a knock at the door, and Deja went to answer it. "Me too. That stuff is sexy as . . . hello, Bash!"

I lifted my head and looked at the door, convinced she was messing with me.

She wasn't. There stood Bash with what looked like clothes in one of his hands.

"Were your ears burning?" Deja teased while Bash looked slightly confused. "I'd love to stay and chat, but Molly and I were just on our way out."

"We were?" Molly protested. "But the latest patch for Halo released today."

"Hush. Don't make me slap you. Come on."

Knowing she was defeated, Molly put down her controller, grabbed her coat, and followed Deja outside.

Leaving me alone. With Bash.

"What are you doing here?" I asked.

"Jess said you wanted to stick me?" He walked over to sit on the bar stool next to me, his legs nearly bumping into mine as he faced me.

What? Part of me was tempted to text Jess and ask her what she'd been thinking. Why had she sent Bash? But the other part of me was excited to have a new vein victim and equally as excited/nervous that he was here. I held up the sterile needle with saline solution. "Stick, as in inject. And I wanted to practice on people because orange peels are nothing like human skin, and the other nursing students in my clinicals have kicked me out of their stick circle."

"Stick circle sounds like an amateur adult video." He held out his hand with the clothes. "I come with gifts."

They were . . . my clothes. How did Bash have my EOL women's volleyball hoodie? "You know what they say about hot guys bearing gifts."

My words turned prophetic when I realized that not only did he have my hoodie and my favorite gray yoga pants, but a pair of red, lacy panties and matching bra. *Mortification* would have been underselling it.

Since I was a baggy-sweatpants-and-hoodies kind of girl, most people would never have guessed that I loved frilly underwear. Soft, satiny, in all different shades. Instead of oversize boxer shorts and faded T-shirts like my roommates, I slept in slinky negligees. It was one part of my life where I allowed myself to go full girly. It was something that was just for me.

Although considering Bash had had them in his possession, it wasn't just for me at the moment.

I knew I was supposed to hand wash this stuff instead of putting it in the gentle cycle in the washing machine. I figured this was the laundry gods punishing me.

"You think I'm hot?" He was teasing me and acting like it was no big deal for him to have had my underthings in his possession.

"You know how you look." I gestured toward his face and his shoulders and then the rest of him, but I was still caught up in my own internal drama. Why was I freaking out? I had bathing suits that showed more skin than this set of underwear. If it had been any other guy in the complex returning my stuff from the laundry room, I wouldn't have thought a thing about it. But there was something there, something specific, some undertone of Bash having his hands on my unmentionables that made me blush all the way up to the roots on my head.

"What I don't know is how you think I look. And we've just established that you think I'm hot." There was a merry twinkle in his eyes that made everything worse.

And, as always, worse had another level.

"What's this?" he asked, reaching for my still open notebook. "Are you writing again?"

Not today, Satan! I pounced on top of my notebook and grabbed it out of his way. I then threw it down the hallway and managed to get most of it through my open bedroom door. "I just had a story idea, and, yes, I did a little bit of writing. But seriously, it's nothing." I was never writing another word again if this was what was going to happen.

We sat in silence for a few moments before he said, "Were you still planning on sticking it to me today?"

"Sticking you. Not . . . never mind. Can you take off your coat?" *And your shirt?* my still-revved-up brain added.

He shrugged off his coat and rolled up the sleeve of the navy-blue sweater he was wearing. "I'm glad you're writing again. I was always in awe of your talent."

His legs were so long that I had to stand in between them to do the injection. I moved my supplies closer and had him rest his right arm against the counter.

I tied the tourniquet around his big right bicep and then handed him a stress ball. "Squeeze that while I look for a vein. Don't worry, I'm good at finding the perfect one. Pretty sure I could find a vein on a former child actor if I needed to. And I don't know how you could say my writing was good. All my stories were so stupid back then." Seriously cringeworthy.

And he was the only person I'd let read them. "Yeah, but you're older now with more education and more experiences. It might be different. Maybe you could take a couple of classes, considering you're already in college."

Maybe I could. Maybe I didn't have to focus only on being a nurse. I could write, too.

I found a vein on the inside of his elbow and tapped it a couple of times while I waited for it to swell. I tried very hard not to think about the fact that we were standing so close or that I was basically stroking his skin like a deranged person. Why did he always smell so good?

"Taking a couple of classes might be a possibility," I told him. I put on my gloves, disinfected the site and then pulled on his skin, making it taut. "Okay, so I'm going in at a thirty-five-degree angle. You should feel a pinch, and then we'll be done."

It was important to keep my hands and the needle steady, which was not easy to do when I could feel his warm breath against the side of my neck. I counted down, "Three, two, one," and then I did it. Another successful injection. He hadn't even flinched, which was a lot different than the time Molly claimed I had killed her and had started writhing around on the floor. I pulled the tourniquet off his arm with my free hand.

"So your new hobbies include writing things I can't see and sticking people with needles."

I slowly plunged the saline solution into his arm. "They were good ones to pick up since most of my hobbies involve eating and complaining that I'm fat."

"You know you're not, don't you?" He put his left hand on my waist, which I was sure went against clinical protocols. But it was a habit we'd both slipped into since we'd started our dance lessons. We spent hours touching and holding each other so that it felt weirdly natural to do it in real life, too. And I liked it too much to tell him not to. "Ember, look at me."

I was thinking about his touch to avoid looking in his eyes. But I never could resist him. I lifted my gaze to his. "What?"

"You know that, don't you? That you're perfect? Tell me you know that."

I took out the needle and quickly pressed down with a cotton ball on the injection site. I grabbed some medical tape to hold it in place. "Leave that on for, like, half an hour," I said. Still ignoring his statement.

Because I didn't know it. I'd spent the last four years thinking that physically I wasn't the kind of woman he wanted to date. That he wanted someone smaller and skinnier and . . . perfect-er.

But he was saying that I was perfect.

I did not know what to do with that.

A subject change was in order. "So how are you doing? Today? How is school?" I didn't say it was a smooth transition.

He frowned slightly. "I got back a test that I thought I'd done well on but ended up with a C minus. I haven't been this disappointed since my mom told me she'd be right back."

My heart caught at the underlying pain in his joke. I rested my hands on his shoulders, wanting to tug him closer, but resisting because I didn't know how he'd react.

His other hand found its way to my waist, too. "So was injecting me the only nursely skill you needed to practice? What about CPR?"

Was I moving closer, or was he pulling me? I couldn't tell. Also, performing CPR on him should not feel so much like a fantasy in my head. "I'm, uh, all good on CPR."

He nodded slowly. "What about a sponge bath? I'll definitely volunteer for that."

Okay, my imagination on that one wasn't my fault. My hands started to slip down his shoulders, and to my surprise he had that look in his eyes from high school, the intense, hungry one that said I was about to be thoroughly kissed. My heartbeat pounded hard as goose bumps covered my forearms.

"Thank you for letting me stick you," I said, my mouth just above his. I only had to lean down, and we'd be kissing. I didn't even care how pathetic that made me, to be wanting him so badly that I was willing to forsake everything else. I had no poker face. Nothing. If he cared to look, everything I was feeling had to be written on my face. The good ship *I'm Immune to You and Your Hotness* had set sail about two minutes ago, and there was no evidence it would be returning.

"You're welcome." His fingers tightened against me, his green eyes turning a smoky gray-green, and the whole world went hazy.

This all felt completely unreal. Like I'd somehow willed this very moment into being, and he didn't really have a say in the whole thing.

Why was I resisting this so hard?

I was totally going to kiss Bash and make a fool of myself, but I. Did. Not. Care.

There was a knock at the door, and then Lauren, of all people, walked in.

"Lauren?" I asked, not sure my brain wasn't trying to trick me into stopping by conjuring up an image of her.

"Well, well, well . . . how fortuitous to find Bash here," she said with a wink, coming over to join us in the kitchen. I pulled my hands from his shoulders, and his hands dropped from my waist. I took several steps back, not able to comprehend what had almost happened or why my sister was in my apartment. "With an elastic rope and needles," she continued. "What kind of weird stuff are you guys into?"

"I was . . . um." I had to clear my throat. I wished I could fan myself or put my head in the freezer. "I was sticking him."

Lauren's eyes lit up in delight. "Really? How felicific."

"I was giving him an injection, Miss SAT Prep."

"Interesting. Did you earn a lollipop?"

"Not yet," Bash murmured the words in a deep voice that made my stomach tighten in response.

"What are you doing here?" I asked my sister.

She grabbed a water bottle from the fridge and then spotted my clothing on the counter. "Why is your laundry out here?"

"I brought it back to her," Bash volunteered. He didn't seem shaken or undone at all. Just his normal self. "It was mixed in with my things."

"Oh, I'm the one who finished up your laundry," she said, the very picture of innocence. Which made me instantly suspicious. "I must have done that on accident."

Ha. On accident? That was the biggest on purpose I'd ever seen. I hadn't put away all of my clean laundry yet, but now I assumed that I was going to find some of Bash's things in there.

I wished Lauren and I were alone so that I could interrogate her. Because what had been her end goal here? Did she think he'd see my bra, and that would be it? He'd fall in love with me instantly? Maybe that might have worked on a boy her own age, but not so much on a guy like Bash.

"What are you doing here?" I asked again. I would get my answer this time.

"I'm here to kidnap you and Bash, so as I mentioned earlier, it's great that you're together. Less time. Come on, Doug, Marley, and Mom are waiting out in the car for you guys."

I was so confused. "For what?"

"It's a surprise. Something for Mom's survivor list. Come on, kids, we don't have all day. Let's go."

I didn't know if Doug had the car's heater on, and I wouldn't want my mom to wait out in the cold because I was arguing with my sister. So I grabbed my cell phone and coat and followed after Lauren, with Bash bringing up the rear.

They had come in their SUV. Lauren climbed into the back seat next to Marley, which left me and Bash to share the middle row. We greeted everyone, and I asked what was going on, but my mother just smiled enigmatically at me. "Didn't Lauren tell you that it's a surprise? You'll have to wait and see. And we're all going to do it together!"

She reached behind her, taking my hand. "I'm so glad you're here. It means the world to me."

"Of course, Mom. You know I'm always here for you."

Mom faced front again as Doug started driving. She turned on some oldies station that she and Doug liked. I was still trying to wrap my head around the fact that I'd almost kissed Bash and now I was off on some adventure with our joint families.

My cheeks flushed as I considered what would have happened if I had kissed him. Lauren would have walked in on us. She would have told everyone. How would they have reacted?

I knew it wouldn't have been good.

But I still wished I'd kissed him. Even if it was only one more time before he stopped me to gently tell me that we were just friends now, and he didn't feel that way about me. I wondered what he was thinking now. If he realized what had almost happened and how he felt about the possibility of that situation.

Lauren leaned all the way forward to stick her head in between us. "Hey, Ember, do you remember when Mom first got sick and you drove me to play practice every day? We were doing *Thumbelina*, and I was the lead, and I didn't want to have to drop out. And you had volleyball, and you would come home every night and clean the house and make us dinner so that Doug could take care of Mom?"

"I remember." What was with her?

I figured it out when she turned toward Bash. "You weren't there so you didn't see it, but she is such a caring person. So devoted to her family and friends."

"Yep, I know that about her. If you call her and need her help, she will always show up." That you're-going-to-get-kissed look was still in his eyes. "I remember, too."

I caught my breath at his words, but Lauren pressed on. "Even now, she's always checking up on my mom. Because she's so caring."

"She's also smart and good at everything she tries," Bash added in. "And she's funny. She always makes me laugh, and I love to laugh."

What was this? It felt like I was on some kind of reverse game show where instead of having me perform some embarrassing task, the other contestants were just going to say really nice stuff about me. Some song came on the radio that apparently Bash didn't like. He grimaced and then grabbed his earbuds from his coat pocket. Once he had them in, I turned around to hiss at my sister, "Stop it, right now. Whatever you're doing. Stop."

"What? Is it my fault if he's already in love with you and knows how amazing you are? I am so married to the idea of you two getting together that I've already picked out our china patterns. Also, I can't decide on Embash or Bember for your couple name."

"How about neither one?"

"Negative. Your ship must have a name. And don't tell me there's nothing going on, because I saw you two when I walked in. There was some serious smoochage about to happen. You are catching feelings. And considering that you're an athlete, that should be easy for you."

"I'm not catching anything! Besides, my job is not to catch but to smack that ball back over the net."

"I don't believe you," she said in a singsong voice. She leaned all the way back, making it so that I could no longer quietly talk to her. I mad whispered her name, but she started talking to Marley and ignored me.

I had a good twenty minutes to sit and freak out over what was going on, what Lauren was trying to accomplish, and how impossible my entire situation seemed.

"We're here!" my mom called out just as Bash took out his earbuds.

"Where?" I asked. We were in an almost empty parking lot near a couple of flat warehouse buildings. It looked like the kind of place where the government would perform alien autopsies.

Cue another big smile from my mom. "It's my surprise. We're all going to jump out of an airplane!"

CHAPTER SEVENTEEN

BASH

Everybody seemed excited as they climbed out of the SUV into the blinding sunlight. Everyone except Ember. Her face looked frozen, like she was terrified but trying to cover it up with a faux smile. Nobody else seemed to notice.

"Hey, are you okay?" I asked her. I wrapped my fingers around her slim wrist and tugged her to slow her down, so that we were behind the rest of the group.

"The only thing on my schedule for today was not dying, and now I'm putting that at risk." She shivered as we walked toward the main office, where Tricia told us we were going to have an hour-long ground-training session before we all tandem jumped out of an airplane.

"It could be fun," I said.

"And totally dangerous. I'm pretty sure there's a negative fun-to-danger ratio here."

"It can't be too bad, or they wouldn't keep letting people do it." My joke fell flat. She looked panicked, and every protective instinct I possessed screamed at me to keep her safe. I tugged on her hand so that she would stop walking.

"You do not have to do this," I told her.

She closed her eyes and shook her head. "Yes, I do. My mom said it meant the world to her."

That just seemed stupid to me, but I knew better than to say it. "I don't care who it's important to. You can stay right here and wave at the rest of us as we jump. I'll even stay with you."

Her eyes snapped open, determined. "No. I'll do it. It's important."

Ember was the only thing that was important, the only thing that mattered to me in that moment. She took her hand away from mine and strode off, following everybody else. I jogged to catch up with her.

"I'm serious about this. You say the word, and I will call an Uber and get us out of here. Your mom will understand."

She just shrugged as her reply.

I tried again, feeling how useless it was. "You can tell your mom no."

"I can't," was the only explanation she gave me. "So let's go carpe this diem."

A very animated man named Skip led our training session, and he reminded me of a television host for a children's program. Everything he said was big and in bold letters. And everything he said made Ember scoot down lower in her plastic chair.

"Our state-of-the-art plane, with comfortable seats and easy exit access will take us up to a cruising altitude of ten thousand feet."

"Ten thousand?" she repeated to me. "That's like . . . fifteen hundred of you."

"Which will give you about thirty seconds of free falling before your tandem partner will pull the rip cord, and you get to float the rest of the way down. While you're free falling, you'll be going at speeds of a hundred and twenty miles per hour," Skip continued.

Ember let out a little moan and then rested her forehead against her knees. "I don't even like driving on the freeway because it feels too fast, and this is twice that."

"It will be fine," I tried to reassure her. "If you want to leave, I will get you out of here right now. But if you choose to stay and jump, I'm going to support you. Whatever you want, I'm on your side."

She reached over to take my hand, and I held it tight, wishing I could give her some of my strength so that this wouldn't seem so scary.

"I've already made up my mind," she said. "I'm going to stay. Even though I'd rather not hurl my body through space and hope it doesn't slam into the ground on impact."

Skip told us that the weather would be about twenty degrees colder when we jumped, and that we might end up landing in some melting snow, which he said would be like jumping into a wet puddle. Ember couldn't have been excited about that.

We watched a training video, worked with our instructors/partners (mine was named Gil, and Ember had been matched with a guy named Albie), and practiced various pieces of the jump and landing. Then we were getting flight suits on and being taken out to the plane. I kept an eye on her, but she just kept going along with it. Everybody else was caught up in their excitement. Which I got, because I'd never been skydiving before, and I'd always wanted to. But my entire focus was on Ember and what she needed.

I reminded her at multiple points that we could stop and didn't have to go through with this. On the tarmac. As we got strapped to our instructors. In the plane as it taxied down the runway. As we climbed into the sky. But then she'd turn and see her mother's grinning face, and she'd tell me she was fine and could do this.

She was so brave it broke my heart.

We reached our cruising altitude, and people started jumping. Tricia went, followed by my dad, then Lauren and Marley. Finally it was just me and Ember. With Gil and Albie.

"I know I sound like a broken record," I yelled at her. "But you don't have to do this."

With her mom already out of the plane, she hesitated. "What if I'm not okay? What if something happens?"

"You'll be great!" I tried assuring her. "Albie here knows what he's doing. And if something goes wrong, Gil and I will air bomb ourselves across the sky like a guy from a spy movie and we'll save you."

Albie responded, "You know that's not possible, right?"

"Dude! You are not helping," I told him.

"It's all good! We got this!" he responded, finally catching my drift. "You're in great hands."

"I'm right behind you," I said. "Wait for me on the ground."

She nodded, and then she was at the door with Albie. One second she was there, then she was gone.

It felt too much like a metaphor for my liking.

Then it was our turn. Gil had me tip my head back and tuck in my feet, and then I was just . . . falling.

Not falling. Flying.

At first the wind was too loud, and my brain couldn't process what was happening. My hands and feet were kind of all over the place. The cold air slammed into me, making it hard to breathe. But as I quickly adjusted and started looking around me, it was like nothing I'd ever experienced before.

It was . . . amazing. Incredible. Exhilarating. There was this total sensory overload, but I'd never felt more like a superhero in my entire life. It was total freedom.

I yelled "Woo-hoo!" into the wind. I wanted this feeling to last forever.

Then Gil pulled the rip cord, and we jerked back until we settled into place. There was this total peace, as if nothing bad ever could or would happen again. I watched as the ground slowly came closer and closer, loving seeing the world from this angle. It wasn't like looking at it from the top of a tall building or an airplane. It was a unique vantage point that I knew I'd never forget.

The rush of adrenaline that was coursing through my body was like . . . coming from behind to score a touchdown and win a game in the last twenty seconds of the quarter.

Then we were landing, and I stuck my legs out while Gil ran at the ground, easing us into a snow pile. As promised, it was like landing in a puddle. My clothes were soaked.

As Gil released me from the harness, I spotted Ember at the edge of the field. She was sitting on the ground with her head between her knees. Once I was free I thanked Gil for the fantastic experience and ran over to check on her.

A staff member hovered over her and looked at me gratefully as I approached. "Is everything okay?" I asked.

The staff member said, "Usually people love this. Even when they're scared initially, they're thrilled after they land. We gave her some peanut-butter crackers and a water bottle."

I crouched down next to her. "We should probably go inside and get dried off."

"Okay." She nodded. "That was terrible, by the way. I felt like I was going to die. On the plus side, I found out that I am definitely scared of heights."

I put my arm around her waist to help her stand up. Her body was trembling, her face completely white.

"Don't worry, Bash. I'm fine. So fine," she tried to reassure me. "I am totally okay now." Her legs gave way, and she collapsed against me.

I put my other arm under her legs and picked her up. "Yep. You totally look like it. Eat your crackers. You'll feel better when you get some carbs and protein in you."

"I'll feel better when I get out of these wet clothes."

I stumbled and almost dropped her at the mental image her words conjured. I tightened my arms around her. "Sorry." I wasn't going to explain for what.

Then she said something that sounded suspiciously like, "This wasn't how I imagined you carrying me," but I decided to ignore it and all the other inappropriate thoughts swirling in my head.

We reached the locker rooms, and I let her down in front of the women's changing room. "Are you okay now?"

"I've got this. Don't worry," she told me.

She went inside under her own power, and I hurried to change so that I could be there if she needed me.

But when she finished putting her clothes on, she seemed fine. Still a little pale, but nothing like before.

"You jumped out of a plane!" I told her.

She gave me a thin smile. "Right. And I should be proud. Only it doesn't really feel like much of an achievement if I had my eyes closed most of the time."

We were joined by the rest of our clan. Everybody else seemed to have loved it, and nobody noticed Ember's lack of enthusiasm as they talked about how much fun it had been. There was some talk about going out to grab some ice cream, but I said that I had some studying to do. That wasn't the reason I'd said it, though. I always had studying to do. What I wanted was to give Ember a break from pretending. We piled in the car, and I kept my eye on her all the way back to school. Dad pulled into a spot at Ember's apartment complex, and I told him I'd get out here. I wanted to check on her, even though she was looking like her old self again.

"Bash, wait," Dad said.

Ember turned to me, questioning, and I waved her on ahead. "I'll catch up."

When she had left, my father said, "There's something you need to know. Your mother has filed for joint custody of Marley."

It was like a gaping hole had opened up in my chest, like a giant wrecking ball had slammed into me and knocked me off my feet. "Wha—what?"

"I guess she got tired of waiting to hear something."

"It's only been, like, two weeks!"

My dad sighed, as if that same wrecking ball had hit him, and he was still carrying the weight of it around. "We'll figure it out. But this means I'll have to tell Marley. It's one of the reasons why Tricia pushed to do the skydiving today. She wanted us to have this one last memory before . . ."

"Before our lives blow up," I finished. "But Mom left us. She gave up her parental rights."

"My attorney thinks I have a case for abandonment, but the judges in our county are keen to reunite kids with their parents. If she really is clean and has her life back together, your mom will be able to prove that she's fit and should be given a chance. Even if it's supervised visits at first."

"And she . . ." My voice caught, and I cleared my throat. "She didn't care about seeing me?"

The love in his eyes was almost too much to handle. "There's nothing she can do about you. You're an adult, and you get to make your own decisions."

If that was true, then I was going to decide that she wasn't allowed to ruin our lives again. My brain buzzed with anger. "Give me twenty-four hours before you tell Marley. I'll call you later."

I stalked off, determined to stop this from happening. I heard Dad calling my name, but I refused to stop. I went straight to Ember's apartment and knocked on her door harder than I'd intended to.

"The skydiving thing didn't make me deaf," she said when she opened up.

"Can I borrow your car?"

The amusement slid off her face. "What? Why?"

"I just . . ." I wanted to punch the wall and yell about Canada. "I need your car."

"Not until you tell me why." She spoke softly and carefully, but I could hear her determination.

"My mom is suing for custody of Marley, and I'm going to go have a chat with her. Now." I had taken a photo of my mother's letter, so I had her home address on my phone.

"I'm coming with you," Ember said, putting her coat back on. "And I'm going to drive."

"I don't need you to do that."

"I need to come. Please."

Too angry to argue, I nodded, and we walked in silence to her car.

"What are you going to say?" she finally asked when we got on the road.

"I don't know." It was true. I didn't know. My brain still buzzed, and that gaping maw in my chest seemed to grow larger and larger. How dare she do this? Who did she think she was to come strolling back into our lives after she had totally upended them once already? I found the address and put it into my GPS app.

Time seemed to fly past us so that the next thing I knew, we were sitting in front of a one-story home that looked a little like a cottage from a fairy tale.

Ember put the car in park. "This is it. You don't have to talk to her. I can turn this car around, and we can just go. Whatever you want to do, I'm on your side."

The same words I'd said to her just a couple of hours ago. "Come with me."

I had fully intended to do this alone, but I wanted Ember with me. Correction, I *needed* her with me. She nodded and we got out.

My heart was beating so loud that I couldn't hear anything else. She stayed a step behind me while I walked up to the front door and rang the bell.

My spine felt like jelly. This had been a mistake. I shouldn't be here. I was about to turn and say as much to Ember when the front door opened.

It was my mother.

Older, but it was her. I would have known her anywhere. It was such a shock to see her again that I was unable to speak.

"Ian? Is that you?" Her gaze darted over to Ember, confused. Probably wondering who she was. "I . . . I can't believe you're here. Do you want to come in?"

"I do not want to come in," I said, the anger swelling inside me like a rising tide. "Who do you think you are?"

"Why don't you come inside?" she tried again, glancing at the street behind me.

"What's wrong, don't want the neighbors to know what a bad mom you are?"

Giving in, my mother shut the door behind her and stood out on the porch. There was a movement in the front window near the door, and two little faces peered out at me. My brother and sister.

Some of my fight left me, but I had come here to protect the sister I already knew and loved. "Stay away from our family," I warned her. "We don't need you. We've been just fine without you."

Her forehead was more lined than I remembered. "I can't do that, Bash. You can make your own choice, but Marley's still a minor. I'm still her mother."

"You gave up the right to call yourself that ten years ago."

She reached out with her left hand. "If you'll just come inside and let me explain and apologize . . ."

Rage exploded inside me. "Oh, I got your letter. I'm not interested in your apologies. I know what you want. Absolution. Forgiveness. I don't have that for you. You can't undo what you did. You left us a long time before you walked out the door. You can't fix me having to make sandwiches for my toddler sister and change her diapers because you refused to get out of bed and take care of her. You can't mend my heart that broke after you left, making me question why I wasn't enough to make you stay."

I felt Ember's fingers lace through mine, and my mother's eyes teared up. "Ian, no."

"Don't call me that! My name is Bash."

She nodded, and her voice trembled when she spoke. "Bash, please."

Something broke in me then, something I feared might never be fixed. "I'm done. I will go to court and testify against you. I will tell the judge every ugly thing you ever did, every way you neglected us, and how little you deserve to be in our lives again. I will fight you to keep Marley safe. It's what I've been doing my whole life."

I turned my back on her, walking away. It didn't feel nearly as satisfying as I'd once hoped it would. Ember and I got in the car, and I slammed my door shut.

Ember drove away without saying a word to me. My thoughts were jumbled inside my head, swirling like a tornado so that I couldn't stop and think and deal with this. I started to shake. She put her hand on my forearm and pulled the car over. I buried my face in my hands, unable to catch my breath.

"Bash." She gripped my arm tighter. "B, please look at me."

I heard her undo her seat belt. "I need to know that you're okay," she pleaded.

A sob tore its way out of my throat. I hadn't cried in a decade, and here I was sobbing. It was like a dam bursting, and all the misery and heartache and pain my mother had caused me came rushing out. Ember climbed over the center console and wrapped her arms around me. I hugged her tight. She rubbed my back, my neck. It had been so long since somebody had held me like this. She kept saying soothing things like, "It will be okay. Everything will be okay," over and over again.

Long after my tears had subsided, we stayed this way, holding on to each other.

I spoke, without meaning to. "Do you know that she's the reason I hate being called Ian? She told me it was her favorite name in the whole world, which was why she chose it for me. Every time somebody used it, it made me think of her. And I hated thinking about her."

"I'm so sorry," she said.

"My mother has ruined so many good things in my life. For the longest time I thought I wasn't lovable. Who could love a guy whose own mom couldn't love him?" I said the words into her neck, as if she could absorb them for me, make the pain go away.

She pulled back, and in the fading sunlight she looked at me so kindly and with such concern that it nearly destroyed me. She stroked the side of my face. "That's not true. When I was seventeen I loved you more than anything else in the whole world. You are such an incredible man. I'm surprised that every woman who meets you doesn't fall instantly in love with you."

Her words pierced me to my core, shining lights on parts of myself I kept hidden. She made me want things I couldn't have. I tried a weak joke. "I guess we're both having some mom issues today, huh?"

"Well, at least yours didn't make you jump out of a plane."

That made me laugh, and I was glad to feel like laughter was still possible for me.

"I kind of want to beat your mom up now," Ember went on. "I'm pretty sure I could take her. You say the word, and I'll go back and let her feel my fists of fury." She balled her hands into fists, and I laughed again.

Ember smiled at me and clapped her hands together, saying, "Okay!" Then she went back to her side of the car, and I felt the loss of her so keenly that it was like she'd ripped one of my arms off and taken it with her to the driver's seat. "I say we drown ourselves in ice cream. You in?"

"I'm in."

After we'd been driving for a few minutes, I said quietly, "Thank you for coming with me."

"Thank you for letting me come."

When my mom left, it had created this hole in my heart that I thought wouldn't ever mend. And it was like I'd spent the last ten years searching for a way to heal it.

It was a person who'd done that. Ember. When I made excuses to myself as to why I wanted to spend time with her, it wasn't just that I missed her or that I liked being around her. While those were true, that wasn't why I needed her in my life. She was the only person who managed to fill that hole all the way up.

The only time I ever felt whole was when I was with her.

CHAPTER EIGHTEEN

EMBER

I drove Bash home that night, not wanting to leave him. He promised me he'd be fine and that he'd call if he needed me. I knew he wouldn't call. Bash was the strongest person I'd ever met, and he didn't like relying on other people. I knew he must have hated that he'd broken down in front of me. And it absolutely destroyed me to see him crying that way. I'd been serious when I'd told him that I wanted to beat his mom into a pulp.

Thinking about his mom made me recall my recent phone call with my own mother. She knew all about the situation with Bash and Marley's mom and said that Doug was planning on telling Marley later on. She then proceeded to spend the rest of the conversation upset because Lauren had been hiding the fact that some of her grades were not great.

"At least I know you don't hide anything from me," she'd said.

Well, just the one thing. And I felt guilty about it, but we had bigger issues.

Like when Doug finally did tell Marley about the letter and lawsuit, and she surprised everyone by saying that she would meet with her mother. Bash was furious, venting about it all through our dance rehearsal. I tried really hard just to listen and be there for him because, while I was a hundred percent on his side, some part of me wondered if maybe he should let his mother explain. Not because I thought she deserved it, but because I thought maybe he needed it.

I tried to cheer him up. "So, I have news."

"Did you get banned from the Silver Trough, too?"

"Too?" I echoed. "You got banned again?"

"After that thing with my mom, I had some feelings I needed to eat. And there are two sides to every story. But you should know that whatever story the management is telling is probably the correct one."

"No, I didn't get banned. I did enroll to audit a night class for creative writing."

Bash's whole face lit up. "Really? Ember! That's so great!"

He grabbed me into a bear hug, and I relaxed into it. Hugging him was like easing into a hot bubble bath at the end of a tough day. He made everything better.

And I was no further along in figuring out the Bash situation. Because on the one hand, I wanted to be his friend. I wanted to support him through this whole thing with his mother. Selfishly, I liked feeling like he needed me. I didn't want to lose that.

But maybe . . . maybe it could be more. After that almost kiss in my apartment, I had convinced myself that things weren't one sided. That Bash, at the least, wasn't repelled by me. It had me questioning a lot of our recent interactions. Wondering if I'd been misreading everything.

How did you bring that up? "Hi, do you like me? Would you enjoy kissing me, or is that something that makes you want to throw up in your mouth?"

So instead I chose silence and focused on our friendship.

When I got home from practice, all of my roommates were home, including Ximena. They were packing a bag.

"What are you guys doing?" I asked in the hallway. Everybody stopped what they were doing to stare at me.

"The exhibition game with Washburn is this weekend. We're leaving in a couple of hours." Molly said this like I was slow.

I'd been so focused on Bash, on his situation with his mom and our rehearsals, that I'd completely forgotten about the game. Coach Manning had told us about it. Washburn was a new junior college about four hours away that had only been open for a year. They had reached out to EOL and asked some of the teams to come and play a game with them as a fundraiser, and to raise awareness for their school in the community.

"It is going to be so much fun," Ximena said.

I raised both of my eyebrows at her.

"What?" she said. "I work hard so that I can enjoy playing hard."

When Deja started laughing, I knew Ximena wasn't just talking about our volleyball game.

"Who else is going?" I asked, suspicious.

"The men's volleyball team, the swim team, men's and women's basketball." Deja ticked off the teams on her fingers. "Oh yeah. And the football team. Apparently Washburn has a very wealthy investor and an indoor stadium."

The football team?

I had a feeling that I knew where this was headed.

"It's like we're getting two girls' weekends in a row," Ximena said.

"Two?" I repeated.

Deja put her hand on her hip and stared me down. "Yes, two weekends. Next Saturday we're going up to Molly's uncle's cabin, remember? I've told you, like, twenty times. Including in our last conversation."

"And I was totally listening," I told her. It sounded vaguely familiar, and I had probably agreed to go.

"We're driving up at noon, but you have that test, so you're going to come up later?" Molly reminded me, and I tried hard not to look guilty.

"Yes. I know." I didn't.

This was Bash's fault. He had been distracting me from everything. I didn't know why we needed a girls' weekend, though. We already all lived together. It was just moving all this to a different location.

But instead of questioning, I went ahead and packed my bag. Bash must not have mentioned going up to Washburn this weekend because, with how my brain was functioning, that was something I would have remembered.

I wondered if I'd get to see him there.

~

We destroyed the Washburn team. They were a new program and looked like they had talent and a good coach; it was just going to take them a while to catch up to a well-oiled machine like ours.

When we got back to the motel we were staying at, I was informed that I would be going out that night to a local club called Slammed.

"I'm wiped. I'll just stay here." And maybe go looking for Bash to see how his game had turned out. No other reason.

"Come on," Molly pleaded. "We're going to get turnt. Or is it lit?"

"What did I tell you about that?" Deja called from the bathroom.

"That you love me, but I'm not cool enough to say that kind of stuff." Molly sighed. "We're still going to have fun!"

Ximena was brushing her glossy, black hair in front of the mirror attached to the dresser. "It's Ember's choice. She doesn't have to come."

There was a knock at the door, and Molly jumped off the bed to run over and open it. It was one of the football players from the team. I couldn't remember his name. Daxton? Dalton?

"You guys ready?" he asked. "I've got us an Uber out front."

"You sure?" Deja asked me as they gathered up their purses and coats.

"Have a good time," I told her.

They all waved and told me good night while Molly explained to the football player that I was being a buzzkill.

I waited about thirty minutes, and then I headed for the second floor, where the football team was being housed. Earlier I'd asked Deja if she knew Bash's room number, and it had taken her all of thirty seconds to track it down. She'd told it to me with a wink.

Taking in a deep breath, I knocked. A few seconds later the door was answered by a disheveled Logan. Whose shirt was on inside out. "Ember. Hi! Bash isn't here."

Jess came to the door, her hair similarly messed up. "He went to that club, Slammed. Without a date. In case you were wondering."

I was starting to feel stupid for having interrupted them and for being so obvious about what I was there for. "Oh, no. I just had a, um, question for him, so you guys don't need to tell him that I stopped by or anything. I'll just . . . see him when I see him."

They exchanged amused, knowing glances, and I walked away without saying goodbye. I went around a corner and smacked right into Keilani.

She put her hands on my shoulder to steady me. "Hey, where are you off to?"

"I was thinking about going to that club, Slammed." I hadn't been, but now I wanted to be there.

"Me too! But you can't go like that. Come with me. I've got some tops you could borrow." I looked down at my ratty hoodie. She was probably right to want to dress me in something else.

We went to her room, which she did not have to share with three other people. "What are you doing here? Exhibition games don't really have anything to do with academics."

She opened her closet and pulled out two slinky tops, one dark purple and the other a shiny silver sequin thing. I chose the dark-purple one. I still had some jeans on as I hadn't committed to changing for bed yet. The top had a drawstring neck and another tie around the back. It kind of felt like wearing a handkerchief.

But then I caught my reflection. I looked amazing in it.

"What size shoe do you wear?" Keilani asked.

I told her, and she told me that she wore the same size. She handed me a pair of black boots. "I'm here because Coach Oakley likes the staff to come along and play chaperone when the players are on the road. To make sure they're not breaking his rules, like no drinking and no drugs."

I brushed my hair out, and then I used some of her lipstick and mascara.

"Okay. Let's go break some hearts," she said with a wink.

Ten minutes later we were at the club, which was apparently filled to capacity. I could hear the bass line in the music thumping hard as we got out of the car. Keilani was ready, full of confidence, and I followed along after her, wondering what I was doing.

We got inside, and like always, I immediately sought out Bash. He was easy to find, given that he was nearly a head taller than almost everyone around him. He had on jeans and a dark, long-sleeved shirt that hugged every muscle in his arms and made his hair look almost white-blond in comparison. He was talking to a woman in six-inch high heels sporting an unnatural shade of red hair.

Keilani followed my gaze and said, "I approve. Bash is wonderful. I've heard good flings come to those who wait."

"No flings," I yelled back. "His dad is married to my mom."

"But you're not related."

"No."

"And you didn't grow up together?" she verified.

"No."

"So what's the problem?"

Right now the problem was he was flirting with another woman, and it was making me twitchy and stabby.

Which only got worse when she pressed herself against him and then kissed him. On the mouth.

When I was retelling this story to the judge at my criminal trial, this would be the point where I said, "That's when I blacked out, and I don't remember what happened next."

Bash immediately stopped the kiss, and when he lifted his head, he saw me. Staring daggers at him. He grinned, said something to the redhead, and made his way over to me. "Hey, I thought you weren't coming."

"I thought you weren't making out with random people. I guess we were both misinformed." I looped my arm through Keilani's and went looking for my girls. I was bound to say something stupid if I stayed near him.

I found my squad, and they all shrieked with excitement that Keilani and I were there. Keilani was like the cool older sister who was fun to hang out with, but would still make you do the stuff you were supposed to.

"Are there any guys here you're interested in?" Molly asked Keilani. "We'll find a way to make it happen."

Keilani grinned at her. "Everybody here is too young."

"Besides," Deja added, "we all know she's in love with Ford." It looked like Jess wasn't the only one with that pet theory.

But Keilani just rolled her eyes. "Yep. That's me. A glutton for punishment and in love with a guy who hates me."

I totally got that. I mean, Bash didn't hate me, but I was completely in love with him and was also a glutton for punishment. By doing things like hanging around clubs where I had to watch him make out with other women.

Deja wasn't bothered by her response. "I don't know what's going on with you two, but Ford hasn't taken his eyes off you since you walked in."

"That's not true," Keilani said with a shake of her head.

I looked and saw Ford, who was definitely eyeing somebody standing near me. Plus, Deja was never wrong about this sort of thing. I would probably text Jess about it later to let her know that her theory had legs.

Deja moved in close to me so that I was the only one who could hear. "Keilani's not the only one who has a man staring her down."

I flicked my gaze in Bash's direction, and it seemed like he was watching me. It made my breathing feel a little shaky. "So?"

"So? Girl, aren't your arms tired from carrying this torch around? Go do something about it."

At the moment the only something I wanted to do was leave. Mostly so I wouldn't have to scour my retinas later if he started kissing somebody else.

"You're missing out," Ximena informed Keilani, providing me a much-needed distraction. "If Ford dated students, he would be my new boyfriend."

Before Keilani could respond, a song came on that was, like, the unofficial jam of our team. Without even speaking, we all moved out excitedly onto the middle of the dance floor. We sang along to the lyrics, dancing and grooving to the beat. For a moment, I forgot. I was just here, with my best friends, living and bouncing and having the best time.

I did a half turn and noticed that Bash was watching me. Fiercely. His hungry gaze was a total kick to the lady parts. He looked at me in a way that made my clothes want to tear themselves off and hope that his followed suit.

Our song ended, and another fast-paced one came on. I kept dancing, my cheeks flushed, trying to pay attention to my friends and not to Bash.

Deja leaned in and said, "I saw someone who looks like an excellent bad decision, so I might be busy for a little while."

We all always liked to check in with one another if we were thinking about heading off with a guy we didn't know. We had our own buddy system. "Make sure your phone is on!" I told her.

She waved and set off. I kept dancing, letting the thumping beat block out any thoughts in my head. Without my wanting it to, my gaze returned to Bash. He set down his water bottle on the table and started walking toward me. He did so with intent, like a giant cat stalking his prey. Which was me.

I was mesmerized by him. Like a cobra and a snake charmer. More accurately, he was the cobra, and I was the poor defenseless charmer about to be bitten.

Was it wrong that I didn't care?

"Don't stop dancing on my account," he said when he reached me. Then, like we were at rehearsal, he put one hand on the small of my back and pulled me in close. Something tightened in my lower stomach. This wasn't ballroom dancing or ballet, but Bash was just as good at dancing to EDM as he was everything else. We danced close, hips swaying to the beat. Little bursts of fire started everywhere he touched me, and then spread out until my entire body felt like it was being consumed. There was heat and sweat and our bodies moving against each other. Everyone around us melted away, and my vision softened, making everything else hazy besides him. There was only us and the driving beat.

He was making me insane.

Until I remembered that he didn't feel the same.

For him, this was just a dance. It was almost like a slap to the face. Or cold water being poured down my back. I gasped and stepped away.

"E?"

I couldn't do this. I couldn't keep doing this to myself. I couldn't hope that he might change his mind and want to be with me. I wanted him so badly even my teeth ached.

"I need to go," I said. "I'm going to go back to the motel and jump into bed."

He moved in close. "Need anyone to break your fall?"

His words were hot against my earlobe, sending exploding fragments of ice up and down my spine. I expected his face to be teasing, his tone to be light. But they weren't. What would he do if I said yes? If I told him exactly what I wanted, even though those feelings were why I was in this mess in the first place?

Instead of answering, I walked away. I grabbed my coat from the coat check and left. I stood in front of the club for a moment trying to decide what to do, and the streetlight out front felt like a giant spotlight. I wanted darkness to think. To hide my warring emotions, maybe even from myself. I headed around to the side of the club and leaned up against the wall. It pulsated from the music's beat the same way fire still pulsated through my veins.

"Ember?"

It was Bash, backlit by the streetlight. I wasn't strong enough. He had melted too many of the walls I put up to protect my heart. "Go away. That's what you do best, right? Leave?"

He came over to me, every step moving in time to my heart. Where his name was seared. *Bash, Bash, Bash,* over and over again. He stopped when he got close. "What is that supposed to mean?"

"It means I'm tired. Tired of fighting . . . whatever this is. Because I know how it ends."

"I'm confused."

I wanted to tell him it wasn't my job to explain it to him, but I did anyway. "Why do you do that?"

"Do what?"

"Act like you want me, when we both know you don't."

In the dim light, I saw his eyes darken. "Why would you say that?"

"That night . . . when we were teenagers. Before you left. You touched me, my hips, my stomach, my back, and then . . . you were gone. I thought I grossed you out or something. You made it obvious that you didn't want me."

He stepped closer until there was barely any space between us. "Not want you? Are you serious? How could you have thought that?"

"The fleeing was my first clue." And even though I was being sarcastic, I couldn't help my voice breaking a little at the end.

Bash reached up and gently stroked the side of my face. "I ran away because of how much I wanted you. And that hasn't stopped. Not for one minute, not for one second."

Then he proved his words to be true. He kissed me. Not tentatively, not gently. But to show me without words what he was trying to say.

And he said it incredibly well.

His mouth was moving against mine before I even realized what was going on. My whole body cried out in a rush of feeling and excitement that Bash was holding me, kissing me, and he wanted me.

I felt a little like Sleeping Beauty. Like I'd been in a spell-related coma, and Bash's kiss was the only thing bringing me back to life. The one man who could breathe embers back into fire.

"Any other questions?" His voice was gruff, sexy.

A thousand questions. A million. But in that moment the only one I could think of was, "When can we do that again?"

"Right now."

His hands were on my face, in my hair, and I made a mental note to tell Deja that he most definitely was a holds-your-face kind of kisser.

I grabbed on to his shirt, wanting him closer. He responded by pushing me up against the wall. I had the cold brick at my back and the wall of his warm torso holding me in place. I wanted to get closer to him. I wrapped my arms around his neck, hoping I could somehow fuse every inch of his skin with mine by melting into him.

I deepened the kiss, and I felt his responding groan deep in his chest. He granted my wish for even more closeness, hitting me with a passion I'd only ever seen from him on the football field.

He moved away from my lips, ignoring my protests, and began to plant hot kisses along my cheek, down to my earlobe. When he drew it into his mouth, I grabbed fistfuls of his silky hair, arching toward him.

I panted at his expert touch, how soft his mouth was as he kissed the pulse just behind my ear, nipping along my neck. He stopped, leaning back, and full-blown panic struck me. He couldn't walk away again. I wouldn't let him.

Forgetting myself and everything else besides how much I wanted to spend the rest of eternity kissing him, I literally threw myself at him. Jumped up on him, wrapping my legs around his waist.

"Don't go," I begged.

"Wasn't planning on it," he said, fully into this new situation. His hands went behind me, to keep me in position, and he had me back up against the wall. My coat began to slip as his hands went to just above my hips, gently massaging my mostly bare back.

I should have been cold, but who could be cold while kissing him?

His breath grazed my exposed shoulder, the heat mingling with my cold skin in a way that was so delicious it should have been illegal. He was turning me into liquid fire, an ember becoming a massive bonfire, lighting up the night.

Then his lips were on mine again, feverish, devouring, consuming. I felt like my whole body was going to shatter from the tension he was building.

This man made me want to howl at the moon.

"Do you know it now?" he asked, his voice low and sexy. "Do you see how much I want you? How much I've always wanted you?"

Why was he talking? I reached for his lips, but he held himself just out of reach. "E. You are the most beautiful woman I've ever known. No one else even compares to you. You are incredibly sexy, and I will always want you."

His words had the opposite effect than what he intended. It made me want to slow down. To think. To figure out what was happening.

"What are we doing? Where is this going?" What would happen past this moment?

He flashed me a devilish smile. "Right now I'm going to nuzzle your neck until you make those panting sounds that I love, but if that doesn't work for you, I'm open to suggestions."

Works for me, my traitorous brain thought as my stomach quivered at his plan.

But I couldn't just be here forever, making out with him outside of a club. With all of our friends inside.

Correction, with some of our friends inside.

"Hey, Ember? When you're, uh, done with being a baby monkey on Bash there, we just wanted to see if you were ready to go back to the motel. Our car is here." Deja stood there with Molly and Ximena, who had her mouth open in shock.

"Ye—yes." It took me a second to make my mouth work properly again. "I'll come with you." I started awkwardly disentangling myself from him, then pulled my coat back up over my shoulders. I certainly felt the cold now.

"You don't have to," Deja said. "I wouldn't."

"Stay," Bash urged me. "We need to have a conversation. I'll get you back to the motel. Or we can go back together so that we can talk."

Much as I had loved every second of what had just happened, it had been too much too fast. "I . . . I need a second. To deal with . . . everything. Can you do that? Can you give me a minute to process this?"

He clenched his jaw, as if barely holding himself in check. "Yeah. Of course. We can wait. Whatever you want."

Right. It wasn't like we hadn't waited an eternity already. I nodded, wrapping my arms around myself so that I wouldn't be tempted to reach for him.

I walked over to my friends, careful not to look back. Because if I saw him standing there, all stoic and masculine, I would turn around. I got into the car, again refusing to look. I worried that my friends were going to tease me or grill me, but instead they talked to each other. I listened as they chatted about their night. When Molly asked Deja what had happened with her potential hookup, she said, "He had a pet bearded dragon lizard. When a guy owns a reptile, usually there's some fantasy TV show that I have to pretend to care about, and I was just not in the mood."

I wanted to be present, to be listening and participating, but my mind was back with Bash. Remembering and reliving every moment. Every touch, every kiss, every caress.

But somehow, it had been better than I could recall. I had an excellent memory and always paid attention to detail, but that . . . that had been otherworldly. Like connecting with him on some astral plane or something.

Bash had wanted to talk, but I was sure that if I'd stayed, there would have been no talking of any kind. Just lots and lots more making out.

It had been everything I'd ever wanted, which made it feel like it couldn't possibly be real.

It scared me that it was real.

What was I so afraid of? Why couldn't I just let myself be in the moment with him and enjoy it?

As I looked at the streetlamps that lined the road, watching as our car passed through each pool of light, I realized that if I were being truly honest, I was afraid he was going to leave me again.

And I didn't think my heart could handle it a second time.

CHAPTER NINETEEN

BASH

Ember canceled the next couple of rehearsals that we'd scheduled. The dance was a week from now, and while we probably didn't need to practice, I wanted an excuse to see her. She'd asked for some space and time, and although it was killing me to give it to her, I knew I needed to do as she asked.

She'd been showing up late to algebra and grabbing a seat far away from me. Which pained me. I wondered what was going through her head, why she felt like she had to stay away.

When we kissed it had been . . . explosive. Incredible. Beyond. But no lines had been crossed. Things hadn't gone too far. At least not as far as I was concerned, especially since I'd wanted to take them much further.

Was it about her thinking I wasn't attracted to her? I thought I'd demonstrated pretty clearly that wasn't the case. And I was still dumbfounded by the fact that she'd ever thought it in the first place. How could she not know how amazing she was? How it was all I could do to keep my hands off her?

After class Sabrina introduced me to a friend of hers. I had been busy watching Ember pack up her things, so I missed the part where Sabrina and her friend had met. The friend's name was Gwen, and once I'd said, "Nice to meet you," Gwen hadn't stopped talking. Like she'd decided, *I was going to exhale anyway so might as well keep saying words.*

I tried to pay attention to what she was saying, not knowing what Sabrina was up to until she stood behind Gwen and held both of her thumbs up, mouthing, *Go for it!*

She was trying to set us up. Me and the girl who would not be quiet. Even when she said, "Wow, I'm talking a lot, aren't I?" and I nodded, she missed that social cue. I liked a woman I could talk to, but also one that I could be quiet with and have it not feel weird. Like what I had with Ember.

I felt a hand on my shoulder, and I recognized the touch and the scent that followed quickly after.

Ember. As if my thinking about her had somehow brought her over to me.

Holding my breath, I turned to face her, wanting to both comfort her and be upset with her about how she'd left me to twist in the wind and be accosted by people who didn't have an off switch.

"Sorry for interrupting, but can I talk to you for a second, Bash?"

I made my apologies to Gwen and walked out into the hallway with Ember. My pulse raced as I waited for her to speak.

"I was hoping we could have practice today. Would that be okay with you?" she asked.

Okay with me? That would be fantastic. "Yeah. I can do that. In about an hour?"

She nodded, giving me a tight smile. I wanted to hold her and kiss that sad face away. I wanted her laughing and happy. Or frantic and passionate. Either worked for me. Anything but this putting me at a distance.

I showed up early to our practice space and felt stupid for having done so. It wasn't like it was going to make her show up any faster. I just wanted to make sure that I was here and ready to listen.

She walked through the door about fifteen minutes later, during which time I'd worked myself up into a frenzy imagining what she might say.

"Hi!" My greeting was like an overenthusiastic puppy, readying to leap on her. "I mean, hey."

"Hey," she returned my greeting. She put down her bag. "Can we sit?"

"Yeah." I sat down against one of the mirrored walls. She came over and sat next to me, but far enough away that I couldn't feel her warmth.

"So, sorry for all the weirdness the last few days," she said, looking straight ahead while I watched emotions flit across her profile.

"I get it." I didn't, but it seemed like the right thing to say.

"That makes one of us," she said with a little laugh. "But Doug came by last night to drop off registration tags for my car that had been mailed to the house, and he seemed sad. I wanted to check in with you and see how you were doing."

Not how I saw this going. "I mean, I'm dealing. It is what it is. It's not what any of us wanted, but Marley seems surprisingly okay with it all, and that's what matters the most."

"I can see why she'd want to get to know your mom."

While I understood, it didn't mean that I approved. But this was Marley's decision to make.

Ember went on. "And maybe . . . maybe you should talk to your mom, too. Tell her some of the stuff you told me. Find out what her story is. It might make things a little easier for you. Especially where Marley's concerned."

If this was some kind of one-person intervention for trying to get me to talk to my mother, I wasn't interested in participating. Especially since all of my recent mental energy had been expended solely on Ember and whatever was or was not happening with us. I felt like I could only deal with one drama at a time. "Okay. Thanks. Should we start practicing?"

"Wait." She put her soft hand on my forearm, and the entire world shrank down to that one touch, as if nothing else could exist outside of it. "There's something else."

"What is it?"

"I've been thinking a lot about what you said and about, um, what we did."

"Me too." My voice sounded gruffer than I'd intended.

Her hand was still on my arm, so I took that as a good sign. "And the thing is . . . the thing is that I've believed certain stuff about myself that wasn't true because I thought you believed it. It's bothered me for years, and it bugs me even more that I wasn't strong enough or self-confident enough to say, 'Screw him' and have my own self-image that wasn't influenced by you."

It still shocked me that she couldn't see how hot she was. How I would have loved nothing more than to pull her into my lap and prove it to her again. Logan had been right. I should have talked to her about it before we kissed. I felt bad that she'd been carrying around all this unnecessary baggage, and even worse about the part I'd accidentally played in packing it up for her. "You are stunning and perfect, and I want to touch you constantly. I wish I could help fix it and undo what I did."

"You've helped. But I can't just flip a switch and feel different about everything. Totally change my worldview and how I see myself in it. Maybe I will, given some time. But I think you know that's not the only issue we have here."

I knew. I nodded.

"If we dated," she went on, "what would we tell our parents?"

I was about to tell her what my dad had said all those years ago, which had been the cause of me leaving, when we heard a commotion out in the hallway.

A woman was yelling. We exchanged glances and then both went over to the door.

Keilani and Ford were walking toward the opposite end of the hall. She called out, "Ford, wait!" He came to a stop, turning to look at Keilani.

"What?" he asked, his exasperation evident in his voice.

"What is your deal with me?" she asked.

Ford crossed his arms. "My deal? Can you just not? Can we not?"

She mirrored his stance. "No, I think it's past time that we did. Could you please just be honest with me for five minutes and tell me what I did to make you hate me so much?"

"Maybe we shouldn't be listening," I whispered to Ember, who just elbowed me in the stomach and told me to be quiet.

"I don't hate you." Ford's voice sounded broken. "I never hated you."

"You did a pretty good job of convincing me otherwise. Why?"

If either one of them turned slightly, they would see us and stop, but they were completely wrapped up in each other and in their conversation.

I felt bad about eavesdropping on this private moment, but it was kind of like a prime-time show I'd been watching for months now, waiting for something to happen in the story line, and it was finally happening, and I couldn't look away, even if I thought I should.

I had to know how it all played out.

He looked down at his shoes for so long that I thought he wasn't going to answer, but then he did. "When I got here, I was one of the youngest QB coaches ever, for any school. I wanted to be taken seriously. And Coach Oakley had that no-dating rule in place, and I thought I couldn't expect my players to follow a rule I wasn't willing to follow myself."

"I don't understand. What has that got to do with me?"

"When I saw you . . . you were so beautiful. I wanted to ask you out. But then I thought about the rule and what would happen if we did go out and we broke up, and then it'd be awkward and we'd still have to work together and see each other all the time."

"That's . . ." She seemed to be searching for the right word. "So stupid it makes me sad. You were worried we'd break up so you acted like you couldn't stand me?"

"It was childish. And selfish. But it was the only way I could stay away from you."

"Oh." She sounded bewildered. "You can't think about dating someone and mentally go on your next thirty dates and predetermine how things will end. What if you were wrong? What if it didn't end badly? What if we were meant to be something more?"

"You think I didn't consider that, too?" Ford asked. "Like when we talked at that Halloween frat party, and I recognized your voice, and I knew you didn't recognize mine. I wanted to prove to myself that I'd been right. That we would fight and pick at each other and get annoyed, but we didn't. It was one of the best conversations I've ever had. It was like we fit together. Like you were a piece of me that I didn't know was missing. And then at the Christmas faculty party, when I let a few glasses of wine impair my decision-making abilities and I kissed you under the mistletoe? That was . . . magic."

She waited a few beats, as if wanting him to go on. When he didn't, she prompted him, "And what? You liked me but didn't want to date me, so you decided to keep being cold?"

"I've had the worst time keeping my distance from you. You're an incredible woman, Keilani. You're so kind and optimistic and beautiful and good at your job and devoted to helping all of your students. How was I supposed to stop myself from falling in love with you?"

"You're in love with me?" Keilani repeating the words made something twist deep inside me. Reminding me that I was in love with Ember but hadn't ever told her.

"How could I not be? And I'm sorry that I'm an idiot. I'm sorry that I thought this was the best way to go about things. I'm sorry that I hurt you, because that is the last thing I would ever want to do. I'm sorry that I ruined any future we might have together. Because of course I want to date you. Of course I want to be with you. I'm sorry that my actions made it so that you'd never want to be with me. Again, I apologize for the idiot part. And I'm so sorry that—"

We never got to hear what else he was sorry for because Keilani was kissing him, and it all felt weird. Both to be watching it and having overheard what we did. It was starting to verge into creeper territory.

Ember sighed, "Aw," happily.

I walked away from the open door, my mind racing. Jess had talked about Keilani and Ford often, insisting that they were in love and the rest of us (including them) just couldn't see it.

Now Keilani was mauling Ford in the hallway, and even I had to admit that Jess had been right.

Telling Jess about what I'd just witnessed would make her insufferable for about a week or so.

Ember quietly closed our door, and I figured Ford and Keilani wouldn't even notice. Then she joined me where I stood, waiting. I wasn't sure for what. For them to leave? For Ember to talk to me again? To start our practice?

She smiled and said, "Wasn't that so sweet? So romantic?"

It was certainly something. "I don't know. I think I liked it better when they threw up at the sight of each other."

She smacked me on my upper arm, but her face was amused.

The problem was, I didn't know how I felt about what I'd just seen. I'd been listening to Jess's conspiracy theories about their relationship for the last few months, and it was weird to see it happen in real life.

But beyond that, I couldn't help but compare their situation to the one I found myself in with Ember. I thought of Keilani's admonishment that Ford couldn't mentally go on their next thirty dates before they'd even gone on one, and it made me recall my dad's thirty-Christmases comment again. It was what had kept me from Ember.

Had I been doing the same thing? Assuming that things with Ember would end and end badly, and then I'd be stuck seeing her for decades at family events, making things hard and awkward on everybody around us?

What if I'd been doing what Keilani accused Ford of? That I'd already mapped out our entire future relationship without even knowing how things would turn out? Ember could be the one. I knew that, in my heart of hearts. I could easily see myself spending the rest of my life loving her.

Was I giving up what could be the most important relationship in my life just to make other people's lives easier?

"Are you okay?" Ember asked, pulling me out of my train of thought.

Not ready to share everything I'd been thinking, I smiled. "Fine. Shall we dance?"

As we moved to our stance, I planned what I would tell her once she lifted her time/space ban. I'd made the mistake when we were teenagers of not telling her everything that was in my heart, and it had hurt her in ways I hadn't anticipated. It made her doubt herself when she was the last person who ever should. I didn't want that to happen again.

I also needed to sort out what I wanted to do. I'd been avoiding all of my problems for so long—that needed to stop. But I still wanted to respect her wishes.

Before I counted us off I said, "E? I know that you need time and space to figure out what you think and what you want to do next. But when you're ready? I'm here."

"Thank you." The words were quiet and heavy.

I only hoped she wouldn't take too long.

CHAPTER TWENTY

EMBER

This was how my Friday was going:

Deja reminded me, like, six times about our girls' weekend trip up at Molly's uncle's cabin. Telling me that I'd been "checked out" lately and we needed bonding time. Which was fair. I'd always prided myself on my ability to show up for my loved ones. But admittedly, I'd been a bit flaky recently without intending to be. Bash was a major distraction.

I was actually looking forward to our getaway now, hoping that once we'd sufficiently bonded that I'd get some time to sort out my thoughts and issues and make sense of what was happening between Bash and me. Because that kiss had thrown everything off balance, and I didn't know what we should do next.

My roommates had left for our cabin trip, and I decided to take a short nap before my test. Which ended up being too long, so I got to the testing center just before it closed, and rushed through my exam. I realized that I probably hadn't done great, given how shaken and flustered I felt.

I'd brought my overnight bag with me and went straight from the testing center to the parking lot. When I got in my car, it started making funny sounds. I stood outside and tried to record the sound of the engine, but it didn't sound the same on my phone. I decided to bring my car home and have Doug diagnose it. As I backed out of the parking spot, I heard a sound, and when I opened the car door to investigate, I saw my cell phone, which I'd left on the roof, lying on the ground.

Where it was, predictably, ruined. The screen was shattered, and I tried to use it, but I couldn't undo the lock because of the messed-up screen.

At least I could kill two birds with one stone—when I got home I'd have to beg my mom to get me another phone. My whole life was on it. I needed it.

But when I got to the house, no one else was there. Both of the cars were gone. Even Roscoe wasn't there. I was going to use the landline to call them but realized that I didn't know anybody's phone numbers. That was why I had them in my contacts list. So I didn't have to memorize them. I didn't even know Bash's, although he had remembered mine. He was who I wanted to call to bail me out. Because I knew if I told him I needed him, he'd be there.

Which was something I decided not to examine too closely.

There was no way I was going to drive to the cabin with whatever was happening with my car. The last thing I needed was for it to break down in the middle of nowhere and for me to end up in a cage in some serial killer's basement.

I logged on to the family computer and opened up my email. In addition to texting me, Deja had made sure to email me the address to the cabin and had left it on a piece of paper on our kitchen counter. If I'd had a fax machine, I was pretty sure she would have faxed me, too. She'd also repeatedly reminded me of the security code they'd chosen, 4155. In case I got there late. Which I had told her more than once that I would not.

Even though that was totally the case now.

I checked the public transportation website. Although there was a stop about two blocks from our house, the closest one to the cabin was a really long walk. Miles and miles.

Then I thought about maybe an Uber or a taxi, but the cost was ridiculously high. Like rent-for-the-next-three-months high.

I was in the middle of figuring out how to find one of my room-mates' cell phone numbers when I heard the front door open and shut.

Finally, someone was home!

I rushed into the foyer to see Bash.

Of course. My ridiculous heart leapt at the sight of him.

"Hey. I'm here to do laundry again," he said.

I blushed just a little as I was reminded of our last laundry encounter. "I'm so glad you're here. I'm having a code red." Was that right? "Or another important color code. I need help." I explained my situation to him, and that I was hoping to use one of the family cars to get to the cabin.

He got out his phone and started texting. "Okay, Marley and Lauren are at a slumber party, and your mom and my dad are at the vet because Roscoe had a funny cough. The vet thinks he's fine, but they're running a couple of tests just to be sure. Dad said he'll check your car when he gets back, but it's probably best if you don't try and use it. He also said if you needed to leave now, you could take the truck."

"The one he's been restoring in the garage?" I clarified. "Isn't that a stick shift?"

"Yes."

I let out a small groan of protest. "I can't drive a stick."

"I can. I can take you."

"It's really far. Like an hour away. I wouldn't want you to have to do that."

He shrugged. "The only plan I have tonight is a hot date with the washing machine. So I have time."

I was so torn. I didn't want to be stuck in a car for that long with Bash with things so unresolved between us, but I also didn't want to deal with my roommates' wrath if I bailed on them.

"I feel bad."

"I'm offering. Come on," he cajoled me. "Let me be a knight in shining armor. It's good to be able to dust off the old armor from time to time, you know? I promise to keep things friendly and casual. No serious discussions need to be had."

He gave me sad puppy-dog eyes, and I sighed. "I can't say no when you look at me that way."

"That's why I look at you that way."

I felt his words burning their way through my entire body, and I tried to brush off the feeling. I really did need a ride, this wasn't my inner teenager scheming to find ways to spend time with him. "Okay. Let's go. But I insist on paying for gas."

"Oh, I was planning on that. Your chariot awaits, my lady."

My stomach flipped over, and I told it to stop. I didn't want to be charmed.

But it was already too late.

~

True to his word, Bash kept the conversation light. He played car games with me, like finding letters on license plates. My stomach was rumbling when he wanted to play two truths and a lie.

"Let's have a snack break instead," I suggested.

"Playing the game could be fun!"

"Lie," I responded, earning me a grin from him.

"I know that you'd prefer to eat—"

"Truth."

"Fine," he said with an exaggerated sigh. "What do you have?"

Obviously, I'd packed a ton of snacks. For me. They weren't going to last long with Bash in the car. I pulled out a package of peanut butter–and–chocolate KIND bars. "How many do you want?"

"Just give me the whole thing."

I studied the back of the box, looking at the nutritional information. "According to their serving sizes, if you eat all of this, you'll be a family of six."

"I like to think of myself as a family of twelve, thanks," he said as I passed him the box.

"That's not very healthy, you know." I said this to him while peeling off the wrapper of a 3 Musketeers.

"Says the woman inhaling her candy bar."

"I went in for a physical, and I'll have you know the doctor said I should be eating more chocolate. Also, I'm calling myself the doctor now."

He laughed so hard I was slightly afraid he might get in an accident. But it was like Bash and I were ourselves again. Laughing, playing, bantering, ignoring the underlying tension that had existed since the kiss.

The soul-burning, lip-melting, madness-inducing kiss.

We were about fifteen minutes away from the cabin, according to the maps app on Bash's phone, when big buckets of snow just started pouring down on us. It was like there was a stagehand just off the side of the road whose job it was to throw puffs of snow at us.

"Did you see anything in the forecast about this?" Bash asked.

"No." I also did not tell him that I hadn't actually checked the forecast before we left.

"If this doesn't ease up, you guys might be snowed in."

"Should we turn around?"

"We'll just keep going and hope the roads stay relatively clear. And if not, well, we'll figure that out when we get there."

If the girls and I got snowed in, that meant Bash was going to be snowed in with us. I was more delighted by this prospect than concerned about it, which made me realize that maybe I had had enough time and space and could accept that I'd misunderstood our interaction back when we were teens. That he was attracted to me and that I was beautiful, at least to him. I'd been building myself up these last few days by thinking about all the things I did like. Like my hair and eyelashes. I had a pretty decent butt. I liked how strong I was, how I could play a sport that I loved and had even earned a scholarship for it. I was usually a good friend and tried hard to be a good daughter and sister. I thought I had a good sense of humor (but to be honest, everybody thinks that about themselves, regardless of whether or not it's true). So my body wasn't perfect. Most people's weren't. Bash being an obvious exception.

Anyway, I still had a ways to go on being kinder to myself, but I figured I'd made a good start.

And I knew our family situation was going to be weird for a while, but shouldn't we give it a shot? Didn't we owe it to ourselves to at least try and see? Because if we moved forward, maybe I could have all this and more. The friendship and the laughter along with the passion.

It still seemed too good to be true.

The snow only seemed to get worse the closer we got. Bash had slowed the truck down to a snail's pace, inching along the road.

I noticed Bash's white knuckles against the dark steering wheel. I reached over and put my hand on his knee, wanting to quietly let him know that I was here and knew that he could do this. He glanced at my hand, then at me, but said nothing as he turned his attention back to the road.

Bash's phone announced that he should turn right, and we went up a snow-covered hill. We fishtailed once or twice, but then we heard the message saying that we had arrived. I noticed that there were no lights on just as he said, "There's no other cars here."

I didn't see a garage, and he was right; I didn't see Ximena's Jeep. She might have parked somewhere else. "Maybe we can't see it. Let's get inside and you can meet everyone," I said. I knew all of my roommates were going to love the chance to spend time getting to know Bash better. Especially since I'd shared so little about him, but they'd all seen that kiss.

"Awesome. I would love to have the chance to be judged by your friends."

Shaking my head, I grabbed my bag and we both ran through the quickly accumulating snow to the front porch, which was covered, protecting us from the heavy snowfall. I knocked. Then again. There was no doorbell, but I did notice the lock with a keypad. I punched in 4155 and heard the deadbolt automatically turn. I opened the door.

"Hello?" I called out. I stamped my feet on the front entry rug and hung my wet coat on the coatrack. Bash flipped on the overhead light and headed toward the back of the cabin. I went upstairs, thinking maybe they'd just parked out of sight, or someplace we hadn't noticed, and somehow all decided to go to bed even though it was still early in the evening.

All of the bedrooms were empty.

I came back downstairs and found Bash in the kitchen. "It looks like somebody stocked the place up. We've got plenty of food," he said.

"They're not here. They left hours before me. This makes me worried." I sat down at the dining table and tapped my fingers against it. "Do you have Felix's number? He used to date Deja. I bet he knows her phone number."

"I don't, but I can get it. Logan probably has it." He set down the package of deli meat he had in his hands and started texting. After a few minutes he said, "Got it."

He handed me his phone, and I called Deja.

She answered. "Hello?"

"Deja, it's Ember. I'm at the cabin. Where are you guys?"

"You're at the cabin? Didn't you get any of my texts or voice mails?"

I explained that I had accidentally destroyed my cell phone.

"We decided to call off the trip this afternoon because Molly checked the forecast. What?" she said, her voice sounding more muffled. "Molly says that her uncle brought by some food this morning. When we told him we weren't going to come, he left it there in case we changed our minds or wanted to come up later."

Bash was in the middle of making himself a massive sandwich. "Yeah, we found it."

"We?" Deja repeated.

"Bash drove me up, and I'm not sure he should try to get out of here."

"Oh, no. Not until tomorrow, at least. The storm is supposed to be really bad."

"Yeah, we saw it. It's not great."

"I don't know, being stranded in a log cabin with a hot man doesn't sound like a bad way to spend an evening to me," she said. "He should definitely stay until the roads get cleared. Which will take hours and hours and hours. I guess you'll just have to find a way to fill that time."

"Okay!" I said, conscious of the fact that Bash was standing right there and Deja's voice tended to carry. "Thanks. I'll talk to you guys tomorrow, I guess. Bye."

I hung up and then stood to bring the phone back to him. He was looking out of the window above the kitchen sink. "It is really bad," he commented.

"Yeah, Deja was saying that's why they decided not to come. Which they tried to tell me, but I had my phone turned off to take my test and then I broke it, so . . . here we are."

"Here we are." He turned around, facing me and leaning against the sink, his arms propped up behind him on the counter.

"She, um, she also said that we'd have to wait the storm out. So you'll, you know, need to stay here tonight."

"Not a problem. I'm going to go look for a thermostat and see if I can get the heat going."

He brushed past me, and my nerves jolted awake, anxious to be touched by him again. I wandered back into the front living room. All of the walls were a light wood color, and the vaulted ceiling went up at least two stories. I guessed the giant windows usually had an incredible view, but right now all I could see was a wall of white.

I went over to the fireplace in the corner. There were some logs in it, including one of those fake ones where you lit the paper on the outside and it burned. I had never operated a wood-burning fireplace before, and I hoped there wasn't anything to it. There were matches on the mantel, and I used them to start a fire. If this place didn't have a heater, at least we could warm up this one room.

And maybe you'll have to snuggle to conserve body heat, my overactive imagination suggested.

Bash returned just as I'd settled down onto the oversize, comfy couch that faced the fireplace. "I turned the heat on. At least we won't freeze tonight."

He sat down next to me, his arm along the back of the couch, almost touching me.

"I thought you were going to get something to eat," I said, watching the flames dance.

"I'd rather be here with you."

He was choosing me over food? That felt profound. Deep in a way I couldn't quite wrap my mind around. The look in his eyes made my breath catch, my heart sputter.

This was it. This was the time to tell him.

"Bash, I think we should talk. It's important."

CHAPTER TWENTY-ONE

EMBER

"Is it about the global water crisis?" he asked jokingly.

"What? No. I mean, that's important, but that's not . . ." I let out a deep breath. It had been difficult to change my mind-set. I'd spent so long thinking of myself in one way, the way I had mistakenly believed he saw me. It would have been nice if once I found out the truth I could have just snapped my fingers and felt differently about my body image. When I'd asked him for time and space, I had really needed it. To not only process the information he'd given me but mostly to try and figure out a way to be happy with myself, regardless of what anybody else thought. "I think I've taken the time that I needed, and I'm ready now. To have the conversation that we need to have."

His lack of reaction surprised me. No smile, no sparkle in his eye, no reaching for me to pull me into a scorching kiss. Instead he just . . . looked at me.

I suddenly felt very stupid. "I mean, if you've changed your mind and don't feel the same, I get it, but . . ." I let my voice trail off, not sure what I intended to say next. Because I didn't want to walk away. I didn't want to lose the chance of us before we'd even begun.

There were several more awkward moments before he said, "You know, I think I finally understand how my parents felt about doing drugs."

Of all the things I thought he might say in response to my statement, that one hadn't even charted. "What?"

"You're like an addiction for me. Only it's not just physical, it's in my soul. In my heart. I want you constantly. I want you in my bed, in my life, all the time. It feels like there's never a point in time where I don't think about you. Want to kiss you. Hold you. Wake up next to you. I want to tell you every stupid thing that happens in my day. When something makes me laugh, the first thing I think is 'I can't wait to tell Ember.'"

His words were like fire, only they burned inside of me. His gaze captured mine, making it impossible to look away. My heart thudded, slow and hard.

"There's something I haven't told you. Something I should have told you a long time ago. When our parents got married, my dad sat me down. He must have seen how I felt about you because he warned me to stay away from you. He didn't want me to break up his new relationship with your mom. He said that unless I could see you and me as a couple for the next thirty years of family get-togethers at Christmas, that I should leave you alone."

I was surprised by the hot tears that suddenly clouded my vision. "And you can't see that."

He reached forward, lacing his fingers through mine. He shook his head. "E, no. That's the problem. I can see the next seventy Christmases with you. I can see forever when I look in your eyes."

I didn't know what to say. Was he saying what I thought he was saying? Forever? And instead of this information easing my tears, it gave them permission to run free, spilling down my cheeks.

"Don't cry," he murmured, leaning close to wipe the tears away with his free hand. "That's the last thing I want."

He reached his hands out tentatively, looking at me for permission. I nodded, and he drew me to him, holding me tight. I laid my head on his broad shoulder, feeling like I was finally where I belonged. I put my arms around his chest and let myself melt against him.

He began to say words against my scalp, causing a tingling sensation. "You're right here, and it's like I haven't been allowed to say or do what I want. It seems so unfair. I try so hard to be good and to do the right thing and keep my dad's rules and Coach's rules, and the one thing, the one thing I want more than any other, I'm not supposed to have. I don't want to destroy our parents' lives. Or Lauren and Marley's. But the thing is . . ." He let out a deep sigh, his warm breath stirring my hair. He put his hand under my chin, lifting it up so that I was staring deeply into his dark-green eyes. "The thing is, E, I love you. Always have."

My heart burst, fizzing and bubbling inside of me, filling my veins with unbearable lightness and hope. Bash had just said he loved me. The darker, insecure part of me wanted to dismiss his words, to count them as lies. But I could see the truth of his words in his eyes. "Are you serious?" It was the only thing I could think to ask. I had to know.

He stroked the side of my face with his fingers. "I'm so serious. This is why I left. Not because I wasn't attracted to you, which, I would like to point out again, I was and still am, but because I was in love with you, and I knew it would wreck everything. And my dad had been sad for so long, and he was finally happy again, and I didn't want to be the reason that fell apart."

"You put your dad's happiness above your own." That was exactly the kind of thing Bash would do.

"I did. Now I realize that I also put his happiness above yours, and that was wrong." He leaned in and pressed a soft but blazing kiss against my cheek. "I've regretted it every day since."

I put my hand against his chest, leaning back. "We were young. It wasn't wrong of you to want to protect your father. Trust me, of anyone, I understand that. But why didn't you say anything before?"

"What could I say? How could I explain this? I don't know that I understood all my motivations until recently, when I forced myself to look at what I'd done and why. You of all people know that I'm all about avoiding a problem and pretending that it doesn't exist and it's not something I need to deal with. All I can say is that at the time, I thought I was making the right choice. But I know now that I didn't just martyr myself. I hurt you and what you thought of us and of yourself."

"I'm working on it," I told him. "I'm trying to see me the way that you see me."

"It's still hard for me to fathom how you can believe that you aren't perfect. I would love nothing more than to worship every inch of you." His words sent a spike of fiery heat straight through my core, and breathing suddenly became something I'd forgotten how to do. His hands began to wander. "I love the swell of your hips, the indentation of your waist, your stomach and the way you tremble when I brush my fingers there." As if to prove his point, he ran his fingertips under the hem of my shirt, then along the skin of my stomach, and just as he predicted, I did tremble.

Then he ducked his head, planting a kiss against my stomach. The trembling turned to miniquakes, even though he had kissed me on top of my shirt, and even though I technically couldn't feel the warmth of his lips, I still felt it. Everywhere.

He lifted his gaze, holding me captive. He explored my face with his lips, speaking softly to me as he did so. "I love your hair, how silky it is against my skin. I love the softness and slope of your neck. I love the curve of your ear. I am ridiculously in love with your lips. With how warm they are, how they feel pressed against mine. And I am also a fan of everything south of them."

As shivers raced around my skin, I let out a laugh of delight, unable to believe that this was happening. That Bash *loved* me.

I realized that I hadn't told him I felt the same and was filled with the need to let him know he wasn't alone in this. "You know, my other theory about why you left that night was because I told you I loved you."

"You loved me, past tense?" He went still. "Do you still love me?"

How could he even wonder? "Yes. I still love you. I can't remember what it was like not to love you." Over the years I had sometimes worried that I always would, that there would never be room in my heart for anyone else.

He kissed me, nipping at my bottom lip. "That's kind of important to share."

I let my fingers run through his hair, dragging my fingernails across his scalp. He shuddered, and his reaction did crazy things to my stomach. "I didn't tell you sooner because I thought you didn't feel the same way about me. You never said it before."

The scruff of his chin gently rubbed against my jawline, and I sighed at the feeling. "I know. I should have. But I knew once I told you, that would be it. There would be no going back for me."

"Going back?"

He pressed a kiss on the top of my nose. "You can't unring a bell. If we cross this boundary, we can't uncross it."

Boundary? What boundary? Did he mean the boundary that was so far behind me I was now on a different continent? I was ready to scale any mountain, swim any body of water, crawl through any swamp if it meant being with him.

But I had to ignore my gut reaction and listen to what he was saying. "You're right. And I'm willing to cross some lines, but maybe the best thing for us to do right now is to go really slowly. I want us to be a hundred percent sure that we're making the right decision first."

"How slow?"

"Really slow. Like maybe we keep it to mostly kissing." Not that I wanted to, but he already muddied my senses and made it difficult to think of anything else just by kissing me. Upping the difficulty factor would only make the situation worse.

I felt his smile against my lips. He kissed me lightly, teasing, and it was all I could do not to grab him out of frustration. But that would be one mixed signal. "That . . . is going to be really difficult."

"I believe in you. Go team!" I said weakly, my bones liquefying from another one of his gentle, light kisses.

"For you, I think I could do anything." This time I got a lingering kiss, one that didn't satisfy me but only whet my appetite for more. "Do you know that kissing you is better than jumping out of a plane?" he asked before he kissed me again.

"Everything is better than jumping out of a plane, so I don't know that that's much of a compliment."

As I said those words against his lips, he chuckled, which I took as an opportunity to explain my slow position. "Anything could happen. Maybe it doesn't work out between us, and it's awkward for a little while. It can't be any worse than you moving to another state just to avoid me. This is part of being mature, right? We can agree that no matter what happens, we'll still be civil and get along. For me personally, I think having sex would make moving on too hard. And I know I'm not supposed to freak out about the future and go on all our dates at once in my head. I'm not trying to see the end before the beginning, because we don't know where this will go."

"E, I know exactly where this is going. But I'm willing to play it the way that you want to. Anything, if I can be with you."

Again, his words thrilled me, shooting little quivers of desire through me. He had one of his hands on the side of my face, holding me while he gently planted kisses up and down the side of my throat. He was making it very hard to think. But there was at least one more thing we needed to talk about.

"Putting how we feel aside," I said, pushing at his chest so that he would sit up and look at me and stop tempting me with his fiery touch, "we also need to recognize that things haven't changed. Your dad still wants you to stay away from me, and my mom is determined to make you feel welcome at your home so that you'll go back more, and she enlisted me to help. To be a good stepsister. She would not be happy if she knew we were dating. *Freaking out* would be an understatement. How are we supposed to overcome that?"

"We don't need to tell them anything while you and I figure this out."

"I . . ." I couldn't even say that I didn't want to lie to her because I had lied to my mother lots where Bash had been concerned. My reasons for doing so had always seemed valid. Was this really any different? "It feels wrong to do that. I don't want you to be my dirty little secret."

His grin was pure sexual magnetism, nearly blinding me. "Even if I don't mind being your dirty little secret?" His fingers were kneading my scalp and making it so I couldn't concentrate.

"We should be more than that," I finally managed to say. "We should be out in the open."

"How would that even work?"

"I don't know." Mostly because my brain functions had ceased. "I was kind of hoping you might have the answers."

"I don't know, either. But we don't have to figure it out tonight." He leaned me back against the couch, into the corner so that I was in a reclining position. He hovered above me, his arms braced on the arm and back of the couch, trapping me. "From my keen observations, it looks as if this storm isn't letting up, and we're going to be trapped here overnight. The only thing we need to decide tonight is who's going to sleep where."

"I'm planning on sleeping in a bed."

"Sounds good. I'll join you."

I smiled up at him, reaching up to run my fingers along his spiky five o'clock shadow. He turned his face into my palm, nuzzling it before he kissed it. "It will be easier to keep this slow if you sleep in a bed and I sleep in a different bed in another room." Possibly a room in another cabin at the rate this was going.

"Okay," he muttered as he lowered his body to mine. "But can we make out a little first?"

"Well, that seems only reasonable."

Then he showed me just how much he agreed.

~

Later, he walked me to one of the bedrooms, his arms still wrapped around me as he pressed me into the doorway and kissed me good night. As he set my entire body ablaze once more, I was tempted to tell him to forget the slow thing. That I had been mistaken.

Just as I opened my mouth to tell him as much, he whispered, "Good night," and kissed me softly one last time. He walked across the hall to what looked like the master bedroom. The room I was staying in had two twin beds, just like what I had in my room in the apartment.

I suddenly felt a chill, even though the heat was on. I'd been glorying in and surrounding myself with Bash's warmth, and now that it was gone, I missed it. As I opened my overnight bag, I realized I hadn't exactly brought anything warm to sleep in. I'd brought a blue silk set; it had a button-up top and a pair of matching shorts, and it had not been designed with snowy nights in mind.

I changed, grabbed my notebook, and got under the covers. Bash and I had spent the evening talking and kissing (admittedly, more kissing than talking), but the conversations we'd had made me believe what he was saying. That we would last. That we could be together forever. I felt too wired to sleep and tried to continue my story about Sven and Julia. I was on the fourth chapter, and they had just arrived in Rome to train Sven to become a gladiator.

I was about to separate my main characters, and I realized that I didn't want to. Not in my story, not in my real life.

Bash was right there, across the hallway. We'd already spent years apart. We weren't going to have another chance like this for a long time. Where we wouldn't have to say good night.

My heart thundered in my ears as I threw off my blankets and headed for his room. I knocked softly on his door and let myself in, closing it behind me. What if he was already asleep?

"E?" he mumbled when I tiptoed over to his bed. Not asleep yet, but almost there. "What's wrong?"

Acting braver than I felt I said, "Could we . . . tonight . . . can I stay here? With you?"

He sat up in bed. He was shirtless, and he absentmindedly rubbed his face. "I thought you wanted to take things slow."

"I do. I'm not offering to have sex with you. I just want to sleep here. I don't want to be apart from you anymore."

I couldn't see his face clearly in the dark, so I didn't know what he was thinking. I was afraid that I'd made a big mistake. I'd almost started to apologize and slink back to my own room when he pulled the covers open and patted the spot next to him.

That was all I needed. I climbed in as he lay down again. I rested my head against his shoulder, fitting perfectly against him. Even though I had my mom and my sister, I hadn't had what felt like home in a long time. We lived in Doug's house, and then I lived in a dorm and then an apartment. All of those places were temporary.

But this? With Bash's arms around me, his warmth enveloping me, this . . . this was my home.

I draped my leg on top of his, stealing my arm around his ridged stomach. I wanted this. A lifetime of nights like this one. I could see forever, too.

"You must think I have incredible willpower to sneak into my room wearing this." His fingers toyed with the hem of my top, feeling the fabric.

"I trust me and I trust you."

He let out a groan. "Great. You had to go and make it about my integrity."

I giggled, snuggling closer. "I can go. I'm not trying to tempt you. I just want to be close to you."

"I don't want you to go."

"I don't want to go, either."

"Then it's settled," he said as he kissed the top of my head. "But I vote that the next time we do this, we do the naked version of it."

"That's a possibility."

His arms tightened around me slightly, and as his breathing grew more even, I felt his chest moving up and down in a rhythmic way that made me sleepy, too.

Right before he drifted off, he said, "I totally knew you were going to sleep with me tonight."

I laughed and held him tighter.

Life was fantastic, and the universe was amazing. As my own eyelids became heavy, I decided things couldn't possibly get any better than they were in this moment.

CHAPTER TWENTY-TWO

BASH

The sun was bright, the sky clear the next morning, and it was beyond hard to climb out of that bed with so much lush warmth and softness waiting for me there. But I wanted to do something special for Ember, so I got up, threw on my shirt, and made her breakfast.

She had just woken up when I returned with a plate of pancakes, bacon, and scrambled eggs.

"What's this?" she asked, and the delight was evident on her face and in her voice.

"I made you breakfast in bed." I situated the tray on her lap. I lay next to her, propping myself up on my elbow. She immediately picked up a piece of bacon, taking a bite.

"This is really good," she said, holding it out to me. "Try it."

I took a bite and couldn't hide my smile.

"What?" she demanded. "What is that look for?"

"You just shared your food with me."

She raised her eyebrows. "And?"

"For you? That's the biggest declaration of love I've ever seen. If I wasn't sure of it last night, now I know you love me."

"All I'm declaring is that I appreciate you doing this, and I was being nice because I know you're hungry, and I was trying to help keep it at bay."

"One tiny bite of food is not going to fill me up. And when it comes to you"—I leaned over to kiss her on the pulse point between her neck and her collarbone, and I felt her soften beneath my lips—"one small taste is never enough. I'll never get my fill of you."

From the darkening of her eyes I knew she felt the same. "Can I tell you something?"

"Always."

"Now that I know how you feel about me and about all this"—she gestured at herself—"it feels a little weird. Like I suddenly feel like I have this superpower over you. As if I could make you lose control with very little effort."

Her words turned my insides molten hot, my body coiled with tension. "You keep talking like that, and you're going to find out how true that is. Besides, didn't anybody ever teach you to use your powers for good?"

"But . . . I think this would be good." Her teasing, seductive smile was back, making my breath catch.

"Stop playing with fire," I warned her. I knew Ember. It would be one thing for her to joke but another for us to move too quickly.

Fortunately my phone buzzed with a message, and I reached over to the nightstand to grab it. "It's from Deja. She said the roads have been cleared and they're on their way up here."

"Oh." Ember pouted a little, making me want to kiss her lower lip. "I was kind of hoping it would just be the two of us today."

I put my hand on top of her leg, still feeling a little awestruck by the fact that I could touch her or kiss her now. "I wanted that, too. I could stick around."

"Yeah, but knowing my roommates there might be a male ritual sacrifice planned for later on this evening. Or they will hound you endlessly with questions."

"I can take a little interrogation."

"This wouldn't be a little interrogation. This would be like . . . a Guantanamo Bay type of situation."

"Well," I said, "in the interest of not being waterboarded, I should probably go dig the truck out." I squeezed her leg. "I hate the idea of leaving you."

"I don't want you to leave, either." Her voice sounded different, strained.

"Hey," I said, waiting for her to look at me. I was surprised to see pain and fear filling her eyes. "I'm not going anywhere. You know that, right?"

"I do. It's just . . . I don't know. I'm being silly." She shook her shoulders, as if she could make her feelings disappear just like that. "I'll see you when I get back to school."

"Right. We've got all the time in the world now."

"Although," she said, that playful tone back, "I liked it better when seeing you didn't involve a shirt."

I reached behind me and yanked my shirt off so quickly that she started laughing. "Is this better?" I asked.

"Much."

"Your wish is my command," I said, crawling over to her. I moved the tray out of the way, down onto the floor. When I straightened up I tugged on her legs until she was flat on her back. Then I braced myself over her. My mouth hovered above hers, loving the feeling of anticipation, the way my abdomen would tighten, how my breathing went shallow, right before our lips met.

"Do you know what I really want?" she whispered as she ran the tips of her fingers along my jawline, leaving trails of fire in her wake.

"Tell me. Anything, and it's yours." If she asked me to bring her the sun, I'd find a way to accomplish it.

"What I really want . . ." she said as she leaned in so that her lips touched my earlobe, sending shivers from my head down to my feet, ". . . is more bacon."

~

I tried to time my departure just before Ember's roommates' arrival so that I could spend as much time with her as possible before I had to go. Her bacon-flavored kisses were hard to resist.

And when the weekend ended and she came back to school we got to behave . . . like any other normal couple. Nobody knew about our other lives, about our parents who would probably have strokes if they saw us together. Instead we held hands during algebra and kissed in the hallways like any other couple who had just discovered they were in love. At practice I was cool with Woodby now. I even felt a little sorry for him. Because that dude had seriously missed out, and I was glad that Ember was mine.

Unfortunately, our other life did decide to rear its ugly head. It was the night of the breast cancer benefit/ball, and Tricia had asked if everyone could come home to get ready and then go to the ball together. Like one big happy family.

Ember and I drove home together, and I stole as many kisses as I could at stoplights, knowing that we were going to have to behave at the dance. "I'm not sure I'll be able to keep my lips to myself." I said the words against her throat before kissing it. She made that sighing sound of pleasure that drove me absolutely insane.

"You're going to have to try hard," she said. "Which, to be honest, may not be easy once you see me in my dress."

"What dress?"

"It's actually the one I bought for prom." Her words hung heavily in the air. The prom that we had planned on going to together. The prom that never happened. "I had been really excited. I bought the dress before you left. I found the perfect one, but I had to get the sales clerk to bring me one from the back in a size for people who ate food. Anyway, I ended up going to the dance with a bunch of my girlfriends, and it was kind of a bummer."

"If I could go back and fix it, I would."

She slipped her hand into mine. "I wish I hadn't been so emotional. I should have enjoyed myself instead of missing you. So my gorgeous dress has had nothing but sad memories. I'm glad I get to give it some good ones. Especially since it's going to be so perfect for our waltz tonight. The skirt is poofy and princessy."

Ember parked in front of the house, and now that we were in non-touching territory I smiled at her one last time before we got out of the car. She placed her new phone on top of the car, and, remembering what had happened the last time she did that, I told her, "Don't forget your phone."

"I'm being more careful now!" she said, grabbing it and walking inside with me. Lauren pounced on us as soon as we walked in the door. "I'm going to help do your makeup!" she told Ember.

With an apologetic look, Ember followed her younger sister upstairs. I went and snagged some leftover chicken from the fridge. I noticed four cellophane boxes. I reached for one and realized they were corsages. My old man could do things up right when he wanted to. I put it back and headed upstairs to my room. They'd left it exactly as it had been in high school. Guilt washed over me again that I couldn't figure out back then how to stay. I grabbed the suit I'd brought with me. My dad was a big believer in having at least one nice suit you could wear to church or a funeral if you needed to. It didn't take me long to get dressed, and I decided to go back downstairs and find something else to eat. When I stepped into the hallway I heard my name. Ember and Lauren were in the bathroom, talking.

"When Bash sees you in this dress, he is going to die. Tongue rolling out of his mouth and onto the floor, eyes bugging out of his head like a cartoon character."

Ember laughed, a sound I adored. "You need to let this Bash thing go."

Did Lauren not know about us? For some reason I thought she did. Probably due to all her little remarks about our relationship.

"Never. I'm ride or die for you two."

"How do you think everybody else would react?"

"Everybody else? You mean, like, Mom?" Lauren asked.

"Yeah. Do you think she'd hypothetically be okay if Bash and I dated?"

"Oh, no. Mom would absolutely flip. Which is one of the reasons I'm shipping you guys so hard. Because the fallout will be epic. She has this whole image in her head of this perfect blended family, and that blending does not include the kind of, you know, blending you're talking about."

Feeling like I'd intruded enough, I went down to the kitchen. Tricia came in wearing a black dress that made her hair look even pinker.

"Bash! You're here!" She came over to give me a hug, which seemed strange. We'd never really had a hugging type of relationship. "I'm glad you were able to make it."

Before I could respond, my dad came in the kitchen behind her. He told her how beautiful she was as they sweetly kissed; it reminded me of why I'd run away in the first place. My dad deserved this. He deserved to be in love and happy.

So do you, a voice whispered to me.

But I was in love and happy. My heart hurt a little that I couldn't share it with the people I cared about most because I knew what their reaction would be. Ember had the right idea. We should just stay quiet about it for now, see where it went. And when the time was right, we'd tell Dad and Tricia and figure the rest out from there.

Dad grabbed the corsages out of the fridge as Lauren and Marley came downstairs. He passed the wrist corsages out. Ember wasn't with them, something Tricia noticed as well. "Where's Ember?"

"Still curling her hair. She'll be down a little later," Lauren said, giving me obvious side-eye.

"I don't want to be late," Tricia worried. "I'm on the committee."

Lauren said, "The four of us can go, and Bash can drive Ember over when she's ready. You can just text him the address for the club."

"I'd be happy to," I responded. Very, very happy to.

"Okay," Tricia said with a slight frown. "I had wanted us to all drive together, but I need to get going. You two have to leave in the next twenty minutes. Promise me you will."

"I promise. I'll pick her up and carry her out to the car if she's not ready."

Lauren shot me an amused grin, which I ignored. Dad handed me the one unopened corsage. "This is for Ember."

"I'll make sure she gets it." I walked them to the front door, again promising to see them soon.

"Ember?" I called up the stairs. "We're going to be late if we don't get going soon!"

"Be down in a minute!"

I considered going upstairs to look for her but knew if I did that, we'd never make it to the ball.

Then I was glad I waited. I heard a noise behind me, and I turned to see her at the top of the stairs. I nearly swallowed my tongue. She looked . . . phenomenal. Her dress was a dark wine color, with a strapless top that reminded me of a heart and a lighter shade for her princess skirt. Her long dark hair hung in waves, and my fingers itched to touch her. My teenage self? His head would have exploded seeing her in that dress.

Wow. Wow, wow, wow.

I couldn't believe she was mine and I was hers. Completely. I would have done anything for her.

She walked down the stairs slowly, her skirt making a rustling sound as she moved. She came to a stop in front of me and twirled around. "Well?"

"You're always beautiful, but you just made me forget how to speak."

"You seem to be doing okay," she teased.

"Maybe on the outside, but on the inside my brain is just saying 'wow' over and over again. Also, that dress deserves whatever happy memories it wants."

She laughed and leaned up to kiss me. "Thank you." She used her fingers to wipe away her lipstick from my mouth. "And thank you for fulfilling my prom fantasy."

"Fantasy?" At that my mouth went dry, and my chest suddenly felt too tight.

"You know, how in the movies the girl comes downstairs for the big dance, and her boyfriend is standing there waiting for her all in love and excited, and you even have the corsage!" I handed it to her, my brain still drooling and therefore unable to think to open the box and put the flowers on her wrist myself.

"I didn't pick out the corsage. Doug got one for each of you."

"But you're the one giving it to me." It was a white orchid with some greenery on it. Ember's smile was dazzling.

Then I thought about something she'd just said. "Boyfriend, huh?"

Her eyes got big. "Oh. Is that okay? We haven't really discussed it."

I drew her close, my hands at her waist. The material was so soft. Velvet. "E, I've been your boyfriend since the first moment I spoke to you."

Then I kissed her much more fiercely than I'd initially intended to, ignoring the fact that my entire body screamed at me to carry her upstairs and blow off this entire evening.

"We should go," I said regretfully, kissing her one last time.

I helped her put her coat on, and then we ran out to her car. I volunteered to drive and helped her into the passenger side, making sure that all of her skirt was inside of the car. She looked like an adorable burgundy cloud.

When we were almost at the country club, I asked, "How long do we have to stay at this thing?"

"We have to do the waltz competition and make sure my mom sees us once or twice, and then we are out of there."

"Sounds like a plan." I gave the keys to the valet out front and offered Ember my arm so that she wouldn't slip on the slightly icy walkway.

We left our coats in a closet up front, and she spotted a table that had a sign saying the waltz competitors needed to sign in. We headed over, and a middle-aged man with a comb-over and paunch belly greeted us.

"Names?"

"Ian Sebastian and Ember Carlson."

He ran his finger down a list until he found our names. "Ember, huh? That's an interesting name. Like a fire?"

I did not like the way he was looking at her, and I was trying to figure out whether his comment was harmless or if I should lean across this table, grab him by his shirtfront, and toss him out into the cold.

"Yes, like a fire," Ember said, taking the number the man offered her. He told us the competition would begin in half an hour and to make sure our number was visible on my back while we danced.

"You've got some real competition tonight," he said, still directing all of his attention to my girlfriend. I couldn't mistake it this time, he was definitely leering at her.

Did he not know how close he was to getting a broken nose?

Ember tugged on my arm, pulling me away from committing assault and battery, and we walked into the ballroom. There were only a handful of people already there, and it felt a little like a prom as far as the decorations went. Round tables with pink tablecloths, pink and silver balloons dotted around the room. There were also some potted trees with pink lights.

"Turn around," Ember told me. She peeled tabs off the paper and then put our official number on my back.

"Like a fire, huh?" I asked her.

"Aw, Bash. Are you jealous of the slightly creepy old man?" Her hand flitted across mine, like she was going to hold it but then changed her mind.

I loved it when she teased me. I wanted so badly to grab her and kiss her but had to refrain because there were eyes everywhere.

"I'm not jealous. I just like that I'm the only one who knows just how hot you burn."

She caught her breath and bit her lower lip, and it was nearly my undoing. Before I could do something really stupid, I heard Tricia's voice just behind me.

"Ember! Ian! I'm so glad you're both here." She hugged Ember hello.

Lauren sidled up to me and whispered, "That's a pretty shade on you."

It took me a second to realize what she was talking about, and then I tried to unobtrusively wipe my mouth. I wondered if anyone else had noticed.

Somebody came to grab Tricia, needing her input, and Marley wanted to show Lauren the chocolate fountain, leaving us alone.

"Does Lauren know?" I asked Ember.

"She thinks she knows everything, but no, she doesn't know about us. She's just hopeful, and it's annoying. I would cut open my own stomach to give her my kidney if she needed it, but sometimes I kind of want to strangle her."

"Perils of being the older sibling," I said.

"You can relate?"

"No, Marley's the perfect kid sister."

Ember nudged me with her elbow while I laughed. Then Tricia returned with my dad in tow, and she wanted to introduce both of us to the people she had volunteered with. It was difficult to pay attention when Ember would move, causing her hair to slide across her bare shoulders, or the way her chest would rise and fall just a bit faster each time she caught me admiring her. Which was often.

I couldn't wait to get her alone.

More people entered the ballroom as the quartet of musicians began warming up. After I said hello to dozens of people whose names I promptly forgot, a woman stepped up to the microphone. She welcomed everyone to the event and then told us it was time for the waltzing competition to begin.

"Shall we?" I asked Ember, and when she nodded, I took her by the hand and led her out onto the dance floor. The music began, an instrumental version of the song Ember and I had practiced to.

I didn't know if it was because we'd decided to be together, to take down those walls we'd built to keep the other one out, but we danced so differently now. We moved together easily, anticipating one another's steps. She followed where I led, and we danced as if we'd been doing it for years.

But we were not professionals, like many of our competitors who were doing elaborate routines and turns.

Nobody else mattered. The competition didn't matter. Just being able to dance, her skirts sliding across my legs, my palm flattened against her waist, her hand in mine. We danced closer than we should have. We had to keep our relationship a secret, but here, in this moment, we belonged to each other. Everybody and everything else faded away.

The song ended, and the judges announced their runners-up and the first-place winners. When we walked off the dance floor, I had to remind myself to let go of her hand when Tricia and Dad arrived to console us.

"You two should have won! I was so proud of you!" Tricia said, and I noticed how Ember lit up at her mother's words.

I overheard Lauren say to Ember, "You know, dancing is a gateway drug to kissing."

"It is not."

"Is too. Especially the way you guys were doing it."

Then we were joined by two older couples who wanted to congratulate us for dancing so well, and they expressed how sweet they thought it was that such a young couple had competed. I didn't follow their conversation. I was counting down the seconds until I could steal Ember away from here.

Her eyes met mine, and I saw her hunger. She was biding her time, too, smiling when she didn't mean it, her intense gaze returning to me again and again, almost like she was touching me. My heart raced in anticipation.

Not much longer now.

CHAPTER TWENTY-THREE

BASH

We successfully snuck out of the ball and went back to the house. As soon as we got inside, Ember kicked off her heels, and I loosened my tie, collapsing onto the couch. It had been surprisingly stressful staying away from her, pretending that we were just friends and nothing more. I needed to touch her again.

I held out my hand, and she put her hand into mine, curling up next to me on the couch. She rested her head on my shoulder.

"Well. Here we are. In an empty house," I said. "Whatever shall we do?"

"We could . . . mop the kitchen?" she offered.

I laughed and pulled her into my lap so that I could kiss her. "No, thanks."

She ran her fingers through my hair, sending waves of pleasure down my neck. "Hmm. We could retile the bathroom floor. Or organize the garage."

"That was not what I had in mind."

She crossed her arms and gave me a very serious look. "If you don't want to do chores, I guess I'll have to come up with something else to do. Because my mom did say it was especially my job to make you feel welcome here."

I ran my hands along her hips so that they came to rest on her back. "I'm not feeling all that welcome."

Ember leaned forward and kissed me softly, once, twice, three times before pulling away. "Are you feeling it now?"

"Not yet."

With a smile, she leaned in to kiss me again. Her lips moved softly and slowly, like she was memorizing what my mouth felt like against hers. Sweet, with a hint of something more just behind it. She moved her mouth back a fraction, hovering just above mine, tantalizingly out of reach. "And now?"

"Maybe a little bit more welcome."

She reached up to run the tips of her fingers along my lips, outlining them lightly. My entire body tightened in response. I lightly bit her index finger and then soothed it with my lips. Then she pressed whisper-soft kisses on my face, on my eyelids, along my cheeks, on my nose, following my jawline. She would move close to my mouth and then immediately move away before I could capture her in a kiss.

Her teasing had my heart throbbing so hard I could feel it in my earlobes.

She kissed my throat, nipping and soothing my skin, just like I'd done with her finger. "What about now?" she asked, the words murmured into my neck.

"Getting warmer." My words were husky, deepened by the harsh undertone of my breathing. What was it about this woman that made me want to completely lose control? To run headfirst into an all-consuming fire?

Ember pulled back, studying me with slightly enlarged pupils, making her eyes look like dark flames. She scooted closer, sending waves of longing and agony through me. She reached up and finished loosening my tie, sliding it slowly off my neck. She undid the top button of my shirt, kissing the skin she'd just exposed. She moved to the next button, and then the next, untucking the bottom of the shirt from my pants so that she could finish. Once she had my shirt open, she smiled and said, "That's better," as she ran her fingers down my chest, causing each muscle to contract as she came into contact with it.

I probably should have felt objectified, but I was down for it. The velvet of her dress felt amazing against my skin as she pressed into me, ready to finally kiss me.

No more tentativeness, no more softness. This kiss was what I'd been waiting for the entire day. Pure, unadulterated passion. Like throwing a lit match into a pool of gasoline—from one tiny ember to a blazing inferno. Instant ignition.

I groaned low in my throat when she deepened the kiss, every cell in my body vibrating with excitement and desire. I kept one hand on her upper back, feeling the way her skin burned beneath my touch, and the other I moved up to her face, then into her hair just so that I could hear her make those breathy, panting noises I loved when I caressed her scalp. She obliged me, and the sound sent blood rushing hot and fast through my veins.

"What about now?" she asked, her warm and sweet breath blowing across my face.

"I definitely feel welcome," I told her. She made me feel like I'd come home, and I was where I belonged. With her.

Then she was kissing me again, leading me to a point where I thought my body might shatter from the tension she created, my stomach quivering with how much I loved and wanted her.

I pulled her face away, waiting for her glassy eyes to focus. I loved that I could make her feel that way. Caught up, lost in pleasure, letting everything else fall away.

But I didn't know what she'd think about what I wanted to do next. "The last time we were here, together, kissing in this house . . ."

She looked so adorably confused it was all I could do not to immediately kiss her again. "What about it?"

"I was thinking we should go upstairs to your room to replace that memory with something better."

"I . . ." She let her words trail off, and I held my breath. I'd respect whatever she decided, but I was heavily rooting for her to choose going upstairs.

"*Slow* is a four-letter word, as far as I'm concerned," I told her teasingly. "But it's your choice, and I'll follow your lead. I don't want to pressure you, and I'll always respect whatever choice you make. I'm just sharing how I feel about it. Personally, I'd like to convince you that *slow* really is a bad word."

"You probably could," she agreed.

Then time slowed as I looked at her, really looked at her. She was so beautiful. Her hair was messy, her lips slightly swollen, her cheeks flushed, her eyes soft and loving. How had I gotten so incredibly lucky?

"What?" she asked self-consciously.

"I just . . . you're so off-the-charts beautiful that I want to remember this moment forever. I'm burning an image of you into my mind."

"I'm in love with you, Bash," she breathed, making the entire image all the sweeter.

"I'm so hopelessly in love with you." Not able to stand not kissing her for a second longer, I pulled her lips down to mine, and she made a sound that was a mixture of thankfulness and relief. Had she always tasted this sweet? How had I ever walked away from this? From the explosive chemistry between us that threatened to burn down the house around us?

The entire world shrank down to this moment, to the sense of weightlessness, of rampaging fire, of Ember's curves and softness pressed against me.

I was about to ask her again about going upstairs when I became aware of a noise near the front door. It sounded like Roscoe.

"This is the greatest thing that has ever happened to me."

Lauren. I turned my head toward the sound, unable to process what had just happened.

Only it wasn't just Lauren. It was everyone. Tricia, Dad, and Marley all stood there, their mouths open, eyes wide.

Ember recovered first, getting to her feet. I pulled the sides of my shirt closed and crossed my arms. Ember pressed the back of her hand to her mouth, and I didn't know if that was out of fear or to stop herself from saying something.

"What is going on?" Tricia finally asked.

Silence filled the void left by her words until Lauren said, not helpfully, "I think everyone knows what was going on and what we almost interrupted."

This was not how I wanted this to happen.

Tricia spoke again, the disapproval dripping from her every word. "I am so . . . shocked. Horrified. How did this happen? How long has it been going on for?"

Ember shook her head, and she ran out of the room, going to the front door.

Cursing, I chased after her, ignoring my dad calling my name. "Ember!" I yelled, catching up to her before she could get in her car. I put my hands on her shoulders. "Stay. Let's talk this out. We can explain."

Tears were pouring down her face. "You heard her. I can't do this."

"Yes, you can." Frustration boiled up inside of me, and then seemed to just spill out. "You don't have to sacrifice your life and the things you want just to make your mom happy. Why can't you stand up to her?"

From her expression I expected her to deny my statement. Then her shoulders collapsed inward, and she hung her head. "I don't know."

"Don't run away." The irony of me being the one telling her to stay was not lost on me. I was the last person on earth who should be telling her not to run.

"I can't." She got in her car, and I stood there, just watching her go. I glanced up to see everybody else either on the porch or just inside the house. I buttoned up my shirt and walked back to face them.

No more. I was done hiding; I was done worrying about everybody else's feelings and sacrificing the woman I loved.

"I'm in love with Ember," I told them. Tricia stared at me, shocked, and then whirled around to run upstairs.

Marley rushed out to me, throwing her arms around me. "If you two love each other, then I think you should be together."

Lauren gave me two thumbs up. "You know I'm on board."

"Son, let's you and I have a conversation. I have the feeling it's long overdue," my dad said. I followed him out to the garage, where we'd had most of our serious conversations growing up. Usually while our hands were busy working on his truck. Today was no different. Despite the fact that he was still in a suit, my father started reorganizing his tools on the pegboard, taking them down one at a time and then moving them to a new spot.

"If you're waiting for an apology, Dad, you're not going to get one. I don't regret anything that's happened between us. I love her. I loved her before you ever even met Tricia. We dated in high school, and were serious about each other."

"Why didn't you tell me then?" he asked as he cleaned a nut splitter. The rough edge to his voice was the only thing that betrayed how he was actually feeling. He sounded hurt, which made me feel horribly guilty, my stomach twisting and turning in response to his tone.

"What would your advice have been back then? If I'd told you, 'Dad, the girl I'm in love with is moving into our house and is going to be sleeping down the hall from me, but don't worry about it, everything will be fine,' you would have told me the same thing. You still would have warned me to stay away from her, wouldn't you?"

He hung the nut splitter onto its new place on the board. "I suspected something was there, but I didn't know that you were in love with her. You were teenagers. I thought it was a physical thing that would pass."

"It hasn't passed."

"I saw."

He sent a pointed glance in my direction, and that's when I realized that I had misbuttoned my top three buttons. With a mutter of "Fetching Canada," I set about fixing it. "I did this for you, you know."

That made my dad pause, his hand hanging in the air. "Did what for me?"

I got my buttons into the right holes. "I gave up Ember for you. For Marley, too, but mostly for you. You were so sad for so long that I didn't want to be the reason your new marriage didn't work out. I left so that there wouldn't be this huge problem with you and Tricia. Like I could give you happiness where Mom had just taken it away."

"I always wondered what it was that drove you to Pennsylvania. But I figured you'd tell me when you were ready." He let out a long, tired sigh. "But it wasn't your job to make up for my mistakes, or your mother's. I don't think I suffered as much as you thought I did."

That information sent me reeling. "What do you mean?"

"I mean, yes, it hurt when your mother left. I loved her. We had a family together, and she walked out. But I focused on you and Marley, and I moved past it. Even before I met Tricia, I had a good life. A life that made me happy. Even now, I only wish good things for your mom. I hope she really is clean and sober and that she's able to build a relationship with you and Marley, if that's what you want."

I couldn't even think about my mom situation right now. She wasn't what mattered. "This isn't about Mom. I'm trying to explain to you what is going on and what happened in the past and why I made the decisions that I did. I thought I was doing the right thing. I was trying so hard not to hurt anyone."

"I know it wasn't your intention, but you did hurt people. Which I understand all too well, because I'm kind of the expert on it. I've spent most of my life hurting people I love, even when I was trying to do the right thing." He shook his head, as if he could just shake those painful memories away. "I am the parent. I should have talked to you about this. I should have told you that running away wasn't a solution. I

242

shouldn't have let you go. But I was trying to respect your independence and your ability to make your own choices for your life."

His words twisted in my gut, like he'd plunged a knife into me and then turned it. "I didn't want to wreck your new relationship and—"

My dad cut me off. "You also never had the power to break up me and Tricia. We made commitments and vows to each other that we intend to keep. Even if the two of you do date and it ends badly, that's not going to affect our relationship."

"That's good. Because you should probably know that I'm not here to ask your permission to date Ember. I gave her up once, and I'm never doing that again. I love her and she loves me, and everybody else is going to have to find a way to be okay with that." By everybody, I meant him and Tricia.

Which he seemed to recognize. I heard a note of respect when he said, "Then it sounds to me like you should go find Ember and tell her what you told me. You can take the truck."

"Thanks, Dad."

It had gone better than I'd anticipated, but even if it hadn't, nothing would have changed. I was always going to put Ember's needs first.

As I headed back into the house to grab the truck keys, I started to think about Ember and her nearly pathological need to please her mother. If Tricia was upset about this and stood in our way, what would Ember do? Would she keep doing whatever her mom asked?

I stopped short, my hand on the car door as a realization slammed into me. Here I was upset that Ember would do anything to make her mother happy, but . . . hadn't I just confessed to doing the same thing? I wanted so badly to make sure that Marley and my dad were happy that I had done what I thought they'd wanted. I'd sacrificed what I wanted, and I'd run away.

Now Ember was running away, but I was going to find her. I knew better than anyone what she was feeling. And this time, I was going to fight for her. Whatever it took, whatever she needed from me, I was in.

CHAPTER TWENTY-FOUR

EMBER

My vision was so blurred by all the tears that I drove into an empty church parking lot not far from my mom's house. My phone kept buzzing and ringing, and I turned it off, not ready to deal with any fallout just yet. Instead I sat in my car and cried. Cried and cried until I felt wrung out and like there was no moisture left in my body because I had sobbed it all out.

I stayed there for hours, my head against the steering wheel as I tried to figure out what to do next. Because now I was in a position where no matter what I did, I was going to hurt somebody.

Once I'd exhausted myself in both body and spirit, I headed back to my apartment. It was only when I arrived that I realized I wasn't wearing any shoes. I'd kicked them off back at the house, and it was only occurring to me now because the sidewalk was cold and I was no longer fleeing the scene, all pumped up on guilt and adrenaline.

I hoped that my roommates were out so that I could go into my room and crash. Unfortunately, I walked in to find Deja studying at the peninsula in the kitchen and Molly on the couch playing a video game.

"Hey, Bash came by a couple of hours ago," Molly said, her eyes still trained on the television.

"Are you pulling a Cinderella?" Deja asked me, surveying me from head to toe. "If you are, you're supposed to be home when the prince comes by. He even brought your coat and shoes home. It was adorable."

"Where did you go again?" Molly asked. "You look like you just got back from a place with rainbow glitter, pastel dreamlands, and birds that help you get dressed."

"The ball. I am kind of like a broken Cinderella, huh?" Limping in with no shoes after midnight, having just run away from the man that I loved, finding out that my mother was against our relationship.

My roommates must have heard something in my voice as they both stopped what they were doing and looked concerned.

My inclination was to burst into tears, but I had none left. I dropped down on the floor, too tired to move another step. Both Molly and Deja hurried over to sit with me.

"Everything is bad."

Molly asked, "Could you, um, elaborate a little?"

They knew about my and Bash's past, what had happened between us and how we'd ended our relationship four years ago. I'd filled them in on all those details after they caught us kissing. They also knew why we were keeping us dating a secret from my family.

I told them how Bash and I had been in the midst of a serious make-out session when both of our families walked in and caught us, and my mom had gotten upset. "Then I freaked out and ran away."

"With no shoes," Molly added, and I nodded.

"And then Bash asked me why I kept sacrificing my own life for my mom. That I was more worried about making her happy than the things I wanted. He asked me why I couldn't stand up for myself and just be honest with her."

Deja and Molly exchanged loaded glances that irritated me.

"What?" I asked.

"You know we love you—" Deja said, and Molly interrupted to say, "You are surrounded by so much love right now!"

"But," Deja continued, "Bash was not wrong."

I was crossing from irritated into full-blown annoyed territory. "What do you mean?" Because my gut reaction had been to say he was a hundred percent wrong. That he just didn't understand the kind of relationship I had with my mom.

"We have been your friends for three years, and again, we're saying this with nothing but love for you," Deja said, putting her hand on my arm. "But every time your mom says jump, you ask how high. Do you know how many times you've canceled plans with us? Or missed a practice or a game because of something your mother needed?"

"She's my *mom*. And she almost died."

"But she didn't die," Deja said. "And no amount of support or obedience or whatever it is you're doing is going to keep her alive. You know that, right?"

Of course I knew that. That wasn't why I did what I did.

"You can't stand to disappoint your mom for any reason," Molly chimed in. "But in another year you're going to be a college graduate and starting your own life. It's not your job to run home every time your mom asks you to."

"You guys don't get it. You don't know what it's like. How afraid I was all the time. And the only way to keep the fear at bay was to be doing something. Helping her. Making her happy."

Deja gave me a sad smile. "There's nothing wrong with your coping mechanism. Only that you don't seem to realize that you don't need it anymore. Your mom is good, and her tests have been clear for years. You don't have to keep operating from a place of fear. I mean, I am still shocked that she got you to jump out of an airplane."

"Right?" Molly said with a laugh. "Remember when we went to the Space Needle to celebrate Ximena's birthday, and Ember threw up in the elevator when we got to the top?"

"Yes, me and my very expensive shoes remember," Deja said. "But making your mom happy is not going to keep her cancer free. You stepped up to take care of your sister and your stepsister, and that is really admirable. You put your life on hold. But you don't need to do that anymore."

Molly put her arm around my shoulders and squeezed. "I mean, you can be a good daughter without being a mindless drone. You might have crossed over just a little into the mindless-drone category."

I wanted to protest and say that they were wrong and didn't understand. But what if they were right? Was I somehow psychologically messed up from dealing with my mom's breast cancer? I hated telling my mother no. I knew that about myself. I had sat and cried in my car not only because of the look of disappointment on Bash's face, but from my mom's shock and anger. If anything, I had probably been more focused on her in that moment, and even I recognized that there was something fundamentally wrong with that.

Because honestly, it didn't matter what Mom thought about me and Bash. It wasn't her relationship, and Bash and I were both twenty-one. We were adults by every definition. It was our decision.

I loved him. I wanted to be with him.

And the only way to prove that, both to myself and to him, was to put him first. His feelings should have mattered more.

I had been wrong, and I needed to tell him. "Why didn't you guys say something before?"

Deja shrugged, like she didn't have a good answer. "I don't know. It didn't really interfere dramatically with your life before. But if pleasing her is more important than the good man you're in love with, that's . . . not great."

"What do I do now? How do I fix this?" I asked. How could I change my own mind so that I didn't automatically default to making my mom's wishes and desires more important than mine or Bash's?

Molly said, "When you're trying to change a behavior, the main thing is to be aware of it. Once your conscious mind recognizes it, it makes it easier to stop. That doesn't mean you'll be perfect at it, but it's just like anything else in life. The longer you practice, the more you do it, the more natural it becomes and the better you'll be at it."

"Now I feel kind of stupid," I confessed. "How did I not notice this before?" I kept thinking of all the times Bash had tried to warn me, without hurting my feelings. Telling me that I could decide things for myself, like whether or not I wanted to be a writer instead of a nurse. Offering several times to take me away from that airfield and the airplane so that I wouldn't have to skydive. Trying to get me to cut my mother's apron strings in the kindest and most supportive way possible.

I seriously loved him. And I didn't want to lose him.

"We don't always see our own shortcomings. It's like a protective thing," Molly explained. "You guys know that my mom's a therapist, so most of our dinner table discussions revolved around stuff like this."

I put my hands over my face. Everything felt like such a mess. I was a mess. But I was going to give myself one last night to feel sorry for myself and my poor decisions. Tomorrow I was going to start fixing them. But tonight, I needed to sleep. To let my brain and my eyes rest, and then I'd start dealing with this stuff.

Thanking my roommates, we hugged, and then they helped me off the floor. Deja unzipped my dress and then hung it up, muttering something about how she didn't want to see it pooled on the floor. Molly pushed me into the bathroom, making sure I washed my face and brushed my teeth. I hugged her again and then went and put my pajamas on. I decided to turn my phone back on.

There were all kinds of notifications from Lauren and Bash. Even a few from Marley.

But nothing from my mother.

I texted Bash, telling him that I was okay and would talk to him soon.

He responded immediately, telling me he loved me. I told him I felt the same, hoping that would be enough to ease his mind for now.

My phone rang. It was Lauren, but I was too tired. I pushed ignore. But then she called again, and again I pushed ignore. When the phone rang for the third time, I knew I wasn't going to get out of this conversation.

"Hi. What do you want?" I asked.

"You answered! I can't believe it. Finally! Marley! She answered! Hey, are you okay?"

"Not so much right now, but I will be. How's Mom?"

There was a muffled noise, and then I heard a door closing. "She hasn't come out of her room since, you know, we saw you climbing Bash like he was a tree. I don't know what's going on. It's all very dark and full of terrors over here. Marley and I have already decided we're both going to sleep in her room tonight."

I was glad she had Marley, because my urge to run home and make this better for everyone else was eating away at me. I acknowledged it and then dismissed it.

"Bash told everyone that he was in love with you." I'd never heard Lauren sound so worried before.

"He did?"

"Yep. Then he had a serious conversation with Doug out in the garage, and he came out of it looking determined and took the truck. I think he went to find you."

I lay down and threw an arm over my eyes. "Yeah. I just got home and heard he came by."

There was a silence that lasted long enough that I thought maybe the call had dropped. "Lauren?"

"I'm here. I was just thinking about when I was twelve years old. I was totally obsessed with romantic comedy movies, remember? The way the heroes and heroines in those movies would look at each other was how you and Bash looked at each other in real life. So I'm sorry if I gave you guys a hard time. My preteen fangirl heart just wanted you two to happen. I also didn't realize how big the fallout would be. I thought there would be some yelling, and then everybody would just get over it."

"Yeah, I feel bad that Mom's basically taken to her bed like some character from a Victorian-era novel." I paused. "She must be really upset."

"You know Mom's not the boss of you anymore, right? You can make your own choices."

"I've realized tonight that I really hate disappointing her."

"Really?" Lauren sounded shocked. "I actually find it very liberating."

I couldn't help but laugh a little. "I wish I felt that way."

"You totally should. Because you get to find out who you are by making your own choices. And maybe Mom's not going to like that, but life usually isn't arranged to our liking. She has her own trials and issues, but you dating Bash shouldn't be one of them."

"When did you get so wise?" I asked.

"We grow up much faster these days. It's all the GMOs and smartphones."

I smiled at that. "Okay, Little Miss Knows Everything, I am going to bed. I have a lot to deal with tomorrow."

"Good. I want to hear as many details as you're willing to share after you chat with Bash. I'm here for you if you need me. And Ember? All I want, all any of us want, is for you to be happy. I love you."

If I'd still had any tears left, I would have been welling up right then. "Love you, too. We'll talk soon."

I hung up my phone, putting it on the nightstand next to my bed. I thought of all the choices I'd been making, just to make my mom happy. Not just where Bash was concerned, but if I were being honest, with my major, too. How I chose to spend my free time. Where I planned on living after graduation.

Family was important, and they would always be important to me, but it didn't mean I had to sacrifice my own life like I was some modern-day reincarnation of Joan of Arc. History had enough martyrs; I didn't need to add myself to the pyre.

It was time to break free. To not run away or to hide behind obligations and responsibilities. And to figure out how to redefine all of my relationships.

Especially the potential one with Bash.

CHAPTER TWENTY-FIVE

BASH

I wasn't able to sleep. The idea of losing Ember . . . it went from a faint fear to all my brain could think about. It whispered that I wasn't good enough for her. That she'd never love me; nobody could. That I should just give up now and stay in my bed for the rest of my life. Ember would be better off without me. These thoughts were like parasites, trying to infect me.

I'd been so good recently about keeping the darkness at bay. Even when I talked to my mom, something that could have easily set me off, I was okay. I knew how to take care of myself.

But this thing with Ember . . . this was different. Scarier. Which made it easier for my lying self-critic to sneak in and make me doubt myself. Make me doubt us.

I took in a couple of deep breaths. I decided to go for another run later since exercise seemed to help. I also held on to the fact that Ember had texted she loved me, too. She was just a person who needed time to process her emotions and make decisions. I could give her that.

I found Logan in our shared room, getting ready for the day. "You were up early today," he commented.

"I went for a run. Things have been a little hard lately. With the whole Ember thing."

His eyebrows knit together in concern. "I heard you tossing and turning last night. Do you want to talk about that?"

So I told him what had happened, how I was in love with and dating Ember without her family's knowledge, but that we'd been caught in a compromising position. "My dad seems to be okay with it, but my little sister informs me that Ember's mom is freaking out. Ember is big on not upsetting her mom, so I don't really know what's going to happen. It's the not knowing that's hard, but I have to wait and see."

"Dude. That sucks. What can I do?"

Sometimes I hated when people asked that question, like I had some internal list where I was just waiting for a volunteer to offer to wash my laundry and then I would suddenly be healed. But I knew the intention was sincere. "Thanks for offering, but all I need from you is to know that I can talk to you."

"I was going to go have breakfast with Jess, but I can cancel," he offered. "Or you could come with us."

I wasn't usually one to turn down food, but there was something I needed to do. I'd been so busy avoiding my problems that I'd forgotten all the lessons I'd already learned the hard way. Like how I couldn't control what was happening around me, but that I could control how I reacted to it. What decisions I made. That if there was something in my life I could fix, I should try.

"Thanks for the offer, but no, thanks. There's someone I have to go talk to."

~

I sat in the diner, waiting. I told the waitress I wasn't that hungry, so I only ordered some onion rings, a double-decker burger, two chocolate milkshakes, and a slice of apple pie with a scoop of ice cream on it.

"I'd hate to see you hungry," she teased. "I'll have that right out to you."

The booth I'd chosen faced the front door so that I could watch people coming in and out. I didn't know if she would show up, not after how we left things. But it was a necessary conversation. I needed some answers.

Right after my food arrived, I heard the door chimes and there she was.

My mother.

She spotted me immediately and came over to sit down across from me. "Thank you for asking me to meet you."

I noticed her hands shaking slightly as she put her purse down next to her. I felt nervous, too. She had nothing to do with my relationship with Ember, but she was a current problem in my life. One I didn't understand, so I had decided to reach out to her, to let her explain like she'd requested. If I didn't like what she had to say, I didn't have to see her again. But I owed myself this. I felt like I couldn't move on with my life until I'd finished up this chapter.

I also had to stop living in a land of delusion where everything would magically resolve itself without me having to make any effort or choices.

"That's a lot of food!" she said. Her smile felt forced, as if she was trying too hard. "You ate all the time when you were small. I thought you were going to eat us out of house and home."

"I do like to eat." I wanted to roll my eyes at myself. Obviously, we were not going to do well with small talk. It already felt weird and stilted. "Look, I asked you to meet me here because you said in your letter that you wanted to explain. I wasn't ready to hear it before. But I'm ready to hear it now."

She gulped, her mouth compressed in a small tight line. As if she was trying to smile but couldn't. She swallowed again before she said, "Back then, I didn't know what was wrong with me. I just felt bad all the time, and the only thing that made me feel better was drinking or getting high. I thought getting married would fix it. Then I thought having kids would force me to quit. And I was able to stop while I was pregnant with you and Marley. Protecting you was the most important thing. And afterward, I told myself it was fine. I functioned just like any other parent, only I wasn't using caffeine and prescription sleeping pills to get through my days."

Her mention of other parents made me think of my father. He had never spoken about his addiction with me, other than to tell me not to be stupid and that as the child of two addicts, I was most likely going to end up an addict myself if I wasn't careful. I wondered how he had started. If he had justified his decisions the same way my mother had.

"I also didn't know that I suffered from depression," she said, and a flare of recognition burst into life inside me. I'd inherited it from her. I felt like I had mine mostly under control now, but there'd been a couple of times in my life when I was sad and overwhelmed. It somehow made me feel better to know that she'd gone through the same thing. It made me feel something for her. Something besides anger or hatred.

She kept talking. "About two years after Marley was born, everything just fell apart. I don't even know how to explain it, but it was like there was this huge boulder on my chest all of the time. I couldn't breathe. Couldn't think. Like you pointed out, I couldn't get out of bed. You had to take care of Marley, and your dad had to take care of both of you."

"I remember." I couldn't keep the bitterness out of my voice. I'd always blamed her, thought she was weak, but now I was having to reassess how I viewed the past because I hadn't known what she'd gone through.

She folded her hands together and placed them on the table. "Things got so bad that my brain told me the only way out of the darkness was to leave. I thought I was doing the right thing. I never felt selfish because I'd convinced myself that you'd be better off without me. That I was somehow actually helping you. I think I was trying to get away from myself. But wherever I went, there I was. It took me a while to sort my life out, to find out what was happening to me, to start going to Narcotics Anonymous and find the antidepressants that worked best for me."

"When you got your life turned around, why didn't you get in contact then?" I asked.

"I was so ashamed. I couldn't imagine how much I'd hurt the three of you because I knew how much I was hurting. I missed you so much." At this her eyes welled up. "I even came to some of your football games in high school. I wanted to see you, even if it was from a distance. I thought I didn't deserve to have you in my life. It took me a long time and a lot of therapy before I got to a point where I finally felt like I was allowed to try and have you be a part of my life again. My husband, Richard, he's the one who encouraged me to seek you out. And I want you to meet Elijah and Evelyn. I want you to be a part of your brother's and sister's lives. And mine."

How was I supposed to react to that? It was hard to stay angry when I, probably more than anyone else in her life, understood what she'd gone through. In Pennsylvania I'd self-medicated when my antidepressants weren't working correctly. I'd gone down a similar path she had, only hers had been more destructive because there'd been more at stake for her than there was for me. The only difference was that it had taken her longer to find what would work for her medically. How could I be mad at her for something that I'd done?

She shouldn't have abandoned her kids. But when that darkness, that dragon, got its claws into you? It didn't let go. And it convinced people that they didn't need help and they didn't need medication, and it took so much effort sometimes to fight. Sometimes it felt easier just to give in.

Just because I'd been able to navigate out of my tailspin relatively easily didn't mean that everyone could.

As if she understood me struggling with this new information, she tentatively reached across the table, putting her hand on top of mine.

I let her.

"I know I don't deserve your forgiveness. And I will understand if you can't forgive me. I'll never be able to tell you how much I regret what I did. If I thought it would make things better, I would spend the rest of my life apologizing to you. Because I am truly, and deeply, so sorry."

For some reason that made the inside of my chest hurt, and a lump formed in my throat. "I'm going to need to think about it."

I saw her surprise, which she quickly replaced with a smile. A real one this time. "Of course. I would never want to rush you into something you weren't ready for. I miss you and your sister so much." She squeezed my hand again before letting go.

"But you're going out with Marley soon, right?" After I came by her house, my mom had dropped her custody suit and had reached out to my dad instead, asking to be able to spend time with Marley. Which my sister had quickly agreed to. Marley had texted me all about it, excited at the chance to finally get to know our mom. She'd had questions for years, but like me she'd been afraid of hurting or upsetting our dad after everything he'd gone through, so she kept it to herself. But now that the opportunity was here, she didn't plan on missing out on it.

"We decided to go get mani-pedis. She sent me a current picture of her. I can't believe how much she's grown up! She's so beautiful."

"She is." At least we could agree on how amazing Marley was. It might be the only thing we had in common for a while.

"Well, what I want is to stay and talk to you, but I think it's probably better if we finish today here. You think about things and let me know what you want to do moving forward. My home is always open to you, and I do want to be a part of your life again. I'll probably text you from time to time, if that's okay."

"That's . . . fine." And surprisingly enough, it was.

"Okay." She stood up and slipped her purse strap over her shoulder. She stood there for a moment, as if unsure what to do. Like she wanted to hug me, but she must have been able to tell I wasn't there yet. Instead she just waved and told me goodbye.

When she walked out of the diner, I slumped against my seat. I crammed three onion rings into my mouth. They'd gone cold, but I didn't care. Relief flooded through me. I'd been almost afraid to talk to her, but that had gone better than I'd anticipated. And it made me understand things about her that I never had before.

It also made me understand some things about myself, too. When I'd left home at seventeen, I told myself it was the righteous, noble move. To sacrifice my happiness for my family. But having heard my mom saying that her depression caused her to believe something similar, and knowing that my medication hadn't been working for me back then, had I done the same thing? Had I convinced myself that all of them, including Ember, would be better off without me? Happier, if I was just gone?

Maybe my depression had been more in control of that decision than I'd realized.

I wanted to tell Ember. It felt like something important that I needed to share with her.

Another thing this conversation showed me was that I could do really hard things. If someone had told me a month ago that I'd be sitting down with my mother while she explained her actions, I would have laughed. Because I wouldn't have been able to conceive of a future where this would have happened, yet here I was.

If I could do this, then I was strong enough to deal with anything. Even Ember saying that things had to be over between us because our families wouldn't accept it. I could do hard things and not let despair win.

I had to choose. And I planned on choosing to try and be happy, no matter what happened.

I chose Ember. I chose her when I was seventeen, I was choosing her now, and I wanted to spend the rest of my life choosing to be with her and only her.

Now I just had to figure out a way to convince her that we deserved a shot.

I grabbed my hamburger and scarfed it down. I raised my hand to flag down the waitress. As soon as I finished this food, I needed to get going.

I had a gift to buy for my girlfriend.

CHAPTER TWENTY-SIX

EMBER

"Ember! Door's for you!"

Molly's voice echoed down the hallway, and my heart raced. Bash? Was he here? What was I going to say to him? I would have to send him away. Not because I didn't want to see him. I did. Desperately. I wanted to explain everything. That I was in love with him and no matter what happened with our parents, I wanted to be with him. But I needed to talk to my mom first, to let her know about the decision I'd made. That I was going to date Bash and that there wouldn't be anything she could say or do that was going to change my mind. I wanted to have everything cleared up. I didn't want there to be anyone or anything hanging over our heads while he and I decided what to do next.

I recognized that it was going to be hard to go against her wishes, but I had to remember that I was doing this for me.

For me and for Bash.

Only it wasn't Bash standing in my living room. It was my mom.

"What are you doing here?" I asked.

"I thought you'd come see me. And when you didn't, I decided to come to you. Can we talk?" She looked very uncomfortable, which immediately made my stomach drop down to my knees. *I don't have to win her approval,* I reminded my brain.

"Oh, I have to go, um, be someplace that's not here," Molly said, disappearing into her room and closing the door.

I went over and sat on the couch, and my mom followed me.

My mom cleared her throat. "I'm sure you know why I'm here."

"I have a pretty good guess." I didn't know how else to respond to it. She'd come to me; I was going to let her lead this conversation.

"How long has this thing been going on with Ian?"

Lauren had told me that Bash and his dad had had a serious conversation. She didn't already have this information? Or maybe she just wanted to hear it coming from me. "Recently? It's only been a few days. And we spent weeks before that dancing around each other, trying to deny our feelings because we were afraid of the exact scenario that happened. But before that? Bash and I started dating in high school, and we were in love back then. We dated for months, and then you married Doug, and Bash left because Doug told him to stay away from me."

It was only now that I could admit that I had somewhat resented Doug. Not for causing Bash to leave; that had been Bash's decision. But for so long my family had been me, my mom, and Lauren. Doug married her, and it had never been the same. Maybe that was another reason why I tried so hard to please her. To reassure myself that I hadn't lost my place in her heart.

"Why didn't you ever tell me about him?"

I was so busy thinking about Doug that it took me a second to realize that she meant Bash. "I don't know. In the beginning it was because he and I chose to keep it quiet. We liked that we were together and nobody else knew. It didn't start out as intentional; I think I was scared he'd figure out he didn't really like me, and I didn't want to be embarrassed. As we got more serious, and I knew it was real, we had plans to share it with everyone. Then you went and married Doug, and that was that."

"But you could have told me after. Especially once he left."

"You got sick," I said, shrugging my shoulders. "And then everything was focused on your cancer and healing, and honestly, I just tried to put him out of my mind because I couldn't have dealt with missing him and being terrified that you were going to die."

"Oh, sweetie, I'm fine now." She took both of my hands in hers.

"I know that. Logically, I know. But I lost my father. He wasn't that great of a father, but he was the only one I had, and he's gone. And I can't even tell you—" My words caught, my voice breaking, and I struggled to stay in control. "I can't even tell you how many sleepless nights I've had worrying about you. You're the only parent I have left, and I think somehow my brain decided that if I was good and did what you wanted and made you happy, you'd stay healthy."

"Neither one of us is in control of whether or not I have a recurrence. In the past, there's been times that I haven't expressed to you how much I've appreciated your help and love. When your dad left I think I internalized the idea that everything had to be on my shoulders. I'd have to be both mom and dad to you and Lauren. That the only person I could count on was myself. I feel . . . weak when I have to rely on other people. Even you."

"Mom, you're not weak. You never have been. You kicked cancer's butt. You're a warrior."

She smiled sadly. "I usually don't feel like it. And when you call to check up on me, it reminds me of a time when I couldn't take care of anyone. I hate feeling that way."

It looked like I wasn't the only one who had issues from my dad leaving us. "I understand. But I think some things between us need to change."

"Like what?"

"Like I'll stop checking up on you so often. I've also recognized that I'm too desperate for your approval. I'm terrified of heights, Mom. And I went skydiving just to make you happy. It was one of the worst things

I've ever been through. Bash was the one who got me through the whole experience and made everything better." Why had it taken me so long to figure out that he was in love with me? He'd been showing me from the beginning, since our double date with other people. I'd been so blind.

"I had no idea! I never would have asked you to do it if I'd known you felt that way."

That actually made me feel better. Like she was really hearing and seeing me and what I needed. "It's not just that. It's affected most of my life. Like I'm majoring in nursing because of you."

Her eyebrows knit together. "I thought you wanted to help people and that's why you chose it."

"I did. I do. But you were so excited and proud of me when I told you that's what I was considering majoring in."

"Of course I was proud of you and your choice. But I would have been proud of you no matter what you wanted to do."

My nerves began to fray as I considered telling her what I really wanted to be. Figuring this was the time, I took in a deep breath before I said, "I think that what I want is to be a writer."

"And . . . what? You think that will upset me?"

I shrugged one shoulder. "It's not like becoming a nurse."

"There is more than one way to help people. When I was going through chemo, it was movies and books that got me through it. That let me forget and took my brain away from my toxin-riddled, nauseated body and to fantastic places with beautiful love stories. Entertainment? That helps people. It can soothe worries and calm fears and let you destress and escape your everyday life. I think that's an incredible way to serve someone who is sick."

Tears had welled up in my eyes, and I let out a short laugh as I brushed them away. "I don't even know why I'm crying. I guess that's not what I thought you'd say."

"I wish I'd been a better mom to you. You've kept so many things from me that you didn't have to. I hate that you felt like you couldn't confide in me. That's not the kind of relationship I want to have with you."

"That's not the kind of relationship I want to have with you, either."

She leaned over and hugged me, and I felt so much like a little kid again, finding comfort in my mom's embrace, that I almost started crying again.

My mom said, "Do you know how much I love you? How all I want is your happiness?"

Then I did cry. I cried for the mistakes we'd both made, for the mis-understandings and the wedge they had created between us. I wanted that to stop, to bridge that gap.

When she released me, she handed me a tissue from her purse. I used it to wipe my tears and then blow my nose.

If I wanted to bridge the gap between us, there was someone else we still had to talk about.

"What about Bash and me dating now?" I asked.

Her answer wouldn't change my mind; I had already decided that. But it would be nice to have her support.

"This is going to be something Doug and I will have to work through as a couple. None of us know what the future will bring. And this is not what we would have chosen because of how messy everything could become."

I wanted to interrupt and tell her how wrong she was. That in my heart of hearts, in a place I barely acknowledged even to myself, I had the feeling that Bash was the one. And the idea didn't scare me, which made me believe in it even more.

But that was something I would share with him before I told her.

"You and Ian are adults. You can make your own choices." Her tone let me know that it was not the choice she wanted me to make.

I didn't care, though, what her choice would have been. I figured that was progress.

"You're right. We are and we will."

She nodded at that and grabbed her purse, as if she was about to leave.

"Do you need to go?" I asked. "If not, I'd love if we could sit and talk. I could tell you all about Bash."

She hesitated for only a second before settling back onto the couch. "Tell me everything."

I grinned. "Let me start at the beginning."

~

After hours of crying and laughing and talking, my mom finally left. I had just gone into the kitchen to grab something to eat when there was a knock at the door. I thought my mom must have forgotten something, and I started to say as much when I opened the door.

But this time, it really was Bash. He stood there, holding a grocery bag with one hand, and it was like all of my feelings demanded to be let free at the same time. So I launched myself at him, arms around his neck, legs around his waist. I needed a full-body hug. To reassure myself that he was here and we were in love and things were all going to be okay.

"Hello to you, too," he chuckled, walking into the apartment while still carrying me and closing the door shut behind him with his foot. He took me over to the couch, and I reluctantly let him go.

"Hi. I love you." I needed him to know that. Before we could talk about anything else, I wanted him to know where I stood. We had a lot of things to talk about, but I wanted to reassure him of my feelings.

I could hear the relief in his voice. "I love you, too."

"I missed you," I said.

"I can tell."

"What's in the bag?"

"Presents."

What could he have brought me? Chocolate? Flowers? He was so thoughtful.

He reached into the bag and pulled out . . . a can of nuts. He handed them to me.

"Um, thank you?" I said, not understanding the meaning. Did he think I was nuts? Or our situation was nuts? Both would probably have been accurate statements.

"They're Blue *Diamond* almonds." He pointed at the brand name. "They'll have to do until I can afford real diamonds. Because that's the kind of gift you deserve. Someday. After I go pro. I'll buy you the biggest and most important diamond of all."

His meaning was clear. My heart melted into about a million tiny puddles. How cute and romantic was he? He made me feel like my whole body was smiling.

And someday he was going to give me an engagement ring. Which I realized was everything I'd ever wanted.

Then he reached back into the bag and pulled out a ham. An actual spiral-sliced, honey-glazed ham. He looked so proud of himself when he handed it to me.

"I was at the store buying you the almonds, and it didn't feel big enough. I wanted you to have something big that would show you just how much I love you, and they don't carry turkeys this time of year. So ham it was. And ham is like bacon, but bigger."

I tried to keep the amusement out of my voice. "It is big. I don't think it's going to fit in our fridge. You know, this isn't really the sort of thing a suitor brings over to his fair maiden."

"Logan brings Jess pizza, and it's her favorite thing in the whole world," he said, as if that explained it.

"I knew I liked that girl."

"Hey, why are your eyes red?" he asked, his voice filled with concern. "Have you been crying? Is everything okay?"

"It's fine. My mom came by to talk."

"Really? How was that?"

"It's been brought to my attention recently that when it comes to my mother, me not being able to say no to her is weird. Which you kept trying to tell me, and I didn't hear. Now I have to figure out my life without her playing such a huge role in it. I need to break that cycle. Just so you know, it doesn't really matter what she says or thinks. Because I've already made a decision. I want to be with you if you still want to be with me."

A happy smile broke out across his face, so bright and brilliant that I fell in love with him all over again. "Ember, of course I want to be with you. You're the most important thing in my life."

His words warmed me, like he'd lit a cozy, perfect fire inside me. How could there be this much happiness in the world? "I've personally witnessed how you feel about food, so I know you must mean it."

"I do mean it. But I want to know how things ended with your mom."

"I told her I can't keep acting like I used to and need to cut those apron strings. It was good. I told her about you and our history. I don't know if she's on board, but she's not going to actively stand in our way or anything."

"How do you feel about that?"

"It is what it is. I may slip up and fall back into old habits, but I'm going to do my best not to. What I do know for sure is that I want to be with you, and our opinions are the only ones that matter."

Before I could finish my sentence, his mouth was on mine, sweet and loving. Like he wanted to convey his emotions with his lips and not his words. When he finally let me come up for air, all I could say was, "Wow."

"I talked to my mom today, too."

I straightened up, surprised. "Seriously? How did that go?"

He grimaced slightly. "Better than I'd expected. I didn't yell, which I figure is a good thing. I think we're on a good path, but I'm not ready to spend a major holiday with her or anything."

"Right. So start with Arbor Day and work your way up?"

He laughed. "Something like that. I also realized that my depression might have played a bigger role in me going off to Pennsylvania than I realized. Her depression is what caused her to leave us. I know it doesn't change anything, but I thought you might like to know that there might have been other forces at play in that moment between us."

That made sense, and while I'd come to terms with the reality of our last teenage encounter, this made me feel even better. "It does change my perspective. Does it help you with understanding why your mom left? Being able to forgive her?"

"It does. But I don't really want to talk about her or get into all that right now. I want to talk about you and about us and what's going to happen next."

I sucked my breath in. Why did that sound ominous? "Okay. Like what?"

"Like why did you run away from my dad's house?"

"I was afraid."

"Afraid?" he repeated. "Of what?"

"At first I thought it was because I was so scared of what my mother would think. That she'd turn against me and our relationship, and I still wanted to please her and make her happy. But when I really started thinking about it and what had made me so upset, I realized that what I was most afraid of was losing you. Afraid that you'd choose your dad and your family over me. Because I am so, so scared of you walking away from me again. I'm not sure I could bear it." My body shuddered with an unshed sob; I struggled to keep it in. I tried to cover it up, but I'd known, deep down and for a very long time, that the fear of losing him was the real driving force behind me wanting to stay away from him. I had told myself it was half a dozen other things because I didn't want to acknowledge how deeply I loved him when he'd left, but the truth was I didn't think I was strong enough to go through it again.

He put his hand under my chin, gently tugging so that I would look in his eyes. "If you'd stayed, you would have heard me telling my dad that I love you and that I didn't care what he thought about us. That you're everything to me. I'm not going anywhere. You don't have to worry about that ever again. I am ashamed of the fact that I ran away from you once. I didn't stay and fight for you like I should have. So now I'm staying. Now I'm fighting. I will be here no matter what."

At that the sob broke free, and he gathered me up, holding me tight against him. His steady heartbeat soothed me, as did his hands stroking my hair and his kisses pressed against my temple, my cheek, wherever he could reach.

When I could finally catch my breath again, I stayed put. This was where I always wanted to be, in his arms. "I'm never going to run away from you again. I promise to always stay and work things out."

"I promise the same thing," he said.

"So . . . are we doing this? You and me?"

"Definitely. You and me. Forever."

I leaned back so that I could look him in the eye. "No matter what kind of obstacles, problems, and other junk we get thrown at us?"

"E," he said, just before he planted a sweet kiss on the tip of my nose, "you jumped out of an airplane, you stood up to your mom, I finally had a conversation with mine, and our parents know about us. We worked out what happened in the past, we've apologized for it, and we know going forward that we'll fix whatever's broken. The scary and hard parts are done. Everything else is just cake."

"Did you bring cake, too?" I asked, excited at the prospect. "Now that I have my own personal and very handsome food fairy, I need to know if I can make requests."

He laughed, the sound wonderful and infectious. "Do you know how much I love you?"

Now that everything was out in the open, now that there were no more secrets between us, now that nothing stood in the way of us being together, I knew exactly how much he loved me and that I always would.

EPILOGUE

EMBER

Two years later . . .

"I thought you might be hungry, because that's usually a safe bet. I brought you cake," Bash said.

"That's why I love you," I told him, taking the plate. "Aw. Only one slice?"

"I couldn't exactly hijack the entire wedding cake for you, E. People would notice."

He looked so handsome in his suit that I'd had a hard time during the entire ceremony paying attention to anything else. I was wearing the pale-pink bridesmaid dress my mother had agreed to after I'd told her I wasn't interested in the electric-yellow dress she'd originally selected. (Lauren and Marley had backed me up.) Doug and my mom had decided to renew their vows and wanted to have the wedding party they'd missed out on the first time around. Lauren and Marley were the other bridesmaids, Bash had been the best man, and two of Doug's brothers were the other groomsmen.

It had been a lovely ceremony and an even better reception. Bash and I had waltzed and danced to almost every song until he had convinced me to sneak away with him and find a spot to cool off.

Our parents had chosen to have their recommitment in the spring at a nearby country club. The same one where Bash and I had participated in the waltzing competition. The trees surrounding the clubhouse were flowering in various shades of pink and white. Our pathway was lined with white Christmas lights, and we found a small bridge that overlooked a tiny but adorable stream. Bash had left me there for a minute while he went back for what he called "supplies." Which turned out to mean cake, smart man that he was.

A flower from a nearby tree came loose and landed in the stream. I watched as it wound its way down, under our bridge and beyond to where I couldn't see. The last two years had felt like that, rushing forward quickly, with us not knowing where things would go or what would happen to us.

I had decided to keep nursing as my major and minored in creative writing. I figured I would need a way to support myself while I tried to become an author. I got my first job at a hospital in Seattle and had joined a local writers' group as I continued honing my craft, almost ready to send my story of Sven and Julia off to some agents. Bash kept telling me I didn't need to work, that he would take care of me so that I could just write all day.

He had chosen to stay on at EOL for another year instead of going to the other Division 1 schools that were recruiting him day and night. I had told him to go to the best one, that our relationship was strong enough to withstand the time apart. We could do the long-distance thing. But he'd insisted that Coach Oakley had such great connections that there was no point in leaving. And of course he'd been right; Bash had been invited to the NFL Scouting Combine his senior year and had been selected for the NFL draft. He was a third-round pick and had been chosen by his hometown heroes, the Seattle Seahawks.

Logan kept saying he was going to fix this and get Bash traded to the Portland Jacks as soon as possible. But we were good with how our lives were going. Maybe that was a possibility someday; Jess and I had also kept up our friendship, and now that she was expecting her first baby, I wished I could be closer to help out.

"Today's been kind of a perfect day," I said to Bash.

"It has been," he agreed. "What did you think about the ceremony?"

"It was nice. I thought Mom and Doug were very sweet." It was obvious that they were madly in love and had actually become nice role models for me.

"Maybe we should have objected," he said with a wink.

"Considering this isn't the eighteenth century, I say no." Especially since our parents had come around to the fact that we were a couple and planned to stay that way. My mom in particular had started talking about how amazing it would be that she and Doug could share a grandchild that would be related to both of them, and thought they should have the priority at holidays. I kept telling her to slow down, in part because we weren't even engaged, and also because she wouldn't be the only potential grandma. Bash had been slowly working to repair his relationship with his own mom, and it had come a long way. He wasn't as close to her as Marley was, but they had made some massive strides. We'd had several dates that had included his younger siblings, Elijah and Evelyn. Elijah reminded me so much of Bash that it was kind of freaky. And although I chided my mom for jumping the gun, when I looked at those two, I could imagine the kids Bash and I would have together.

"You should try the cake. It's really good," he encouraged me in a strange voice. It made me think he was keeping things from me, something we'd promised not to do.

"Why are you being so weird?" I asked.

"Try it and find out."

Shaking my head I speared my fork into the multilayer chocolate cake.

"Spending time with my dad today . . . seeing how happy he and Tricia are . . . it made me think. Really think. About what I wanted. About what is most important in my life."

His gaze was focused on my cake. What was up with him? "At least you figured out that cake is very important," I teased as I went to get another bite. But my fork hit something solid, which fell onto the plate. I looked up to see Bash down on one knee.

I realized that the piece of fallen cake had a ring.

A ring with a diamond big enough to be seen from outer space. I gasped, fished the ring out of the piece, and started sucking the chocolate cake and frosting off it.

Giddy love bubbled up inside me, while glitter bombs exploded. He was *proposing*!

"Ember, maybe here and now is not the best time to propose to you. But I can't wait anymore. I love you, and I want to spend the rest of my life eating bacon and cake with you. I want to laugh and joke with you and have extremely tall children. I promise to never make you go to the top floor of any building and to be your sounding board for every story idea you ever have. I will support you and love you forever and ever. Will you marry me?"

I couldn't help it. My feelings overwhelmed me, and I started laughing. It was so like my adorable Bash to propose with food. "You do realize you gave me a choking hazard, right? If it hadn't fallen out, I would have eaten it and choked to death."

He looked playfully offended. "I wouldn't have let you eat it."

"Are you sure about that?" I had actually seen cases like this in the emergency room before.

"I was carefully watching you. I'm always careful!"

"Respectfully disagree." I loved teasing him and was so glad that I was going to spend the rest of my life doing just that.

"You know I wouldn't have let you eat your ring."

"I know." I finally let up. "And I love you for it."

His eyes lit up, his mischievous grin making my heart flutter. "That sounds suspiciously like a yes. And like I did an awesome proposal and you're admitting that I wouldn't have let you choke. Am I right?"

He knew how much I hated admitting that I was wrong. "You were right, and I was less right."

"But were you wrong?"

I sighed dramatically. "I could have possibly been wrong. And this cake is really delicious. I will even share it with you."

He got up and sat next to me on the stone wall of the bridge. "Now I know that's a yes." He took the chocolaty ring and slid it onto my finger. Perfect fit. I wasn't ever going to take it off again. I mean, after I cleaned the remaining chocolate off. Then it would be stuck there for life.

I kissed him. "It's a yes. It's always been a yes and always will be. For the next seventy Christmases."

"For the next seventy," he agreed, and then he kissed me, a kiss full of promises and cake and love and Christmases yet to come.

AUTHOR'S NOTE

Thank you for coming along on this journey with me! I hope you enjoyed Bash and Ember's story. If you'd like to find out when I've written something new, make sure you sign up for my newsletter at www.SariahWilson.com. I most definitely will not spam you. (I'm happy when I send out a newsletter once a month!)

And if you feel so inclined, I'd love for you to leave a review on Amazon, Goodreads, the bathroom wall at your local watering hole, on the back of your electric bill, any place you want. I would be so grateful. Thanks!

ACKNOWLEDGMENTS

For everyone who is reading this—thank you. Thank you for your support, for your kind words, and for loving my characters as much as I do!

To Alison Dasho, thank you for all the opportunities and the support and for all your suggestions. It's been such a joy working with you! Thank you to Megan Mulder for getting me the contract for this book. Thanks to the entire Montlake team for all that you do for me and my books (Anh, Kris, Kelsey, Le, Laura, and Lauren)! A special shout-out to those Montlakers who hang out with me at conferences and let me chat their ears off—Adria Martin, Jillian Cline, and Colleen Lindsay. And a special thank-you, as always, for Charlotte Herscher—for finding the story I want to tell and for helping me make everything better.

Thanks to Erin Dameron Hill for the beautiful cover, and thank you to all the proofreaders and copyeditors (including, but not limited to, Hannah, Laura, and Claire).

Thanks to the writing friends who support me, chat and hang out with me, and generally make my life better, both personally and professionally. (I'm not naming everyone here for fear of leaving someone out, but you guys know who you are!)

Thank you to Sarah Younger just for being awesome and for totally getting my snark and believing in my dreams, and to everyone at the Nancy Yost Literary Agency for supporting me.

For my children—I love you three thousand.

And Kevin, I may run out of ways to say it, but I'll never stop loving you.

ABOUT THE AUTHOR

Bestselling author Sariah Wilson has never jumped out of an airplane or climbed Mount Everest, and she is not a former CIA operative. She has, however, been madly, passionately in love with her soul mate and is a fervent believer in happily ever afters—which is why she writes romances like the End of the Line novels, the Royals of Monterra series, and the #Lovestruck novels. After growing up in Southern California as the oldest of nine (yes, nine) children, she graduated from Brigham Young University with a semi-useless degree in history. She currently lives with the aforementioned soul mate and their four children in Utah, along with three tiger barb fish, a cat named Tiger, and a recently departed hamster who is buried in the backyard (and has nothing at all to do with tigers). For more information, visit her website at www.SariahWilson.com.

Made in the USA
Monee, IL
28 June 2024

60790705R10166